LETTING GO

Also by Pam Rhodes

WITH HEART AND HYMNS AND VOICES
(Lion Publishing)

THE TRESPASSERS

WHISPERS

TIES THAT BIND

LETTING GO

Pam Rhodes

Hodder & Stoughton

Copyright © 2001 by Pam Rhodes

First published in Great Britain in 2001
by Hodder and Stoughton
A division of Hodder Headline

The right of Pam Rhodes to be identified as the Author of
the Work has been asserted by her in accordance with the
Copyright, Designs and Patents Act 1988.

2 4 6 8 10 9 7 5 3 1

All characters in this publication are fictitious
and any resemblance to real persons, living or dead,
is purely coincidental.

A CIP catalogue record for this title
is available from the British Library

ISBN 0 340 76539 9

Typeset in Centaur by Hewer Text Ltd, Edinburgh
Printed and bound in Great Britain by
Clays Ltd, St Ives plc

Hodder and Stoughton
A division of Hodder Headline
338 Euston Road
London NW1 3BH

Chapter One

'Do I look enormous in this?'

Meg and Val dutifully stared at the vision in green framed in the kitchen door.

'Fine, you look just fine.'

'No, I don't. Everything wobbles. And in this outfit, I'm not just pear shaped, but pear coloured. Green has never suited me.'

'Well, I like it,' said Meg. 'It's fresh and bright.'

'Too young, you mean. Mutton dressed as lamb.'

Val sighed. 'Sandy, you look great, and the outfit's terrific. Now grab a knife, would you? That lettuce needs cutting.'

'I should have gone for black. Black's classy. And slimming. I always feel slimmer in black.'

'You ARE slimmer,' said Meg, walking over to inspect the green trouser suit in more detail. 'Half a stone lighter, didn't you say?'

'That was last week, before the Mars bar. I've put on four pounds since then.'

'Well, this fabric is gorgeous. It hangs beautifully. I think the whole effect is really flattering on you.'

Sandy looked doubtful as she smoothed the material against her. 'My legs look like tree trunks in these trousers. They're far too wide.'

'That's all the fashion,' retorted Val, as a cucumber disintegrated into slices under the vicious cut of her chopping knife. 'Hides a multitude of sins.'

'Like my huge bottom, do you mean? I knew it! I'm going to change this minute.'

'What does Dave think?'

'It's no good asking him. He never notices what I wear.'

'That's probably because you always look good to him.'

'Any woman under the age of seventy looks good to him. That's the problem.'

'Dave adores you!'

'Not for long, if I can't stick to a diet and my legs look like tree trunks.'

Val turned then, knife in hand, and taking Sandy by the shoulders, shook her firmly.

'Darling Sandy, in Meg and me you have friends who care enough to tell you nothing but the truth. You don't wobble. Green suits you. Your husband has eyes for no one but you. So stop the angst, and come and give us a hand. The guests will be here in less than an hour.'

Sandy's eyes were enormous with disbelief. 'Are you sure? You would tell me if I looked really ridiculous.'

'Of course.'

'Fair enough,' grinned Sandy, pushing up her sleeves as she marched over to the work surface. 'What shall I do first? Pineapple chunks or sausages on sticks?'

'Mum, Dad says do you want candles on the table?'

'Great idea,' replied Meg, turning to face her son as she spoke. 'The red ones in the sideboard, third drawer down. And has he got that fire alight yet?'

'Nearly. It's smoking a bit.'

'Oh no, not today. The wind must be in the wrong direction. Does he want help?'

'Do you want help, Dad?' Ben yelled through to the lounge.

'No,' came the distant answer. 'It's catching now.'

'Take the dustpan and brush through to Dad, love. He'll need it. And the bottle opener too. Put it near the glasses. And that waste-paper bin should be emptied. Bring it through when you come, will you? Oh, and Ben, have you seen Emma? She's not still in the bathroom, is she?'

'Probably.'

'Well, go and give her a knock, and tell her that if she's not down here pulling her weight in five minutes, then that new sound system she's got her eye on for Christmas will be in severe jeopardy!'

'She'll only tell me to shove off.'

'Just do it, Ben. And make sure she knows I mean it!'

Val turned to watch as Ben dragged himself reluctantly upstairs. 'So how's Emma's romance going? Still on?'

Meg grimaced. 'I don't dare say another word, because that will only make her more determined then ever to stay with him. But Alan's livid about it. He doesn't like the thought of his darling daughter in the clasp of a grease monkey who works in a garage, rides a bike that's downright dangerous, and doesn't seem to wash a lot.'

'Doesn't he?'

'No idea. Never fancied getting close enough to find out.'

'But Emma's hooked, is she?' asked Sandy as she scraped egg mayonnaise off her knife and popped it into her mouth.

'Completely smitten. Apart from her time at school, she seems to spend every waking hour either out with him, or talking to him on that blessed mobile. I hope he's ringing her, because we pay the bill for that phone of hers.'

'How did she meet him then, if they're not at school together?'

'They were apparently. She's in her last year of 'A' levels now, and he was at the same school until the summer before last. He flunked all his GCSE's, she tells me.'

3

'So what does she see in him?'

Val grinned over at Sandy. 'Well, I don't think it's his mind . . .'

'Even I can see he's cute. I get my car serviced at his dad's garage, you know.' Sandy's eyes sparkled as she spoke. 'When I saw him bending over to inspect my engine the other day, I certainly got an eyeful of his best features!'

'Oh, don't!' groaned Meg, 'I can't bear the thought of what the two of them get up to.'

'How old is Emma now? Eighteen?'

'Not yet. Not for another few months. Far too young to be getting involved with just one person. And definitely far too young to be—well, you know . . .'

Val stopped buttering bread to look at her. 'For heaven's sake, Meg, you know what we were like when we were seventeen!'

'No, I don't – and I didn't.'

'Yes you do – and I bet you did. We all did.'

'Definitely not. You were a hippy. I came from Theydon Bois.'

'Well, Emma's generation are definitely more like me than you. Just make sure she knows what she's doing, and that you've got the Kleenex handy when it all goes wrong.'

'I'm going to pick up the rest of the wine.' Alan popped his head round the kitchen door, then spotting the quiche Meg was cutting up, put his arm round his wife as he reached through to pinch a piece. 'Do you need anything else while I'm out?'

'Yes, some lemons! And a couple of French sticks would be useful too.'

'Right.'

'Oh, and is one jar of olives enough, do you think? You know how the vicar and his wife tucked into to them at our last party.'

'I like them too,' interrupted Sandy.

'They're fattening,' said Val.

4

'But it's Christmas,' wailed Sandy. 'I think another couple of jars would go down a treat today with the mulled wine and mince pies.'

Alan turned to hug Sandy affectionately. 'You will have your olives, Sandy! And don't forget what you promised if I found a bit of mistletoe!'

Meg was chuckling as she turned to look at them. 'You'll have to join the queue for Sandy in that smashing outfit she's wearing. She's not sure about it, but help us convince her. She looks great, doesn't she?'

'Always!' said Alan, holding Sandy at arm's length so that he could take a proper look. Over the top of her head, he spotted the time on the cooker clock. 'Must go.'

'Don't forget to pick your mum up on the way back!' yelled Meg after Alan's disappearing figure.

'Will do!' was the reply – and he was gone.

'Right.' Meg reached out to grab a towel. 'That's done. I'm going up to get my glad rags on, or those guests will find me still in my dressing gown.'

'And I'll be back with the fruit salad and Christmas cake in about an hour. OK?'

'Thanks, Val. You've been brilliant. Who's coming with you? Chas or Jay?'

'Both. It's Sunday, the one day of the week they're prepared to share.'

Sandy chuckled. 'Whoever heard of two husbands sharing one wife!'

'Ex-husbands,' corrected Val, 'and I'm nobody's wife, not at the moment, anyway.'

'Well, I think it's wonderful that you all get along so well,' grinned Meg. 'Very modern and civilised.'

'Oh, I'm good at choosing husbands. I just don't want to keep them. Back soon then. And Sandy, that green really suits you!'

Disappearing before her friend could argue the point, Val banged the front door behind her.

Quarter of an hour and a quick shower later, Meg squeezed herself into her seasonally red trouser suit, and stood back to stare critically at the woman she saw reflected in the mirror. Not bad for forty-three. Waist a bit thicker than it once was, her face paler and more rounded, but her hair had kept its blonde highlights, complementing the hazel eyes fringed by thick lashes which had always been her most striking feature. She slipped her feet into heeled shoes, and turned to inspect the back view of her outfit. It was amazing how much more confident a couple of extra inches in height made her feel. It had always been that way right from her school days. She smiled at the memory of how Katherine, who had simply been born tall and elegant, would hug her affectionately whenever Meg got in a state about being 'dumpy as well as spotty'. By the time the spots faded, Meg had discovered high heels – and felt instantly grown up. The confidence those shoes gave her then had never left her. Neither had Katherine. All these years on, although their lives had taken such different paths, their friendship was as intimate and special as ever.

'Mum, where's my white blouse? I need it.' Emma burst into the bedroom to confront her mother.

'Which one? You've got about six white blouses.'

'The one I put in the wash.'

'When?'

'Last night, I think.'

'You put it out last night, and you expect me to have it washed and ironed by this morning? Didn't it occur to you that we are having a big Christmas party this lunch-time, and I might just have other things to do?'

Emma's expression was a picture of exasperation. 'Mum! I've got to have it!'

6

'Then perhaps you should have thought about it earlier. As it happens, it is washed, but still in the tumble dryer.'

'It will need ironing!'

'Then iron it.'

'I can't iron as fast as you – or as well. Please, Mum, please!'

'Emma, we have sixty guests arriving in half an hour. I have a million and one things to do. If you'd come down to help me this morning, maybe I'd have had time to iron your wretched blouse for you. As it is, I'm busy – and if you want it, you'll just have to iron it yourself. Better still, why don't you wear something else? The new jacket you bought?'

'I wore that last weekend.'

'And it looked really nice on you.'

'If I can't wear my blouse, then I'm not coming to this stupid party.'

'Emma, this is one of the few family occasions when Dad and I ask that the whole family be together.'

'If you want me to come, you should have asked Matt too.'

'He wouldn't enjoy it, love. He doesn't know any of this group.'

'Well, how's he ever going to get to know them if you don't invite him?'

'Emma, not now – and not again! We've had this conversation, and I'm getting very tired of it. Now sort yourself out. Iron that blouse, if you want to. Wear something else if you don't. And I could do with your help in the kitchen. It wouldn't hurt you to do something occasionally to earn your pocket money.'

At that moment, Emma's mobile phone rang. Glaring at her mother, she put the phone to her ear, her voice echoing behind her as she marched out of the room.

'Matt, this party sucks. I knew it would. Believe me, you're not missing much . . .'

Sighing, Meg applied a final coat of lipstick, plumped up her hair, took a deep breath, then started down the stairs. On the way, she met Ben coming up.

'OK, love?' she asked deliberately, making sure her lips could be clearly seen by her son. Meningitis when he was five had nearly claimed his life. He recovered, stone deaf in one ear, but all the more precious because for several worrying days, they'd thought they might lose him forever.

Ben nodded without comment.

'Are you going to get changed?'

He glanced down at his jeans and sweatshirt.

'Do I have to?'

'How about your new jumper? That would be nice.'

'I'm not dressing up.'

'You don't have to. Just change your sweatshirt, and you'll be fine.'

'Do I have to be down there all the time?'

Meg sat down on the stairs so that their faces were level as she ran her hand through his soft, sandy-coloured hair.

'Not your scene really, is it?'

He shook his head.

'Daniel will be here, you know. His mum and dad are definitely coming. And I expect Rebecca and Alice will come along too.'

Ben's nose wrinkled with distaste at the thought of GIRLS on his home territory.

'But do we have to stay downstairs, or can we come up here and play on the computer?'

'You do whatever you feel like doing. We want you to have a good time.'

With a wordless shrug, Ben carried on up towards his room. Meg watched him go, worrying for the umpteenth time about the change in him since he'd started senior boys' school just over a year earlier. Her bright, talkative son had become withdrawn and self-contained. She had hoped that a different, more mature environment would bring new friendships and opportunities. Instead, he'd become a solitary figure, reluctant to be drawn on the subject of school at all.

At that moment, the front door opened, and Alan appeared ushering in his elderly mother before him. Now in her early seventies, Jean Barratt had a mind as bright as a button locked inside a body crippled with aching joints. With one hip already replaced, and the other some way down the waiting list for operations at the local hospital, she shuffled painfully towards the lounge where she sank down on a high-backed chair by the table.

'What needs doing?' she asked without preamble. 'Glasses polished? Serviettes folded? You know I'll only be trouble if you don't put me to good use.'

Meg smiled with affection at her mother-in-law, then pushed a pile of dishes and bags of nuts and savoury nibbles across the table towards her.

'That lot in those dishes, please. I'll put them round the room later. And thanks, Mum. It's good to see you.'

'Right, that's all the red wine out,' said Alan, 'and the white is already in the fridge. Oh, you look nice!'

Meg stepped into his embrace, laying her head against the solid comfort of his shoulder. But then Alan was a solid sort of man. Stockily built, attractively greying at the temples with a square, kindly face that expressed laughter or concern with equal ease.

'Did you get the French sticks?'

'They're in the kitchen.'

'The lemons?'

'By the bottle of gin and the ice cubes.'

'And the olives?'

'Couldn't find them. Mind you, I rushed round that supermarket so quickly.'

'Sandy will be disappointed – not to mention the vicar!'

'Then we'll know what to give him for Christmas. Apart from that, are we ready? What about the kids?'

'Ben's on the computer. Emma's in a sulk in her room.'

'I've just seen her in the kitchen.'

'You have? Don't tell me she's come down to help!' Meg broke away abruptly, stopping at the sight which greeted her in the kitchen. Piles of clean washing had been turned out of the wicker basket on to the floor. Plates carefully arranged with food were shoved together at one side of the work surface, while a selection of blouses, skirts and trousers took up all the other. And in the middle of the room was Emma, red-faced and furious as she bashed the iron ineffectually over a particularly skimpy white blouse.

'For heaven's sake, Emma, you can't do that HERE! The guests will be arriving any moment! Why didn't you take the board upstairs?'

Without looking at her mother, Emma slammed down the iron. 'I've finished now.' And leaving clothes, board and iron in chaos behind her, she snatched up the blouse and sailed upstairs.

Meg didn't see Emma for at least a couple of hours after that. By then, the house was packed, and lunch in full swing. It was as Meg balanced a plate of hot sausages in one hand and mince pies in the other that she spotted Emma sitting on the stairs, mobile phone glued to her ear. Without even asking, Meg knew it was Matt on the line. It was always Matt. For months, she and Alan had hoped that Emma's attachment to the garage mechanic would cool and fade. No such luck, judging by the flush in her daughter's cheeks whenever she spoke to him. Best to say nothing, and keep their fingers crossed that a more suitable partner might suddenly seem devastatingly attractive to their lovely, clever, strong-willed girl – a partner who shared her intelligence and ambition, who would encourage her in her 'A' Level studies, and recognise her potential – someone absolutely the opposite of Matt, who seemed to have no interests except his motorbike, and no acknowledgement of how important study was to Emma at this crucial stage of her life.

Katherine was standing to one side of the table as Meg manoeuvred the two plates on to the heated tray.

'Well?' hissed Meg in her old friend's ear, 'what do you think?'

'About what?' Katherine's face was a study of innocence.

'About whom, not what – and you know perfectly well who I mean. He's a successful businessman, got a bob or two, all his own teeth, and he's on his own again since his divorce.'

'How do you know?'

'Know what? That he's on his own?'

'No, that he's got his own teeth.'

Meg grinned. 'Well, they look real enough to me – from a distance, you understand. Get a bit nearer yourself, if you want to check.'

'You don't give up, do you?'

'Look, you're my dearest and oldest friend.'

'Not so much of the old.'

'My dearest and best friend then. Look at you – absolutely gorgeous, successful in every way – and you're on your own! I just can't understand it.'

'Perhaps that's the way I like it.'

'Nonsense. You forget how long I've known you. You're quite capable of BEING on your own. You're brilliant in your own company. But I don't believe you want to live alone for ever. You've been searching for your soulmate as long as we've been friends.'

'Oh, Meg . . .'

'Don't "oh Meg" me! We both know I'm right. It's time you found someone to adore and cherish you. You deserve nothing less.'

'Actually, dearest Meg, you may not believe this but I'm not short of men who want to cherish me.'

'You aren't? Why haven't you mentioned them?'

'Because I have never felt the wish to adore and cherish THEM.'

'You've not met the right one then, have you.' Katherine didn't answer.

'You need a man like my Alan, dependable and steady, someone you can really rely on.'

Katherine reached out to pick up a dry roasted nut, glancing over towards Alan, who caught her eye as he stood chatting to a group of neighbours.

'And Robert Masters could be just that man. He's not bad-looking. Well, I don't think so, do you?'

'It's not just about looks though, is it?'

'Well, how are you ever going to know if there is more to him than just good looks if you won't let me introduce you?'

Katherine sighed. 'Meg, you're a darling, and I know you mean well, but I'm really not interested in being touted around as a prospect.'

'You're not. I simply think that he's on his own, and you're on your own – so why shouldn't the two of you be on your own together?'

'Tell you what, I'm going to talk to my god-daughter instead. Where is Emma? I've not seen her yet.'

Meg's lips tightened. 'Last seen perched on the stairs glued to her mobile, telling that dreadful boyfriend of hers what an awful mother she has.'

'I see,' laughed Katherine. 'What have you done to her?'

'The usual. What was it she yelled at me the other night? That I'm out of touch, tightfisted, puritanical and I treat her as if she were one of my eight-year-old pupils.'

'Typical teenager stuff then?'

'She used to be such an angel. What happened to that friendly, funny little girl?'

'Hormones.'

'Does that mean I've got another thirty years of this?'

'Probably.'

'Were we like that at sixteen?'

'Absolutely not. We were perfect in every way.'

Meg grinned. 'And we still are. Oh, there's Sandy. I need to see her. Do me a favour and please go and talk to Robert Masters. Not for any particular reason if you're really not interested, but he does look uncomfortable there on his own.'

At that moment, Alan also realised that Robert was out on a limb, and collecting a glass of white wine for them both en route, made his way over to join him. Work had brought the two men together, not particularly as friends, but as colleagues who occasionally met because they were both involved in the banking business. Robert was on the board of an up-and-coming investment house in the City. Alan's company specialised in providing software programs individually created for the accounting needs of large banking institutions. Over recent months, they had been working together to create a new computing package for Robert's business, and during that time Alan had become aware that Robert was going through a painful and messy divorce. As it turned out that his ex-wife and children lived only a few miles away from Alan and Meg, an invitation to their annual Christmas lunch-time party seemed an excellent way of getting him circulating again.

'So,' began Alan, 'what are your plans for Christmas?'

Robert took a gulp of wine before answering. 'A bit unsettled really. Wendy seems adamant that I shouldn't have the kids with me even for Boxing Day. You'd think I was a child abuser or something, with all the vitriol she's throwing my way.'

'That's rough on the children too. How old are they now?'

'Well, Jonathan is nearly fifteen, so he's fairly sensible about all this. But Naomi is only six, and I do worry about the way Wendy is poisoning her against me.'

'How often do you manage to see them?'

'Not enough. Once a week if I'm lucky, and that's just for a few hours on Friday evenings. It's tough if work comes up and I can't get there for four o'clock. The door is shut in my face, and that's it for another week.'

'Why is Wendy so bitter?'

'Money mostly. She thinks I'm hiding assets from her, although honestly I'm not. I only want to be fair about all this, make sure she and the kids are all right — but I have to be able to live too. I think she'd like to see me in a tent on the side of the motorway, just to make sure I'm suffering enough.'

'Was there anyone else involved in your break-up?'

'Initially, yes. Wendy and I hadn't really been getting on for years, and although that's no excuse, I admit that in the end I got myself involved with a woman at work. Lovely girl. Everything that Wendy wasn't.'

'So you left the family to be with her?'

'It wasn't like that. I didn't mean to leave the family at all. Wendy did a bit of snooping, and the whole thing just blew up in my face. There was no discussion about it, no question of counselling, nor recognition of the fact that the problems in our marriage were certainly created by both of us, not just me. It felt as though she was relieved to see me go — and from the moment I was out the door with my bags flying around my ears after me, she went for the jugular — all joint property, and very little access to the children.'

'How long were you married?'

'Eighteen years.'

'We beat you by one year. It's our nineteenth anniversary tomorrow.'

'Well, you and Meg seem happy enough.'

'We are.'

'Then it must be hard for you to understand what it's like to marry a girl who seems sweet and bright and devoted at first, only to see her turn into a bossy, demanding nag the moment the children come along. I got to the point where I made excuses not to go home, and then it was all too easy to let a work relationship slip into becoming more than it should be. She was beautiful and intelligent, and listened for hours as I poured out my troubles to her. When you're feeling low and alienated from your partner, that kind of response is hard to resist.'

'Must be,' agreed Alan, emptying his glass. 'So where will you be for Christmas? Not on your own, I hope.'

'Would you believe I'm going back to my mum's? She's in her seventies now, so you can imagine how devastated she is to see our family break up after all these years. But we'll be at my brother's for Christmas Day, so I'll combine staying at the old family home with her for a few days and then the two of us will go over there for lunch, which will be nice – but odd. And it means I'll be with my brother's children on Christmas Day, not my own. The thought of Naomi opening her presents without me beside her really cuts me up.'

'You wouldn't like to join us? You'd be very welcome, you know.'

Robert's smile transformed his long, slightly tanned face. 'That's kind, but unnecessary. And who knows? Wendy might relent at the last minute and let me have the youngsters on Christmas Eve or Boxing Day. Mum's house is not far from theirs, and I want to be close at hand if there's even a chance of that happening.'

'I understand. Another drink? And have you tried some of that delicious gammon joint? Heaven knows what she does to it, but gammon is Meg's speciality.'

'The thing is,' Simon Foster was saying as the two men brushed passed him on their way to the food table, 'there's a good deal of jealousy amongst the other primary schools in the area about the reputation we have for our stage productions. All thanks to Meg,

15

of course. Where she gets the inspiration from year after year, I'll never know, but she pulls rabbits out of hats every time. I've seen children who are desperately shy and gauche really blossom under her guidance and encouragement.'

'Are your ears burning?' asked Sandy as Meg came to stand next to Val and join in with their conversation. 'Your head-master is waxing lyrical about your theatrical achievements.'

Meg grimaced towards Simon. 'Well, this production might ruin our success rate forever. We're running really late on rehearsals, and the scenery is still in pieces. And the children have been so busy with school trips and national tests just lately, we'll be lucky if they've learnt their words in time for Easter, let alone the Christmas show.'

Simon's smile was confident. 'You'll manage. You always do. And our show will once again knock spots off the efforts of every other junior school in the area.'

Meg frowned. 'Hardly. And I couldn't manage without the help of all the staff and parents, especially my trusty team here. Thank goodness for Val and her costume-making skills! By the way, is there any news on that donkey outfit yet?'

'County definitely haven't got one, and the hire shop told me theirs is already booked out for next week. We've got an offer of a donkey suit from the local operatic and dramatic group, but when they last used it, two six-foot fellas got inside. Can't imagine our ten-year-olds in that somehow.'

'We'd have to tie the legs up with ribbons,' giggled Sandy. 'You know, Meg, my Jason is desperate to be the back legs. He's only nine, but he's pretty tall for his age. Is there any chance you could choose him?'

'You have no idea how many lads are queuing up for that role. I've decided that if we do manage to get a costume, we may have to put all the names in a hat, just to make it fair.'

'Aah,' observed Simon, who always seemed to be rubber-necking to check if there was someone more interesting to talk to, 'I see you've invited Neil Miller from the high school. I wasn't aware you knew him.'

'A neighbour. His son, Daniel, is good friends with our son, Ben.'

But Simon was already on his way over to the other side of the room where the company was suddenly more enticing.

'How do you put up with him?' asked Sandy as she watched him greet Neil Miller with enthusiasm. 'He's such a snob.'

'But a good headmaster. He gets things done.'

'Only because he's terrified some other school might achieve something he hasn't thought of yet.'

'Maybe.' Meg went silent as she took a moment to gaze around the collection of people now filling her living room.

'It's going fine,' said Val. 'The food's great, the wine keeps coming and the conversation is flowing nicely. What more could you ask?'

'Do you think everyone's mixing OK?'

'Well, if you want me to mix with that good-looking chap over there talking to Alan,' suggested Sandy, 'just let me know. Who is he, by the way?'

'His name is Robert Masters. He's a work colleague of Alan's.'

'Where is his wife?'

'His ex-wife doesn't speak to him.'

'He's footloose and fancy free?'

'Probably too early for that, from what Alan tells me.'

'How delicious! He's available.' Sandy looked around the crowd. 'Now who would suit him?'

'What about your friend, Katherine?' asked Val.

Meg shook her head. 'Not interested. She was quite definite about it.'

'Pity I'm spoken for,' sighed Sandy. 'I wouldn't mind helping him over his loss.'

'The marriage broke up because he went off with someone else.'

'Oh, did he now? I thought he had shifty eyes. Thank goodness I'm a happily married woman!'

'What did Dave think about your outfit?'

'He said he likes it.'

'Well, of course!'

'But whenever I ask him if he likes what I'm wearing, he always says he does, so I can't trust either his judgement or his opinion.'

'For heaven's sake, Sandy, whatever your poor husband says he's bound to be wrong.'

'Look, he said he liked that red dress I wore to the school disco, and we all know I looked hideous in it.'

Catching the exasperation in each other's face, Meg and Val simply dissolved with laughter.

Slipping away from the crowd, Daniel Miller followed the intriguing computer sounds up to Ben's room. He pushed open the door to find the room dark except for the patch of bright, flashing light which came from the computer screen.

'Smart! That's Rally Masters, isn't it?'

When Ben didn't answer, Daniel remembered that unless he could see lips moving, the younger boy didn't actually hear very much. Bit rough on him, really. No wonder most of the boys at school thought he was a bit of a space case.

Ben jumped with a start when Daniel pulled up a chair beside him. Then with a small nod of recognition, the two boys stared at the screen as Ben skilfully manoeuvred his way through a particularly difficult race track at high speed. At last he sat back with satisfaction. 'Want a go?' he asked.

'Wicked!'

It soon showed that Ben had had lots of practice with computer games because five minutes later, Daniel had crashed the car several times, sending it rolling into brick walls and tumbling on to grass verges. Hooked now, he was determined to improve his technique.

'Want a Coke?' asked Ben, rising to go downstairs. 'I'll grab a bowl of crisps while I'm there.'

'Cool.'

In fact, the bowl of crisps was joined by ham sandwiches and two plates of ice-cream when Ben returned, by which time Daniel was ready for a break. For some seconds, the two lads downed their Cokes in silence until Daniel sat back to pull his sandwich apart and study it in minute detail before he actually took a bite.

'What you getting for Christmas then?' Daniel's mouth bulged with sandwich as he spoke.

'A couple more computer games, I hope.' More munching. 'You?'

'I'd like a decent CD player, but my mum says that if I want to go on that ski ing trip with the school, I should have my ski clothes for Christmas. Makes me think I'd rather not go really.' Ben reached out for a handful of crisps as Daniel spoke again. 'Are you going on the ski-ing trip?'

'Nope.'

'Don't fancy it?'

'Not really.'

'I thought you might. I remember when we used to go to the skating rink, you were the best out of all of us.'

'That's because the others we went with were girls. It was easy to be better than girls.'

'Funny though, I thought you might have wanted to go on that school trip.'

The dregs of his glass of Coke disappeared noisily down Ben's throat.

'I wonder,' continued Daniel, choosing his words carefully, 'whether it's the ski-ing you don't fancy – or the group you'd be with?'

Ben shrugged and turned back towards the computer screen.

'How's it going, Ben? School, I mean?'

'All right.'

'Only I saw you the other night, you know, when Michael Smith was walking home behind you . . .'

'It doesn't matter.'

'It does. It must do. He shouldn't be allowed to talk to you like that. He's just a bully.'

'I don't care.'

'Yes you do.'

'Even if I did, I can't do anything about it so it doesn't matter.'

'Have you talked to anyone? Mr Elliott or someone?'

'Nope. No point.'

'There might be. They've got rules about that sort of thing.'

'It would only cause more trouble.'

'But it might help. Mr Elliott is a fairly decent bloke, I reckon. I'm sure he'd . . .'

'I'd rather not. But thanks all the same.'

'Would you like to walk home with me? That might put them off.'

'They'd only pick on you as well.'

'Why is he doing it? Have you done something to annoy Michael Smith?'

'I didn't need to. It's just me being me that irritates him.'

'You mean, because of your . . . your . . .'

'Deafness?' Daniel nodded. 'He thinks because I'm deaf, I must be dumb. I'm an easy target. I'm used to it. I don't care any more.'

'I know you do. I can tell you do.'

'They'll get bored. Eventually they'll find someone else to make fun of. I'll just have to lump it till then.'

'Have you told your mum?'

Ben looked surprised at the suggestion. 'No!'

'Why not? She's a teacher like my dad. She'd know what to do.'

'She'll want to march in there and fight my battles for me. I'd hate that. No, I just want to keep my head down and do this my own way.'

Daniel watched quietly for a while as Ben restarted the game, before asking, 'Did you know Tom Benson?'

Ben shook his head, not stopping the flow of his game. 'Should I?'

'Maybe not. He was at junior school with me. He hasn't gone to the boys' school here though. He's been sent to some private school about twenty miles away, so his mum told mine.' Ben made no comment. 'He changed schools because of Michael Smith. He was being bullied too, just like you.' Ben carried on playing almost as if he wasn't listening.

'The thing is, it got really bad for him. A whole gang of them laid into him after school one night. They broke his glasses and his nose was a real mess. Someone said it was broken.'

'Why?' asked Ben at last.

'Because he had alopecia – you know, where great chunks of your hair falls out?'

'They picked on him for that?'

'Well, he had a couple of big bald patches, and his hands were shaking all the time.'

'Was he always like that? I mean, was he ill or something?'

'No, he used to be fine, but I think it was when his dad died it started. Tom's the oldest in his family with about three younger brothers and sisters, I think. Just got a bit much for him, I suppose.'

'Poor bloke.'

'Well, it wasn't until he got beaten up that the school had any idea what was going on. They gave Michael a warning then. Said if anything like that ever happened again, he'd be suspended. That's why I think you should talk to Mr Elliott now. I know it's a different school but maybe if you . . .'

'Maybe if I did, he'd go and talk to Smith to find out if there was any truth in it, and Smith would deny it all – and he'd get me for it later. Thanks, Daniel, but I really don't fancy that.'

'Look, I know we're not in the same form but I'm quite happy to hang around with you whenever I can, if you think it would help.'

For the first time that afternoon, Ben almost smiled. 'Thanks, Dan.'

'I mean it.'

'I know you do and I'll think about it, OK?'

'Cool.'

'Want a go on this? Or would you rather play Resident Evil Three?'

'Wicked!'

Their two heads crowded towards the screen in complete concentration, until before long they became aware that they'd been joined by a gaggle of other youngsters bored by the adult company downstairs: Sandy's children, Jason, Darren and Joely, and another couple of brothers whose dad worked with Alan. It occurred to Ben briefly that he was the centre of attraction, and whenever that had happened in recent months, it had usually meant he was in the middle of a hostile crowd led by Michael Smith. But this time was different. This time the group around him were admiring, respectful and on his home territory. It was a good feeling, even if it was only here – and only now.

Half an hour later Alan came across Emma sitting outside on the garden seat huddled in her favourite fake fur coat, smoking a cigarette.

'Hello Goose. I wondered where you'd got to.'

Emma looked up at him with the rare smile kept only for her dad. She thought he was over-protective; he thought she was growing up too fast and often made wrong decisions – but the love between them had always been special and strong.

He sighed. 'I wish you wouldn't smoke.'

'I wish you wouldn't drink so much.'

'If I were your age, I would decide not to drink or smoke at all.'

'If I were your age, I'd know you never learn from other people's experience.'

In spite of himself, he chuckled, reaching out to take a cigarette from the packet she offered him. Together they sat in companionable silence, until he shivered slightly. Emma gave him a sideways glance.

'Why didn't you put a coat on to come out here?'

'Didn't know I was staying.'

'Shouldn't you be inside entertaining your guests?'

'Shouldn't you? They're guests of the whole family. You've known most of these people your whole life.'

'Was I allowed any say in the guest list? No. So why should I bother to be polite to people who bore me stiff?'

'For me? For your mum?'

Emma snorted with indignation before dropping her cigarette and stubbing it out viciously with the toe of her platform shoe.

'It's just one day of the year, Goose. It won't be long before you leave home to go to university, and then you might find your thoughts as you look back on your Christmases at home are very different from what you feel right now.'

'Rose-coloured specs, eh?'

'Not really. I just think we don't value what we have until it's not there for us any more.'

'Our generation is different from yours, Dad. We're more mature, more worldly-wise than you ever were. I can't wait to leave home, and I'll be fine, you know I will.'

'I don't doubt that. Your mum and I have brought you up to

be independent and self-sufficient when the time comes. But don't rush towards that time too fast, love. What's here and now is precious too. Precious to us as well as you.'

'Well, if my feelings matter so much, how come Matt wasn't invited to this stupid party?'

'If it's so stupid, why would he want to be here?'

'I wanted him to come.'

'But would he have enjoyed it? Would he have liked these people, felt comfortable in their company?'

'Why shouldn't he? He's a really bright, interesting guy once you get to know him. But you'll never get to know him, will you, because you think he's common, not the right class for your precious little girl?'

'I don't . . .'

'Yes you do. You and Mum are just snobs, too wrapped up in your own comfortable lifestyle to recognise that even if other people may look and live differently from you, they're still more worthwhile than you'll ever be!'

He drew breath for a few seconds before answering. 'How about,' he ventured at last, 'Mum and I taking you and Matt out for a pub meal during the week after Christmas? I'll be at home for a few days then, so we can take our time about it.'

He laughed to see Emma's eyes narrow, looking for the catch in his suggestion. 'I mean it! You're right that we haven't given Matt a chance – although to be fair, he's not exactly given us much chance to meet him either. It will be an opportunity for us all to make amends, a new start for the New Year. How about it?'

'Do we get to choose the pub?' He nodded in agreement. 'And no restrictions on what we drink?'

'Within reason.'

'And you promise not to embarrass me in any way at any time?'

'What? Like bringing out that picture of you wearing nothing but your birthday suit in the paddling pool?'

'Exactly.'

'You were only two years old.'

'It's embarrassing, Dad!'

'Agreed. No embarrassment from us, and no sarcasm from you either. Best behaviour on both sides. Agreed?'

'Done!'

'I'm frozen. And your nan would love to see you. She's been asking for you all afternoon. Coming?'

And without another word, she got up to link her arm through his as they walked back into the house.

'A mince pie, Mary?' Plates were still being handed round as Alan and Emma made their way into the lounge. Mary, Alan's fifty-something, ultra-loyal, highly efficient secretary, was chatting to his mother, Jean, as Emma slipped into the seat beside them to hug her grandmother with affection.

'What's good to eat, Nan? I haven't got near the food table yet.'

'You don't eat enough to keep a fly alive,' retorted Jean, eyes dancing with pleasure to see Emma again. 'Look at you! There's nothing to you but skin and bone!'

'That's all the fashion, Nan. Not skinny, but slim. Not boney, but svelte.'

'You should come and see me more often. I'd get some good, nourishing dinners inside you.'

Emma chuckled. 'I wouldn't do very well with guys if I pile on the weight.'

'You show me a man who says he doesn't like curves on a woman, and I'll show you a liar!'

Watching the good-natured sparring with amusement, Alan and Mary finally moved away a little as Alan helped himself to a mince pie.

'Any plans over Christmas, Mary?'

'Just going to my sister's, as usual.'

'And you really don't feel you'd like a few days' holiday between Christmas and New Year? I've no intention of going into the office over that period, you know, so there will be very little for you to do.'

'Good, that will give me a chance to catch up. I've been meaning to turn out that filing cabinet for months. I'll be able to start the New Year with at least one of my resolutions intact.'

He felt a gentle tap on his shoulder. 'I must go,' said Robert. 'I'm hoping to take a detour and call in on the children on the way home.'

'Of course. It was good of you to come. And I hope everything works out for you over Christmas.'

'I hope so too.'

'Don't forget we're only a phone call away if you need company.'

'That's kind.' Robert's expression softened as he spoke. 'Thanks, Alan. I'll just say goodbye to Meg before I leave.'

'She's in the kitchen, I think.'

Meg was indeed in the kitchen, loading the dishwasher. Sandy was up to her elbows in the kitchen sink. Katherine was drying delicate wineglasses with a tea towel.

'Oh, goodbye Robert,' said Meg getting to her feet. 'I'm sorry I've hardly had a chance to talk to you. And I don't think you've met my trusty assistants – Sandy . . .'

Sandy's flirting smile was accompanied by a soapy hand wave.

'. . . and Katherine.'

As Katherine struggled to extricate her hand from both wineglass and tea towel, Robert looked approvingly at the woman who greeted him. She was slightly built but quite tall, her slim figure enhanced by a simple, well-cut suit, with chin-length dark hair tucked neatly behind dainty ears decorated with elegant pearl studs. But it was her eyes which fascinated him most – brown, almost black, with a direct stare at once challenging and defensive.

He took her outstretched hand, holding it for just a second too long before taking his leave.

'Well!' whispered Sandy, 'You certainly made your mark. And he's gorgeous, absolutely gorgeous!'

Katherine went back to her drying up without comment.

'But he hasn't got your number! Of course he can always ask Alan for it, can't he? How exciting! I BET you get a call from him. I just bet you will!'

Ten minutes later, Robert pulled into a lay-by, dug out his mobile and phoned his wife's number. Could he possibly pop in and see the children for a quick half-hour or so? Perhaps it was the unexpectedness of the call that made her so tetchy. Perhaps it was just that anything he suggested irritated her beyond belief. Whatever the cause, what he had intended to be a short phone call was plainly destined to turn into a lengthy and acrimonious conversation. Gritting his teeth, he settled down into the seat, and got on with it.

Katherine looked at her watch before turning to wave goodbye once again to Meg and Emma as they stood framed in the doorway. This dear group of long-trusted friends were the nearest thing to family she felt she had. Apart from a much older brother who now lived in France, her own relatives had all passed away. Nowadays it was rare that she even thought of them – except perhaps at Christmas when sentimentality overtook the whole human race, including her. As she hurried down the path towards her car, a sudden longing for her mother shuddered through her, deeply felt, soon buried again and forgotten.

She pulled away from the kerb, taking a final glance at the lit door of their house. How she loved them all! Did they know that one of the soundest comforts in her life was the knowledge of their totally accepting and fiercely loyal love for her?

Her mind too full of thoughts to bother with the radio, she

almost missed him as she drove down the long straight road towards the motorway. At first, she thought she must be mistaken, but then a good look into the rear-view mirror confirmed her first impression. That was Robert Masters she'd just passed, walking alone along the pitch-dark edge of the road.

Her heart sank. She didn't want to stop, but then obviously something was wrong, and he was an acquaintance, if not a friend. Carefully, she pulled up on to the grass verge, opening the passenger door as he approached her car. It was then that she saw the petrol can in his hand. 'Can I give you a lift?'

'That would be great. I'm not even sure where I'm headed. Can you think of a petrol station likely to be open around here at this time on a Sunday?'

Katherine thought for a moment. 'Perhaps. Hop in and we'll drive till we find one.'

He folded his large frame into the seat beside her, and she pulled out on to the road. For a while neither spoke, unsure what to say.

'I should have checked,' he said at last. 'I knew I was low, but I thought I'd fill up at the service station on the motorway.'

'That must be ten miles away.'

'You're right, and I'm an idiot. Sorry.'

She smiled. 'You didn't get very far.'

'Well, I stopped to make a phone call which went on a bit, and then when I tried to restart the engine nothing happened. In the end I just started walking. I can't tell you how glad I am to see you.'

'No harm done. You're welcome.'

'Where are you heading?'

'I live in Hampstead.'

'Really? I'm in St John's Wood. We're practically neighbours.'

She didn't reply as she pulled off the main road towards a supermarket sign. They were in luck. The garage was still open.

Minutes later, can full, they were making their way back towards his car.

'Thank you, Katherine, I am in your debt. Can I repay your kindness by inviting you to dinner one evening soon?'

She hesitated. 'That's a generous thought, but probably complicated with the Christmas break coming up. And there's no need really. I was pleased to help.'

His eyes held hers in the darkness for a moment before, with a wave of his hand, he started back towards his own car.

But the next morning, with the incident almost forgotten, Katherine opened her front door to accept delivery of a beautiful Christmas bouquet. The card read:

> Merry Christmas to my kind neighbour,
> with love and thanks, Robert.

And the vision of his long, intelligent face and surprisingly warm eyes slipped into her mind as she arranged the blooms, and placed them beside her bed.

Chapter Two

'We've got one!' Val came rushing into the staff room during morning break the following day to show Meg. 'It's a bit tatty, and I'm going to be up half the night shortening the legs, but it's ours for the rest of the week!'

Meg was already dragging a shapeless bundle of tatty grey fur out of the enormous carrier bag Val was clutching. A small crowd gathered round in the staff room, no one quite sure what to say as they stared at the misshapen head and lop-sided eyes. It was Sue, the newest and youngest member of the teaching team who started to giggle first.

'You're sure that IS a donkey?'

'The chap at the operatic and dramatic group told me they call it Daffy.'

'So this is their pantomime costume?'

'I think they'd almost forgotten they had it. One of the wives made it for them years ago, and they've only used it a couple of times since, when they did a spot of fund-raising by carol singing with a wind-up organ in the town square.'

'I remember,' said Margaret Best, the deputy headmistress (affectionately known as Second Best), 'and now you mention it, I remember this costume too. It looked pretty dreadful even then.'

'I don't care.' Meg was trying to push Daffy's left eye back into position as she spoke. 'It's the dress rehearsal today, and already Class 8's head-dresses have drooped on me. Why on earth didn't we use REAL feathers? And did you hear that Katy Mitchell twisted her knee over the weekend, and I only chose her to be the Angel Gabriel because she does ballet and has got the costume.'

'Well, brace yourself,' said Hilary, the school secretary, 'Peter Dalglish hasn't come to school today either. Flu, his mum said when she rang in.'

Meg's eyes widened in disbelief. 'Oh, for heaven's sake, we can't manage without him! Whoever heard of a school Christmas concert without Joseph?'

'Could one of the other boys stand in?'

'I suppose they'll have to. Joseph's got a lot of words though. That's why Peter got the part in the first place. He's reliable.'

'Then maybe rather than miss the concert, he'll make it tomorrow night even if he is feeling rotten?'

'You know what a stickler Simon is about children not coming in with colds and flu.'

'Well, if we're desperate, he'll just have to bend the rules on this occasion.'

'Did I hear mention of school rules?' Simon walked into the staff room at just that moment to get a cup of coffee.

'Peter Dalglish is off with flu today. We were hoping he might be well enough for the performance this week.'

'Probably not, if it really is flu. I don't want the whole school contaminated, especially just before Christmas.'

'He's got a big part — a lot for another child to take on.'

Simon took a small sip of coffee as he looked directly at Meg. 'We'll rise to the occasion. At Heaton Road Junior Mixed, we always do. And as usual our show will be a triumph. Ah, the bell! Don't forget the staff meeting at lunch-time today, everyone, to discuss the new pupil assessment forms.'

'More forms?'

'Pupil assessment is vital,' snapped Simon. 'How else can a successful school be properly recognised?'

'Because the pupils are happy and well adjusted, and the teachers aren't sinking beneath a mountain of paperwork?' suggested Val.

'Constant monitoring,' was Simon's curt reply. 'That's the way forward. Make sure our pupils are reaching their potential – and our targets. Now don't forget to wash your cups, everyone! And . . .' His eyes fell on the untidy heap of fake fur draped over the plastic settee. 'What exactly is THAT?'

'Oh, that,' retorted Val over her shoulder as she left the room, 'is Daffy. And if she's going to reach her potential, Simon, you might feel like targeting her eyeball. It's falling off.'

He recognised her voice immediately when she answered the phone.

'Katherine, this is Robert Foster.'

'Oh, I've been thinking about calling you, but realised I didn't have your number.'

'I know. An oversight on my part.'

'The flowers were lovely. Very enterprising of you considering you didn't have my address or phone number.'

'I'm glad you liked them. Just a small token for rescuing me the other night – seeing as you turned down my offer of dinner, of course.'

'It was no trouble. And really, the flowers weren't necessary.'

'But you liked them?'

'Very much. Thank you.'

'It was a nice party.'

'Alan and Meg always have a good Christmas get-together.'

'Such a well-matched couple. Have you known them long?'

'Seems like forever. Meg has been my dearest friend since we shared a bedsit while we both took degrees in English.'

'English? But you're in finance, aren't you? That's what Alan said.'

'Public relations, but specifically aimed at the financial markets. I did a second degree in business management.'

'Impressive.'

'So he was talking about me, was he?'

'Alan? Well, I managed to prise the odd fact out of him, in addition to your contact details, of course.' She could hear the smile in Robert's voice as he replied. 'He seemed rather alarmed that I was asking so many questions about you.'

'At the party?'

'No, last night on the phone. I rang to thank him and Meg for inviting me, and told him how we met up later. It was he who gave me your number.'

Katherine didn't reply.

'Anyway,' continued Robert, 'I have another reason for ringing.' Still silence. She certainly wasn't helping him with this conversation. 'Alan may have told you that I'm on the board of SM Finance.'

'I've heard of them. Quite a small investment house, but they've had a noticeably successful run lately.'

'So successful that a take-over bid is looming.'

'Really? From whom?'

'Well, I'd rather not discuss that on the phone. Suffice it to say that any aggressive moves towards our company will be strongly resisted.'

'I see.'

'And that's where you might be able to help us. We have need of an imaginative and highly professional public relations campaign. From what Alan tells me, you might be exactly the person to help us.'

Katherine's voice changed immediately from slightly wary to definitely interested. 'That's possible. How urgent is this?'

'Very.'

'Then we should meet to discuss the situation in detail.'

'I agree. Dinner tonight?'

'Surely a meeting at your office would be more appropriate?'

'Certainly. Could you be here about four-thirty? We'll spend a couple of hours going over the current position, and then we can plan strategy over dinner. OK?'

She hesitated – but only for a second.

'OK.'

'But sir, it really hurts. Look, I can't put my weight on it.'

Chris Elliott didn't lose his rhythm folding up the school football team sweatshirts as he answered. 'Really, Steven? Then I must have been witness to a miracle about ten minutes ago when I saw you chasing down the corridor after David.'

'That was before I tripped and twisted it again, sir.'

'I see. And how come it was the other ankle you were limping on before that?'

'Was it?'

'Definitely.'

'They both hurt, sir. I'm in agony, honestly I am.' Steven Manson's round face bore a theatrically pained expression as he bent his podgy frame to cradle first one ankle, then the other.

'Now, let me think,' mused Chris, folding the last shirt thoughtfully. 'What is it about the next lesson that you're anxious to avoid? You're down for football today, aren't you?'

'No sir, rugby.'

'Well, that's OK, isn't it?'

'I hate rugby, sir. Always seem to end up under the scrum, not round it.'

'That's because you don't run fast enough. Perhaps you need more practice. Five laps round the school field might get you into shape.'

'No, sir, please . . .'

'Would you feel happier about doing gym?'

'A bit, sir. Not much.'

'Swimming?'

Steven's eyes lit up.

'Right, here's the deal. You do rugby today, because if you don't you'll let the rest of the lads down, and sport is all about not letting your side down. But starting next term, you can change sets on Monday afternoons, and do swimming instead. How's that?'

'Brill, sir!'

'But I'll be watching you. If I catch you slacking at swimming even once, you'll be on double detention for a month. Understood?'

'Understood.'

'Push off then.' Grinning from ear to ear, Steven hared off down the corridor. 'And Steven!'

'Sir?'

'You forgot to limp.'

'Oh, it's much better now, sir. Thanks for asking.' And with a loud chuckle, he disappeared round the corner.

Chris smiled to himself as he made his way through the changing rooms towards the gym. It was heaving with activity, as twenty or so twelve- and thirteen-year-old boys balanced on bars, crawled up wall frames and tumbled on to huge rubber mats. He made his way over to where an older member of the PE teaching team was supervising. 'I'll take over now, Frank. The rugby lads are all out on the pitch waiting for you.'

'This lot are half asleep,' replied Frank. 'Demob happy, I suppose, with the end of term just four days away.'

'Aren't we all?' grinned Chris, before giving a blast from his whistle which brought the class to attention. Five minutes of detailed instruction later, the boys were divided into four groups, each tackling movements on one section of the apparatus before moving on in rotation to try the others. Chris made steady progress around the hall, correcting here, advising there, his eyes constantly scanning for opportunities to give praise, correction or prevent an accident.

He loved his job. He had always loved this job. Since he had been little older than the boys in front of him now, he had known that this job would be perfect for him. If he had been more talented, or perhaps more dedicated in his teenage years, he would have liked to have competed in athletics. Somehow school studies and home life had got in the way. With a widowed mother and a younger sister in the house, money never stretched far. He had started his job in the corner grocery store on his fourteenth birthday, and somehow never got round to leaving. What had begun as a Saturday job developed into a seven day a week commitment, which saw him rushing home from school every evening to put in four hours at the shop before finishing at eight o'clock. That meant he was never around for after-school activities – and as most sporting clubs were at the end of the school day or on Saturdays, he was excluded from them.

He had no regrets at the time though. He had never forgotten the swift cruelty of the illness which claimed his father's life. Chris had been just nine years old when he stood beside his mother at the funeral. He felt her weight against him as she leant on him for support, and knew that from that moment, he had to be the man of the house. His mother had never been strong. Her slight frame and pale prettiness made her more decorative than maternal. Children bewildered her, especially her own. There was no doubt that she loved them, but when it came to practical care, her skills were sadly lacking. Often the cupboards were empty, and washing piled up in the corner of the bathroom until Chris returned from his evening job with supper in his rucksack, and the household chores still to do before he began his homework.

His long hours of work meant that he never fitted in with any particular group at school. He was an oddball, introverted and self-contained, and the fact that he was 'different' led to him being on the receiving end of bouts of bullying which were still painful memories for him all these years later. At the time, he told himself he didn't care. He was too busy for that. In fact, when it came to the decision about whether to stay on at school to take 'A' levels, he was unsure where his priorities lay. It would be more practical for him to leave at sixteen to take on a full-time job somewhere.

His mother, however, wouldn't hear of it. What she lacked in practical skills, she more than made up for in love and ambition for her children. By that time, Chris's younger sister, Gilly, at fourteen, was a talented ballet dancer, constantly needing money for lessons, exam fees and costumes. The demands of her dancing schedule left little time for her to take up the offer of evening work at the store, which meant Chris was busier than ever.

School studies throughout the day, sport at lunch-times, shop and house work every evening, followed by prep each night, left little time for anything other than exhausted sleep. Even the girls who noticed his long-limbed muscular body, thick, dark blond hair that inclined to curl, and long, angular face which tightened with determination whenever he was working or competing on the athletics field, found that their flirting glances in his direction went largely unnoticed. He seemed cool and distant, which made him more attractive than ever. Little did they know that his apparently detached manner was in fact a lack of confidence with members of the opposite sex. He certainly noticed them, but chose to kept his distance because he couldn't imagine he'd have anything to say which could interest them.

Not surprisingly for a young man to whom hard work was simply a way of life, Chris did well in his 'A' levels. His form tutor wanted him to study Maths or perhaps Physics at one of the top universities, but that would have meant him moving away from the area. Instead, Chris chose to combine his love of sport with his need to be the provider at home.

The local college ran a three-year teaching diploma in

Physical Education for secondary school level on which he was accepted immediately. It combined both academic and practical skills – and Chris loved it. Most of all, he enjoyed the teaching practice. The first time he stood out in front of a class of youngsters, their faces turned to him in a range of expressions from anticipation to boredom, he felt he'd come home. The challenge of keeping them interested, stretched and involved in sporting activities fascinated him from the start. His own enthusiasm coupled with an easy rapport with his young students made him a natural teacher. As staff went, Mr Elliott was cool. Even reluctant sportsmen like Steven with the Limp thought Mr Elliott was just about all right.

He had never married, although he would have liked the right partner to come his way. He'd thought he had found her in Debbie who had shared his life for five years until she first discovered personal fitness training, then the fitness trainer whose sessions were so personal that he married her six months later. For Chris, other girls had come and gone. Some he loved. Others he didn't miss at all.

In the meantime, there had been some surprising developments within his own family. When his sister, Gilly, finally realised that at the height of five foot eight, a career in ballet was no longer an option, she turned her attention to ballroom. Within months, it became clear that this was the form of dance in which she had been born to excel. Because of the strength, grace and co-ordination she had gleaned from years of formal training, she took to the sinuous, body-contorting moves of the samba and tango with skill and discipline combined with a releasing sense of abandon. Gone were the pink tights and neat leotards, replaced by skimpy, figure-hugging scraps of costume in glittering, see-through shades of pink and orange. She was soon noticed by Colin, son of the Director of Dance at the Hubert Scott Academy. On an individual basis, Colin and Gilly were both outstanding dancers. As partners, they were superb, a fact proved beyond doubt as they won first the county championships, then some time later the South of England final. Several years on when they finally clinched first position in a national Latin championship, they turned professional to take up a life which had consisted ever since of travelling the world, giving demonstrations and lessons. They were dancing partners, but never a couple – constantly in each other's arms, but not lovers. On the other hand, Chris's mother, Maureen, who had tirelessly sewn sequins on her daughter's costumes from her earliest dancing days, had finally fallen into the arms of Colin's father, the widowed Hubert Scott, who adored, cosseted and eventually married her. Chris was delighted – and free at last from the role he had assumed of playing parent to his own mother.

An unusual movement in the middle of a gaggle of boys on the other side of the hall suddenly caught Chris's attention. As he moved across towards them, one small body hurtled headlong across the mat, landing in a thudding, angular heap at the other end. Loud, derisive laughter broke out all round as Ben Barratt clambered painfully to his feet.

'That's enough!' Chris's voice broke through the din. As dazed and disorientated as Ben obviously was, it was clear that embarrassment was what worried him most as he quickly dismissed his grazed elbow and badly bruised knee when Chris inspected them.

'Michael Smith!'

'Sir?'

'Have you anything to tell me about what's just happened to Ben?'

'Me, sir?'

'Come here! And the rest of you boys, get on with what you were doing!'

Chris was aware of Ben shrinking and sliding behind him as together they watched Michael Smith slouch over to join them.

He was unusually tall for a boy who was just thirteen, his broad shoulders and neck supporting a head which seemed unnaturally large in spite of the cropped haircut. Perhaps because of his long limbs and undoubted strength, he was an excellent athlete, especially at sprinting and cross-country running – but his recognition of his own easy talent made him arrogant and dismissive of others. Eventually he stood before Chris, his expression a mixture of boredom and defiance.

'I saw you, Smith. As Ben ran past you, you deliberately put out your foot to trip him up.'

'You must have been mistaken, sir. It wasn't me.'

'No mistake – and don't you dare answer back when I saw you quite clearly.'

'You couldn't have done, sir. I was talking to Spoogy at the time.'

'Spoogy?'

'David Sutton, sir.'

Chris eyed him thoughtfully, before turning his attention to Ben. 'Well, Ben? Have you anything to say? I did see exactly what happened.'

'Nothing happened, sir.'

'Bullies are not tolerated in this school, Ben. That's something Smith here plainly hasn't grasped.'

'He fell over his feet, sir, because he's a wimp,' retorted Michael. 'He doesn't need anyone to bully him.'

'But you ARE a bully, Smith. Both Ben and I know that, don't we Ben?'

Ben shook his head nervously, staring at his feet rather than face the venom-filled stare of Michael Smith. 'I'm fine, sir, honestly I am. Nothing happened. I just tripped.'

'Ben just tripped,' said Chris slowly, 'while you were talking to David Sutton. Well, talking during class isn't allowed either, Smith. You and Sutton can report to me in the staff room at lunch-time. The PE cupboard needs a good clean-out, so the two of you can work IN SILENCE in there until it's completely straight. Do you understand?'

'That's not fair, sir! I didn't do any . . .'

'And I expect two hundred lines from you before you leave this evening. I MUST STOP TALKING IN CLASS AND NEVER ANSWER BACK. Is that completely clear?'

'My mum will be mad, sir. We're going out tonight. I can't be late.'

'Then you'd better start writing, Smith. Tell your mother she's welcome to come in and talk to me. In fact, I think a few words with your mother might be an excellent idea.'

Petulantly, Michael turned away, although the hatred in the stare he shot in Ben's direction was not lost on either Chris or the quivering boy beside him. Putting an arm around Ben's shoulders, Chris gently turned him away from the curious eyes of the rest of the class. 'Do you get a lot of this, Ben?'

'Sir?'

'Boys like Michael Smith make themselves feel big by picking on others who aren't able to stand up for themselves. And I bet he's only like that to you when he's surrounded by a group of his cronies. He thinks it makes him look clever in their eyes. But it's not big or clever. It just shows him up as inadequate and cowardly.'

Ben didn't reply.

'You don't have to put up with this, and it's my job as your form tutor to make sure you are protected from behaviour of this sort. But you have to be honest with me, and tell me exactly what's happening.'

'Nothing to tell, sir.'

'He's threatened you, has he?'

'He doesn't need to, sir.'

Chris nodded with understanding. 'Ben, I think you need help, but I can do nothing unless you tell me what's going on. Think about it, please. Now's not the moment, but how about we have a quiet chat after school?'

The boy stared at his shoes in miserable silence.

'All right, you could do with a plaster on that elbow. The lesson's nearly finished. Why don't you get changed, then go to the office and ask Mrs Anderson to clean and dress it?'

The boy disappeared from the hall in an instant, and as Chris watched him go, he made a mental note that a talk with Ben Barratt's parents might not go amiss either.

At four o'clock, Katherine packed the final papers into her briefcase, switched on the answerphone, and stole one final glance at herself in the mirror before she closed the office door behind her. She took in the neat dark suit and dove grey silk blouse, the immaculate cut of her almost black hair which framed the creamy skin of her oval face. She looked good, business-like and efficient – just right for the meeting ahead.

Her thoughts shifted to Robert Masters. Since his phone call that morning, Katherine had made a few calls of her own. SM Finance was certainly well thought of in the city, a small investment company with sound management and good prospects. Moreover, it was generally agreed that Robert himself was the guiding hand behind the success of SMF. Of any potential take-over bid, she had heard not a whisper; but she knew enough of the fickleness of the finance world to know that even the most apparently impregnable companies could find themselves suddenly and unexpectedly vulnerable.

She was due at his office at half past four. If she left now, she would be bang on time. Then they could talk business. He could explain his company's need for an improved, probably slightly massaged image in the light of any take-over approach, and she would prove her worth by explaining the service she could offer, and how much it would cost him. And then they could continue their discussion over dinner.

Unless, of course, her niggling suspicion was correct, and this possibility of work was simply a way of enticing her to go out with him. She had deliberately shown little interest in his offer of a date after Meg and Alan's party, and Robert Masters was plainly the sort of man who wasn't used to being turned down. If this turned out to be merely a ruse, how would she react?

Katherine smiled to herself as she started down the stairs. Then she'd have dinner with a newly eligible, highly entertaining, attractive man, that's what she'd do. After all, tonight of all nights, why on earth shouldn't she?

'Mum, it's for you!' Emma threw the phone on to the hall table, ignoring the fact that Meg was plainly loaded down and in need of help as she staggered in through the front door. Dropping an armload of costumes, a pile of books to be marked, and her bulging bag on to the floor, Meg reached for the phone, glaring icily at her disappearing daughter. It was Alan.

'I'm on my way, but the traffic's dreadful. Could take me a couple of hours.'

'No rush. I've only just got home myself. The dress rehearsal was a disaster.'

'You always say that about every school production.'

'This time I mean it. I'm NOT going to produce the school show next Christmas, and that's that.'

He laughed. 'Look, put your feet up for a bit. Have a bath or something.'

'Put my feet up? Do you know how much I've got to do this evening?'

'Do you know what evening this is?'

Her voice softened a little. 'Yes, but after nineteen years, do we really need to go out and celebrate on the actual night? Couldn't we leave it, and perhaps find a more convenient evening next week?'

'Meg, if I'd known you felt like that, I wouldn't have

bothered to come all this way back from London when I've got so much work on. For heaven's sake, it's our anniversary. We ALWAYS go out on our anniversary.'

She sighed. 'You're right – and I'm just a tired old grump in desperate need of a cup of tea.'

'Well, at least you won't have to cook tonight. Where have you booked for us to eat?'

'I haven't. Was I supposed to?'

'Never mind. Let's try that new Italian in the market place. The menu looked promising.'

'OK. See you when you get here.'

'And Meg?'

'Yes?'

'Happy anniversary, darling.'

Meg smiled as she gathered up all the bags and bits she'd dropped hurriedly on the floor, and was just moving away when the phone rang again. With a moan of exasperation, she let it all fall back to the ground as she reached for the receiver.

'Mrs Barratt?'

'Speaking.'

'Ben Barratt's mum?'

'That's right.'

'Mrs Barratt, it's Chris Elliott here, Ben's form tutor.' For a second, Meg's blood ran cold with anticipation that a call like this could only mean bad news. What now? 'Look, I don't want to alarm you unnecessarily, but I'd appreciate the opportunity to chat with you some time.'

'Why? What's wrong? Has something happened to Ben?'

'Not so much happened, as happening. I think he's being bullied in a way that's affecting his whole performance at school. We know he's bright, and we expect more from him than he's giving. He's seriously underachieving . . .'

'I know,' interrupted Meg, 'I've been desperately worried about him. I'm a teacher myself, did he tell you?'

'Ben won't tell me anything. He doesn't speak up in class, and spends most of his time trying to make himself invisible.'

'Bullying?' Meg's voice was choked with concern. 'Do you know who's involved?'

'I've got a good idea, but if Ben himself is unwilling to talk to me, there's little I can do to help unless I'm actually on hand to see.'

'I understand. You know, of course, that he's completely deaf in one ear? Bullies always pick on someone who's different, unable to defend themselves.'

'Perhaps you could have a quiet word with him? Or if you think it would help, the two of you could meet me after school one evening so that we can plan the best course of action?'

'He'll hate it if you single him out for protection just as much as he'd hate me for interfering or trying to fight his battles for him.'

'Of course. That's why I wanted to talk to you. I don't want to make a bad situation worse.'

'Mr Elliott, I really appreciate your call. Yes, of course I'll have a word with Ben, and yes, I'm sure we should both come in and see you at the start of next term. Thank you for being so thoughtful.'

'It's no trouble. Goodbye, Mrs Barratt.'

Meg's hand remained on the receiver for several seconds as she thought through the implications of the call. Then shaking herself into action, she loaded herself up once again with bags, books and costumes, and staggered through to the living room.

'I can't, not tonight. I'm BABYSITTING.' The disgust in Emma's face as she said the word was reflected in her voice. She was lying face down on her bed, holding the mobile to her ear, legs kicked up behind her.

'Ben doesn't need a babysitter, does he?' asked Matt. 'He's thirteen years old.'

'Mum says he does.'

'So how come you're both on your own this evening?'

'It's their anniversary.' Matt digested this information without comment. 'And it gets worse. Dad's going back to London as usual in the morning, and then Mum's got her school show tomorrow night.'

'Don't tell me you've got to babysit Ben on both nights!'

'Well, I'm trying to persuade him to stay with Daniel tomorrow, but I don't suppose Mum will approve of that if he's got school the next day.'

'Can't I just come over and keep you company?'

'Oh, Matt, I wish you could, but you know what they're like.'

'Have you told them about the place yet?'

'You're kidding!'

'We've got to do something about this, Em. They need to know how we feel about each other. I'm not going away. They have to get used to me being around.'

'I know.' She rolled over to hug herself into a ball, smiling as she held the phone even closer to her ear. 'Do you know how much I love you, Matt Bawdon?'

'If last night was anything to go by, yes, I think I do.'

'When did you know? That you loved me, I mean.'

'Well,' he said slowly, 'it might have been that night in the club when you were dancing with the geek, the one with spots. I took one look at him and another at you, and knew you needed to be rescued.'

'So you waded in . . .'

'You didn't seem to mind.'

'He did. He came round the next morning to tell me how upset he was, and how we ought to go out again so that I could make it up to him.'

'He was giving you another chance – and you didn't take it?'

'I hate spots.'

'I love you.'

'I love you too.'

'Tea's ready, Emma!' Meg's voice came floating up from the kitchen. 'And it's hot, so I mean NOW, not in half an hour's time!'

'Got to go.'

'I miss you already.'

'I'll ring in about half an hour.'

'That's ages.'

'I know. I'll eat fast. Love you, love you, love you . . .' And reluctantly she switched off the mobile.

Downstairs, Ben was already sitting up at the breakfast bar where their plates of lasagne and salad were waiting. A ring of the doorbell announced the arrival of Sandy.

'I couldn't help myself,' she wailed. 'They had Christmas dinner on the canteen menu today, and I just couldn't say no. The pudding was bad enough, but brandy sauce too! I've put on POUNDS!'

'Sandy, you haven't. You're just panicking. Anyway, you've been so good at watching your weight recently, you can afford the odd slip. It is Christmas, after all.'

'I'll never get into that dress now. I bought it specially for Christmas Day. We always dress up, don't you?'

'You mean you're wearing that new outfit?'

'I bought it a size too small as an incentive.'

'Well, couldn't you nip back and change it for something more comfortable?'

'I could – but I CAN'T. I just can't!'

'Why ever not? You're naturally a size sixteen. You look good in size sixteen. Dave loves you BECAUSE you're a size sixteen.'

'How could he? I was size ten when he married me. He fell in love with a size ten, and look at me now!'

'For heaven's sake, Sandy, you've had three children since

then, and Dave adores them! He wouldn't change a thing about any of you!'

'I've seen women look at him. They always fancy men in uniform, don't they — and policemen most of all. It's because they look so solid and reliable as if they know what they're doing. Women always throw themselves at masterful men — size ten women, that is!'

'Oh, Sandy . . .'

'It's all right for you. You're skinny. You don't understand how I feel.'

Meg looked down at herself critically. In truth, her figure wasn't bad for a woman celebrating her nineteenth wedding anniversary. Being fairly short, she found that any extra weight around her middle was accentuated, but her busy lifestyle and the odd keep-fit session had kept everything vaguely in proportion. Hardly any boobs, of course. She'd never had much in the way of a bust, and after two children, 'hardly any' became 'virtually non-existent'. She caught sight of her reflection in the glass of the kitchen cabinet. Shortish blondish curlyish hair around a small face with clear eyes and a nose that turned up impishly at the end. Not bad. Not particularly good but, all things considered, it could be a great deal worse.

'I could try a corset.'

'Really? What would Dave think of that?'

'It could be a pretty corset.'

'With suspenders, do you mean?'

Sandy giggled. 'Now there's an idea . . .'

'One of those frilly jobs, in red because it's Christmas.'

Sandy's eyes were alight with possibilities. 'Must go then. Oh yes, and have a nice night yourself!' And with a wink, she was gone.

It was nearly half past seven when Alan arrived, his mobile glued to his ear. With a cheery wave in Meg's direction as she sat in the living room marking books, he continued his business conversation all the way upstairs and out of earshot.

'Please, Mum!' pleaded Emma as she poked her head round the living room door. 'Can't Ben go to Daniel's just once?'

'Not on a school night – and we've had this conversation. You know the answer is no.'

'Then why can't Matt come round here and keep me company while I'm babysitting?'

Meg looked at her daughter coolly. 'Because it's a school night, Emma. Have you done your homework?'

'I haven't got any.'

'With "A" levels coming up, I hardly think that's likely.'

'It's the end of term, Mum. We break up on Thursday.'

'Emma, PLEASE! Just give me a break. You can see I'm busy, and Dad and I are rushing to get out. It IS our anniversary, after all. That may not mean a lot to you, but it happens to be important to us. We don't ask much from you, but tonight there's no argument. Do you understand?'

'You treat me as if I'm still a kid!'

'You act as if you're still a kid!'

'None of the other mothers are mean and unreasonable like you. Sally Beeson's mum goes out all night and leaves Sally on her own.'

'Good for Sally Beeson's mother. Unfortunately, yours feels differently.'

'I HATE it here! And I HATE you!'

Meg sighed. 'I'm not all that keen on you at the moment either. Now just clear off, Emma, if all you want to do is argue.' But she was talking to herself judging from the way the wall shook as Emma slammed the door behind her.

After that, Meg found it hard to concentrate on her marking. She knew she handled situations with her daughter badly, but these days the two of them seemed to be constantly at loggerheads. It was all right for Alan. He was away for most of the week, and didn't see his darling 'Goose' at her wicked worst. Nevertheless, Meg recognised that as a trained teacher, she should be able to deal with Emma's teenage tantrums and emotional outbursts with more patience and understanding. In fact, they seemed to be getting worse, the gulf between them becoming more entrenched each day. Perhaps the Christmas holiday would help, the season of goodwill and all that? Maybe, with both the term and the school show safely behind her, she wouldn't feel so exhausted all the time? Meg closed the last exercise book with relief. She certainly hoped so.

There had been no sign of Alan since he had disappeared upstairs about a quarter of an hour before. Meg glanced at her watch. Did she have time to nip next door to Val's to check on Daffy's progress? Probably not — but she'd go anyway. Yelling up the stairs in the hope that Alan might hear, she slammed the front door shut behind her and made her way up the path round to the back of the neighbouring house. She found Val sitting cross-legged on the floor, the donkey costume spread out lifelessly around her.

'How's it going?'

Unable to speak because of the pins gripped between her teeth, Val nodded encouragingly. It was at least a minute later before all the pins were safely installed and she sat back to rub her aching shoulders. Meg grinned at her friend with affection.

Val and she had first met years before during their teacher training days. They had taken degrees in their specialist subjects — English for Meg, Fine Art and Textile Design for Val — at different universities, but had met up on their year's postgraduate teacher training diploma. At the time, they weren't close, as it would have been an odd friendship between the neat, more conventional Meg, and Val, who was bohemian in dress, style and spirit.

Even now, twenty years later, her hair remained uncut, although the thick waist-length curls were more grey than the dark copper they had once been. She wore no make-up, her shoes were always either lace-up Doc Martens or open-toed sandals, her legs were bare even in the worst of winter weather. Her arms rattled with bangles and ears with long dangling hoops and beads. She was warm-hearted and practical – and one of a kind.

For years, she and Meg had gone their separate ways, only to meet unexpectedly when Val joined the staff of Heaton Junior four years earlier. At that time, her second marriage was just breaking up; at least, she and Jay had finally chosen to live separately, if only for part of each week. When the house next door to Meg, with its original Victorian features and light airy rooms, went on the market, Val snapped it up. Within weeks, she had filled the place in her own distinctive style with drapes and voile, candles, chimes and incense sticks.

'Nearly done?' asked Meg.

'Three legs down, one to go, the odd seam to repair in her tummy – and her eye, of course.'

Meg chuckled. 'Yes, it was rather alarming at the dress rehearsal to see two eyes looking in completely opposite directions. No wonder she kept falling over.'

'That had more to do with Jason mucking about in the back end. I hope you're replacing him for the show, or there'll be an accident.'

'She's looking much better. You've really worked hard.'

'Oh, I had a bit of help. Jay is good at things like this.'

'Of course, it's Monday.' Val was nothing if not loyal. She had been married twice, first to Chas and then to Jay. The marriages had failed long ago, but in both cases, the love remained. An arrangement had emerged which seemed to suit them all. Jay came on Monday night, Chas on Tuesday. Wednesday was Val's night for a rest and yoga. Thursday night belonged to Jay, Friday to Chas. Then after Saturday to herself, both of them arrived for lunch and the rest of the day on Sunday. It was a very cosy system. It worked for them, even if it raised a few eyebrows in the conservative tree-lined avenue in which both Val and Meg lived.

'Where is he?'

'Gone for a Chinese. He's come up with a good idea though. Look at this.' Val's arm disappeared inside the voluminous costume — and suddenly Daffy's tail began to wave in a most expressive way, stiffening along its length to look indignant or haughty, bending at the end as if peering around a corner, then coiling round itself with bashful shyness. 'What do you think?'

'It's great! Brilliant!'

'Jay's good at things like this.'

'Thank him for me, will you? Look, I've got to rush.'

'Aah, the anniversary . . .'

'Alan will be furious if I'm not ready soon.'

'Get going then! Don't keep him waiting.'

'Will you have a chance to look at Class 8's head-dresses too?'

'Go, will you!' replied Val with a grin. 'Forget about all this for just one evening! It will do you the world of good.'

Alan was indeed waiting impatiently as Meg slipped back into the house. 'For heaven's sake, it won't be worth us going at all if you don't hurry up. You're not even changed!'

Meg groaned. 'I don't have to dress up, do I?'

'You aren't seriously thinking of going out for our anniversary dinner in your jeans, are you?'

She grinned. 'Do you think the romance has gone out of our marriage?'

'Romance? There won't even be time for a meal, let alone romance if you don't get a move on!'

But he smiled back as she reached up to brush her lips quickly across his before racing upstairs two at a time.

The waiter led Robert and Katherine across to the far side of the restaurant where a table for two was tucked away in a quiet corner. Once settled, the two of them spent several minutes discussing the menu, selecting mussels in wine and steak Diane for him, deep fried goat's cheese and grilled sole for her. They discovered they shared a taste for fruity red French wine gleaned from holidays in the same area of Burgundy. They both loved opera, but fell asleep during ballet. They realised they had been at the same Proms concert earlier in the year, and missed each other by a day at Wimbledon. They exchanged stories of childhood and travel and ambitions. He was charming and attentive while the wine flowed as freely as their conversation.

'You never married?' he asked at last.

Katherine ran a finger round the top of her wine glass as she answered. 'No.'

'I can't believe you were never asked.'

'Not by the right person.'

'Have you met the right person?'

'It's never quite as easy as that, is it?'

He sat back in his seat, eyeing her carefully. 'I thought it was. I thought I'd found the right person in my wife, and that our marriage would last the course.'

'How long were you together?'

'Eighteen years.'

'Were you faithful?'

'Mostly.' He grinned as her eyebrows went up. 'Completely, in fact, until the last year. I believe that affair was a symptom of what had gone wrong in our marriage, rather than a cause.'

'Children?'

'Two.'

'And you still see them?'

'Whenever I can. Whenever Wendy will let me.'

'Are you divorced now?'

'Just.'

'How sad.'

'I agree – but finding myself single again does have its compensations.'

'Oh?'

'I can ask a beautiful woman out for dinner with a totally clear conscience.'

'Tell me something, Robert . . .'

'Uh-huh?'

'Is there even the remotest chance of your company being taken over?'

'None at all.'

'So this evening has simply been an elaborate ploy . . .'

'. . . to get to know you better.'

'I see.'

'Do you mind?'

She took a long sip from her glass, her eyes fixed on his. 'I'm not absolutely sure. I'll let you know later.'

And raising his glass to meet hers, his smile was warm, intimate and intriguingly dangerous.

Raising his glass to touch Meg's, Alan drank appreciatively before settling back into his chair. 'I can't believe I've finally stopped. Today has been manic.'

'For me too. You know what they say about a bad dress rehearsal meaning a great first night. I hope it's true.'

'That Swedish contract came in today – a week before Christmas, I ask you! However am I going to get their system up and running before the New Year with Christmas in the way?'

'You should see the wonders Val has worked with that old donkey costume. She's given it such a comical expression, and Jay has come up with a really good idea for the tail.'

'I suppose I might have to go over to Sweden next week, in spite of the rotten timing. That may be the only solution.'

'And worst of all, my Joseph fell ill today. I rang his mum

tonight, and she says he's determined not to miss the big night tomorrow.'

'It wouldn't be so bad if I didn't have my books absolutely full at the moment anyway. I suppose that's what comes of being at the cutting edge of the banking business. Everything lands on your plate at the same time — and of course, I'm not complaining.'

'You'll be up in London tomorrow night, won't you? Of course you will, it's Tuesday.'

'I'm hoping I won't end up working on that contract right over Christmas itself. Mind you, I may have to put some extra hours in if I'm going to get it done.'

'Only Emma wants Ben to go and stay with Daniel tomorrow, because I'm out at the school show for two nights.'

'I honestly don't know how I'd manage without a secretary like Mary. She's an absolute treasure.'

'I don't think it's a good idea though, do you? Not on a school night. No, I just think that Emma must take her turn at babysitting. It's not as if we ask her to do much round the house.'

'She's planning to work right through the week after Christmas, did I tell you?'

'Emma? I don't believe it. School work, do you mean?'

Alan looked at Meg blankly. 'Mary. I'm talking about Mary.'

The puzzled expression on Meg's face slowly changed to laughter. 'We should try listening to each other a bit more. You first. Work's going well for you then, is it?'

'If we carry on at this rate, my department will be fifty per cent up on our profit from last year with four months still to go before the end of the accounting year.'

'And you were so worried about going into the banking software business, do you remember? How long ago was that? Eighteen months?'

'More than three years. I started at the company on Emma's birthday in May.'

'Gracious. Was it that long ago?'

'I've taken on a new department, had two pay increases, three bonuses and shares in the company since then. Not bad, eh?'

'Not at all. I'm very proud of you.'

'Funny really. I never imagined myself employed in this sort of line.'

'All that training as an accountant only to end up designing computer software programs for other people's banks. Do you ever regret not having your own business as an accountant?'

'I regret not having my own business, but have no reservations at all about the area I'm working in. Nowadays banking is all about information technology. We're at the forefront of it. This is ground-breaking stuff, and I've always been drawn to innovation because it's the way to make progress.'

Meg smiled over at him as their conversation was interrupted while the waiter served their starters.

'Actually,' continued Alan popping a garlic-coated mushroom into his mouth, 'I have been thinking about setting up on my own, perhaps later next year.'

'Don't you need a lot of money behind you to do that?'

'I think I could find backers.'

'Would it mean being in competition with your current employers?'

'Yes, but only in the specialist area of banking in which I'm working at present. But I have such good contacts with customers, I think quite a few of them would come with me.'

'Sounds rather risky to me. With the children still so young, I don't think we should think about taking risks with our security at this stage in their lives, do you?'

'Frankly, Meg, if I don't take risks at this stage of my life, I wonder if I ever will. I've always wanted to be my own boss, you know that.'

'We've got a huge mortgage. Emma costs us a fortune, and that's even before she's got as far as university. And we talked about a new car in the spring. It's hardly a time to be going out on your own.'

'The financial rewards could be tremendous . . .'

'Eventually, once you've built up the business. But what happens before then, especially if customers are not as keen as you hope they'll be?'

'Well, you're working. That's a buffer for us.'

'You could hardly call a primary school teacher's wage much of a buffer.'

'And we've got a bit put by.'

'How long would that last if you're not able to earn properly for a year or two?'

'I hate working simply to make a profit for other people, Meg. I know there's money in this. That's why I've had so many bonuses over the past few months. I've given it a lot of thought, and I really think I could make a go of it.'

Meg sighed. 'I'm not convinced – but in fairness, I don't understand a great deal about your business. Why don't we decide to talk about it again in the spring? We'll have a clearer picture by then of where we're going as a family.'

Alan looked at her in silence for a while, before shrugging his shoulders and carrying on with his garlic mushrooms.

By the main course, their conversation had moved on to safer ground. The family's Christmas presents, arrangements for picking up Jean, Alan's mother, for Christmas dinner, the fact that the car could do with a service and Ben needed a haircut were all up for discussion.

It was over the dessert and coffee that a smile crossed Alan's face as he reached into his inside pocket to draw out a small package.

'Happy anniversary, Meg.'

Surprised and curious, she lifted the lid of the elegant velvet box to reveal a gold ring studded with a row of diamonds.

'An eternity ring! Alan, how lovely! Did you know how much I've always longed for one of these?'

'Of course. Try it on – but look inside first. You might find something special.'

Peering closely at the inner circle of the ring, Meg read the italic inscription out loud. '*Forever, Alan*. Oh, darling, it's beautiful. It fits perfectly, just look! How clever you are – and how wonderfully thoughtful.' She reached across to take his hand in hers, the ring sparkling against her wedding band. 'And I love you too.'

'Not a bad pair, are we?'

'A pretty good couple, I'd say.'

'Let's go home, shall we?'

'So early? It's not bed time yet.'

'Oh yes it is,' he grinned, signalling for the waiter to bring the bill.

Their coffee cups were refilled twice before Robert and Katherine finally left the restaurant. Somehow, although she kept glancing at her watch, they never quite managed to finish their conversation until they became aware that the waiters were rather pointedly watching for them to leave.

She had been careful to bring her own car, preferring to be independent about travelling home. It was too early to invite him on to her own territory. He walked beside her as they strolled towards her Audi, their hands not quite touching, their step in perfect unison.

She opened the driver's door, then turned to face him before she climbed in. 'Well, thank you. it's been lovely.'

'For me too.'

She was very aware of him as he stood close to her in the darkness, his breath warm, his eyes on hers, lips disarmingly close. Without thinking, she slipped to one side, managing to place the door between herself and him. 'Goodnight then.'

He reached out to trace the line of her cheek very softly with his index finger. 'Sleep well, sweet Katherine.'

And then he was gone, leaving her wondering if he thought her odd to be so nervous about saying goodbye — and what it would feel like to kiss him.

Meg took special care about how she looked as she got ready for bed that night. In the bathroom, after a particularly vigorous brushing of her teeth and a squirt of breath freshener, she didn't take off her make-up as usual, adding a touch of blusher and a smudge of lipstick instead. She sprayed herself with deodorant, then tipped a drop or two of the perfume Alan liked so much behind her ears. With a quick brush of her hair and one last look in the mirror which took in the sparkling ring on her finger, she smiled back at her reflection before snapping the light off behind her.

The moment she entered the bedroom, she knew he was asleep. She tiptoed over to stare down at her husband's face, peaceful and careless in slumber. 'Alan!' she whispered. 'Alan, are you awake?'

No answer. She knew there wouldn't be. With a sigh, she climbed into bed beside him, checked the alarm clock, plumped up the pillows and switched off the light.

Chapter Three

'But miss, they're GIRLS' tights!'

If the clock hadn't said twenty-five minutes to curtain-up time, and if she hadn't been at her wits' end and in desperate need of a gin and tonic, Meg might even have laughed as she stared down at Jake Barnes, tears perilously close to his huge blue eyes as he stared dolefully up at her.

'Just put them on, Jake, and stop making a fuss.'

'But they're PINK, miss.'

'You're a flamingo. Flamingos have pink legs.'

'Girls wear pink, miss. Can't I have black legs with trousers on?'

'Jake Barnes, have you ever heard of a flamingo wearing black trousers? Now, either you put those tights on yourself, or I'll get three of the girls to put them on for you! Do you understand me?'

That was it. The first tear plopped noisily on to the floor between them, as Jake's fists shot to his eyes, and he began to sob dramatically. Quick as a flash, the deputy head Margaret Best was at Meg's elbow to lead away both the sobbing boy and the offending pair of tights.

'Mrs Barratt?' asked a nervous voice behind her. 'Mum says I'm not allowed to take my vest off.'

Meg spun round to see one of the smallest girls in Class 7 eyeing her timidly. 'You're a fairy, Jessica. You're wearing a glittery frock with sequinned straps. How can you wear a vest under that?'

'I don't know, miss . . .'

'Do you think fairies wear vests, Jessica?'

'No, miss.'

'Then neither must you. Go into the girls' toilet if you want to change without all the others seeing you.'

'But I've got a cold, Mrs Barratt. Mum always tells me to keep my vest on if I've got a cold.'

'Is your mum coming tonight?'

'Yes, miss. And my aunty Pat, and my nan.'

Meg sighed, and knelt down until her face was level with the worried little girl beside her. 'Do you WANT to wear your vest under that lovely costume?'

'No, miss.'

'Then I'm going to leave the decision up to you. You can blame me, if you like. Tell Mum that I said all the fairies HAD to look the same.'

'She'll tell me off, miss, I know she will.'

'Then if you must wear it, you must – but I'll back you up if you decide not to. You can bring her to talk to me after the performance, if you like.'

'Really, miss?'

'Of course.'

Jessica's face broke into a toothless grin, before she turned to skip off in the direction of a cluster of chattering, twinkling fairies. Meg looked over towards the other corner of the room where Val was on her knees with her box of pins, totally surrounded by a gaggle of shepherds and two Wise Men. Where on earth was Myrrh? And Sue, the newest and youngest member of staff, was spooning out to a deathly pale 'Joseph' the correct measurement of Calpol, supplied with copious instructions by his anxious mother. Peter Dalglish had turned out to be a trouper after all, dragging himself in for his moment of glory in spite of his heavy cold and bleary eyes.

This year, as in all previous years, each class had been asked to devise and prepare their own contribution to the Christmas show. All the individual class performances appeared within the framework of a play acted out by the ten-year-old pupils now in their final year of junior school. This Christmas, each class's performance would be introduced by Peter Pan, Wendy and Captain Hook, who would lead the audience to first one scene then another, as they took a look at how people in other times and countries celebrated the festive season. The flamingo appeared in the jungle scene devised by Class 3, along with the snake, lion, a few apes and something which could have been an elephant or a rhino, but no one was quite sure. The Red Indians in Class 8 were looking splendid in their crêpe-paper feather head-dresses after a bit of nifty last-minute repair work with cardboard stiffening. Bless you, Val, thought Meg gratefully, remembering how her friend had still been hard at work into the wee small hours of the night before.

The grand finale for the whole performance was the traditional nativity play, performed mostly by the four- and five-year-olds who had recently joined the Reception Class. Meg made her way towards their classroom, to discover thirty excited youngsters with tea towels on their heads and cheeks pink with excitement as angel wings were pinned on, woolly sheep tucked lovingly under arms, and coffee jars cunningly disguised in metallic paper to become 'precious gifts'.

'Ten minutes to go!' Simon Foster's only contribution to the evening seemed to be his gracious welcoming speech to the parents when they arrived, his even more gracious 'thank you's' to the children and staff at the end – and these minute-by-minute countdown announcements in a thundering voice that panicked the children and ruffled the teachers before the show had even started!

'Never again,' mumbled Meg under her breath so that only Val could hear. 'It's someone else's turn to organise this show next year.'

Val glanced up in her usual calm, totally organised way. 'It will be fine. Everyone's ready. YOU'RE ready. It will be fine.'

Meg would have grinned in gratitude if it hadn't been for the tug on her sleeve.

'Mith, Thimon's been thick in the boyth's toileths. It'sth gone all over hith shoeth.'

Val nodded over towards the door. 'Look, the caretaker is already on his way with the mop. It will be fine, Meg, believe me! Now, go and get this show on the road!'

Two hours later, as the parents sipped cups of tea and munched mince pies at the back of the hall, everyone said it was the best Christmas show they'd ever seen. Did it matter that Joseph's voice disappeared completely, or that after constant wobbling and pulling throughout the whole nativity play, Mary finally yanked out her front tooth and held it out to show her mum at the back of the hall, at exactly the moment when an adorable, golden-haired angel announced that 'Baby Jesus had come down from Devon . . .'? Of course not! And when the donkey wagged his tail – WELL! It was brilliant, just brilliant! However could they better that next year?

Eventually, flushed with success and excitement, the youngest members of the cast began to look suddenly glassy-eyed with exhaustion, as doting parents gathered up the remains of their picnic tea and carrier bags of discarded school uniform, and headed for home.

'Christmas Assembly in here tomorrow at half past nine sharp!' The staff groaned as Simon Foster's clipped voice rang out across the hall. 'We need this place shipshape before we leave. Can't ask the caretaker to take on extra work at this time of night. Meg, can you manage that pile of chairs on your own?

They need to go down the end there. Let me know if you need help.'

'I need help. I've got enough on my hands sorting out this staging without doing domestic furniture removal too.'

'Well, you start on the chairs, and I'll come and give you a hand when I've finished in the office.'

'When he's finished a game of Solitaire on the office PC, he means!' hissed Hilary, the school secretary, in Meg's ear. 'Look, I'll sort out the chairs. A couple of the dads are still here. They'll give me a hand.'

It was a good two hours after the finish of the show before Meg wearily squeezed herself into the passenger seat of Val's beloved old mini. With the nativity and fairy costumes stashed in the boot, and Daffy the Donkey unceremoniously dumped across the back seat, the two women sighed with relief as the engine turned over on the third key turn. It wasn't far to their road – hardly more than fifteen minutes' walk – but neither Meg nor Val had the energy to stand, let along put one foot in front of the other ever again after the evening they'd had.

'Alan away?' asked Val as she wound down the window and lit up a cigarette.

'Until Friday. When's Christmas Eve? Sunday, isn't it? So I suppose he's at home all next week, and isn't due back in London until after the New Year. Do you know, I'm not sure exactly what he said now.'

'If he's not around, come in for a nightcap. You look as if you need it.'

Meg smiled at her in the darkness. 'Thanks, but I must get back for Ben. Emma's babysitting. You can imagine how pleased she is about that!'

'Emma?' Val caught sight of something out of her side of the car, and looked back over her shoulder to check what she'd seen. 'You mean, your daughter Emma who's just come up for air from a snogging session with Matt the Mechanic back on the wall there?'

'You're joking!' Meg was fumbling furiously at the door handle even before Val brought the car to a standstill in her driveway. 'The little madam! How dare she! I don't ask her to do much – and I can't even rely on her for a simple piece of babysitting!'

'Calm down, Meg. She's a teenager. And Ben's not a baby. He's OK for an hour or two on his own.'

'He's thirteen years old, and going through a rough patch at the moment. Emma knows I'm worried sick about him. And that's not the point anyway. I asked her to perform a simple task – and as usual, she's completely ignored me and done exactly what she wants to do. Well, this time she's had it! I'm just not in the mood tonight!'

Val put a restraining hand on Meg's arm as she tried to open the door. 'And it's exactly because you're not in the mood that you might say things you regret at the moment. Why don't you go indoors and put the kettle on, and I'll have a word with Emma?'

'Val, I appreciate your offer, but I can handle my own daughter, really I can. I'll see you in the morning.'

'Ring me. If you need anything – if you just need to let off steam – ring me.'

'What night is it?'

'Monday – and it's all right. Jay knew I had the school concert tonight, so he's gone out with the boys instead.'

Impulsively, Meg leant over to place the peck of a kiss on her friend's cheek. 'Thanks for everything, Val, especially all your work on the costumes. You made the show tonight!'

'Don't lose your cool with her. You know you'll get nowhere if you do that.'

'Night, Val – and thanks again.'

Meg considered for a second whether she should tackle Emma straight away, without at least going into the house first to empty her armfuls of costumes. Her daughter was hardly going to take her seriously while she read the riot act with Daffy Donkey's head lolling against her shoulder! In the end, she was too angry to care as she started to march down to the road towards the low garden wall from which Emma started defiantly at her mother, her hand resting possessively on Matt's thigh.

'Where's Ben?' Meg demanded.

'In bed, I suppose. Or playing on his stupid computer.'

'And why aren't you in the house keeping an eye on him, as you were supposed to be?'

'Because I can still keep an eye on him from here. Because if he tries to sneak out of the house, which we both know he'd never even think of doing, I would see him. Because I asked him if it would be OK for me to sit out here with Matt, and he was totally happy about it.'

'That's not the point, Emma. Once again, I find that I can't trust you to do as you're asked!'

'Look, Ben is fine. I'm sitting just yards away from the house. Everything is perfectly OK – so get off my back, will you!'

'How dare you speak to me like that! Is this how you speak to your parents, Matt?'

Matt stared at her coolly. 'I don't need to. My parents don't treat me as if I'm five years old.'

'Well, perhaps they should, when you encourage my daughter to behave in such an irresponsible and childish way!'

'Your daughter is no longer a child, Mrs Barratt. If you took the trouble to get to know her, really find out what she's thinking and feeling right now, you'd know that.'

Meg nearly choked with anger. 'And how long have you known Emma, Matt? Six months, is it? A week or two longer? Well, I've known her from the second she was born and I can assure you that there is very little I don't know about my daughter.'

He was infuriatingly calm as he gazed steadily at her, then

turned towards Emma, reaching up to cup the side of her face in his hand as he spoke. 'Will you be all right?'

Emma nodded wordlessly.

'This is it then. Just do it exactly as we said. OK?' Another nod, before she leaned forward to place a deliberate kiss on his lips, well aware of how much it would infuriate her mother. 'Ring me when you're ready.'

'I will,' she agreed before getting up abruptly to stride towards the house with her mother trailing behind with as much dignity as Daffy the Donkey would allow her. Meg reached the house just in time to hear Emma's door slam shut and the key turn in the lock. Good, thought Meg. Best place for her! She can just get on with sulking in her own room!

Dropping Daffy and the other costumes and bags in the study and shutting the door firmly on the mess they made, Meg pushed the knob down on the kettle before going upstairs to see Ben. Emma had been right. He was huddled in front of the computer, totally engrossed in a noisy game in which two fantasy warriors were fighting to the death with futuristic guns. Meg went over to ruffle her son's hair, knowing that he wouldn't have heard her come into his room. He acknowledged her without taking his eyes off the screen, continuing for several seconds until one of the warriors died a dramatic death, and he pressed the pause button.

'It's gone ten o'clock. You've got school tomorrow.'

'It's the end of term. We're not doing much this week.'

She smiled at him. 'Well, as a teacher myself, I'm not sure that's strictly true – but I do think you should get to bed now.'

He leaned back and stretched his arms high above his head. 'All right. This game is just about finished now anyway.'

'Did you do your homework?'

'Haven't got any.'

'How long have you been on your own this evening?'

'Don't know. I've been in here all the time.'

'Emma was supposed to be looking after you. I'm sorry she was so hopeless at the job.'

'I wasn't worried. She was cool.'

'She was irresponsible, Ben. She should have been in the house, not outside with Matt leaving you on your own. Anything could have happened.' He shrugged without comment. 'Do you want a drink before you go to bed?'

'Like what?'

'Hot chocolate and a bowl of cornflakes?'

Interest flickered in his eyes. 'Cool!'

'You get into your PJ's then, and I'll bring it up on a tray.'

It was heading for eleven o'clock before Meg had brought the tray back down from Ben's room and tucked him in, then taken a long and rambling call from Sandy congratulating her on the success of the show that evening.

'Of course,' Sandy had said with a giggle, 'I thought the back legs of the donkey stole the show!'

'I don't know how your Jason kept his balance with Craig Stevenson charging across the stage at that rate! I don't think he realised that the front end can only move at a speed the back end can manage!'

'And apart from having to keep up, Jason was working the tail too, of course. That was terrific!'

'Great sense of comic timing!' agreed Meg with a laugh. The donkey costume worked a treat after Val put so much work into it.'

'Oh yes, that reminds me,' continued Sandy, a sudden edge in her voice. 'Tell me about Miss Creaven.'

'Sue?'

'Our Darren's new teacher, I understand.'

'Yes, she is. She only joined in September, but the kids seem to like her, and she's plainly a very good teacher.'

'So I'm told.'

'Come on, Sandy, out with it! What's eating you?'

'She made such a beeline for my Dave. Absolutely blatant! Not surprising really, seeing as he couldn't take his eyes off her!'

'Oh don't be ridiculous. She's ten years younger than him!'

'And twelve years younger than me! And blonde! And slim!'

'And she's got a very nice boyfriend . . .'

'Well, she should be ashamed then, throwing herself at other people's husbands like that!'

'Like what? What exactly did she do?'

'Laughing up at him, she was, all coquettish and giggly.'

'They were probably talking about Jason and his wonderful tail technique!'

'They probably were. But did she have to gaze up into his eyes like that? And there was no need for him to stand quite so close either!'

'Did you ask Dave about it later?'

'Pretended he didn't know what I was talking about.'

'Perhaps because there was nothing to talk about. Look, I know Sue well. She's a lovely girl . . .'

Sandy snorted.

'. . . totally devoted to her boyfriend. They're apparently thinking of getting engaged on her birthday in April.'

'Well, I hope her fiancé knows what a flirt she is.'

'No, she's not.'

'You should have seen her, Meg.'

'If I had seen her, I probably would have read the situation completely differently. They may have been talking to each other, but I'm sure it was totally innocent. Poor Dave! If he as much as glances in the direction of another woman, you're convinced he's having an affair!'

'If I didn't watch him like a hawk, he would be. I'm certain of that.'

'Why? Have you got any proof that he's ever played away from home?'

'Not exactly. Just call it woman's intuition. I know the man I married. I know the kind of women he likes.'

'Yes, a woman just like you – warm-hearted, loving, a great mum, a smashing wife . . .'

'Look, face facts! I've had three children. I've got a face full of wrinkles. I'm forty in two months' time.'

'Hmm,' agreed Meg with a smile, 'completely over the hill. I do see your point.'

'Don't patronise me, Meg! It's all right for you, so petite and attractive and settled with your husband.'

'Dave is perfectly settled with you too!'

'A lot of divorced women thought that before their husbands upped and left them.'

'Sandy, Dave is not going to leave you – unless you drive him away!'

'I can't trust him, Meg. I know I can't. I don't believe any man is beyond temptation. It's the nature of the beast.'

'Don't be ridiculous . . .'

'Including your Alan. Don't you ever wonder about him, when he's away in London so much?'

Meg laughed out loud. 'No! I honestly never give it a thought.'

'Why not?'

'Because we're married.'

'So?'

'Because we love each other. I trust him.'

'Then you're a bigger fool than I am.'

Meg chuckled at the ridiculous thought. 'Besides, who'd have him? A workaholic with a gammy back, who falls asleep in the chair the moment he stops work in the evening!'

'You're being naïve, Meg.'

'You're being neurotic, Sandy.'

'I'm being realistic.'

'So am I.'

Sandy sighed. 'Then I hope you're right.'

'Kids in bed?' asked Meg, hastily changing the subject.

'Yes, but Jason has only just dropped off to sleep. He was so excited after the performance. That's show business for you!'

'Is Dave there?'

'Night shift tonight. He went on duty at ten. He won't be back until eight in the morning.'

'Have a good sleep yourself then.'

'I will. You too.'

'I could sleep on a washing line, really I could! It's such a relief that the show's finally over.'

'Just Christmas to organise now!'

'Oh don't! I'm going to soak for a good half hour in a tub of something hot and soothing.'

'Good for you! And well done, Meg. The show was brilliant. I knew it would be.'

Sandy's compliments about the show were still ringing in Meg's ears as she ran the bath and dripped in a generous helping of sweet-smelling body oil. It was as she crossed towards her bedroom that she met Emma on the landing. Meg was just getting over the surprise of seeing the large rucksack Emma had hooked over her shoulder when she also realised that her daughter was wearing outdoor clothes.

'Em?'

'We need to talk. Then I've got to go.'

'Go? Where?'

'I can't stay here any longer. I'm leaving, Mum.'

'At this time of night?'

'It doesn't matter what time it is. I can't live here any more. I don't want to.'

'So where exactly do you plan to go? Round to a girlfriend's house? Does Mel's mother know that you plan to land on their doorstop at half past eleven at night?'

'I'm moving in with Matt.'

Meg's jaw dropped.

'I've been planning to move in with him for weeks, but we thought we'd leave it until after Christmas. But I don't care now. I just want to go.'

'And what do his parents think about this?'

'They're fine about it. HIS parents are nice, reasonable people.'

'Unlike YOURS, do you mean? Will they be quite so reasonable when they hear that you're planning to move in with them?'

'I'm not. Matt's got his own place now.'

'His own place?'

'It's nothing much. We'll need to do a bit of work on it, but we won't mind.'

'Emma, you're just seventeen years old. You have your 'A' levels in six months' time. You've had three offers already from universities who want you as a student next summer. The plan has always been that you'll live at home with us until you go off to university.'

'I'm not going to university.'

'What!'

'I'm not taking my "A" levels either.'

'Don't be ridiculous! The school thinks you'll get straight "A" grades. Of course you'll be taking your "A" levels! Now stop this nonsense, take that stuff back to your room, and go to bed before I ring your father!'

'Ring him if you like – but I'm leaving anyway.'

'You can't live with Matt! Even if he were a suitable partner for you, which he most certainly is not, you have such a lot going for you. I wouldn't expect a garage mechanic with no qualifications at all to understand the potential and responsibility of an excellent intellect such as yours, but I'm not going to let you waste your talent, young lady – especially not after all your father and I have invested in your education! I'm afraid that Matt has another think coming if he believes for one moment that you're going to give up all that for a silly little boy like him!'

Emma's stare was cold and dismissive. 'That "silly little boy" is the man I love.'

'Love! What does he know about love? If he truly loved you, he'd hardly be planning to ruin your life like this now, would he!'

Emma picked up her bag and started to walk down the stairs.

'Emma! I forbid you to leave! Come back here this instant!' The girl didn't slow her pace, neither did she look back. 'Em, I'm sorry! I've done this all wrong! I'm a bit tired after the show tonight. Why don't we have a cup of tea and sit down in the lounge to talk about this?'

'No point.'

'You can't live with him! I can't have a daughter of mine living in sin! Whatever would your grandmother think?'

'Gran's more realistic about these things than you are.'

'I doubt that very much.'

'Then ask her. I have.'

'You've talked to Jean about this?'

'At the party on Sunday. We talked for quite a while about it.'

'I don't believe you.'

'Well, you've got to start listening to what you're told, Mum. You've got to start realising that other people have plans and opinions which are just as relevant as yours. And you've got to understand that Matt and I love each other, and plan to marry just as soon as we can.'

'Marry? You can't marry without our consent!'

'Then we both hope you will give it – but if you don't then we'll just wait until I'm eighteen.'

'But university? You're planning to be a doctor . . .'

'YOU planned for me to be a doctor. I'm not sure at the moment exactly what my plans are, but being a doctor is hardly likely to be part of them. A family perhaps? Matt and I would like children of our own pretty soon.'

'Emma, for heaven's sake, you're little more than a child yourself! And what about school? You've got all your studies to do for your "A" levels in June.'

'I've decided not to bother with them. I really don't think I'm going to need them.'

'Of course you'll need them! You've been working towards those exams for years!'

'Perhaps that's why I don't want to work on them any more. I've had enough of studying. I'd like to find a job which pays real money which is mine, and not just the pocket money with strings attached that you and Dad give me. I want to have my own home, earn my own wages, and live my own life. It's that simple really.'

'Emma, this is preposterous. You'll be at school at nine o'clock tomorrow morning!'

'I dropped a note into the headmistress's office this afternoon to tell her I was leaving. And as I don't plan to return after Christmas, there hardly seems any point in going in for these last two days of term. I've left school, Mum. That's it.'

'I'm going to ring your father! Let's hear what he has to say about all this.'

'I can imagine exactly what he'll say – and I really don't care. Bye, Mum!' Emma was already at the front door.

'Wait! Where are you going?' Gathering her dressing gown around her, Meg hurried downstairs towards the open door in time to see Matt at the garden gate taking Emma's rucksack from her. 'Emma! Don't do this! Matt, you must see this isn't right for her! Please, both of you, come inside and talk about what you plan to do!'

There was no answer as Meg watched her daughter sling her leg over the back of Matt's motorbike. Rushing down the path towards them, Meg's outstretched fingers almost touched the bike as it roared into life, its headlight flaring into the darkness. Emma didn't look back as Matt pulled away sharply, disappearing round the corner and out of sight in seconds.

Meg wasn't sure how long she stood there staring at the empty street corner, willing them to re-appear. Somehow her eyes couldn't shift their stare, her legs wouldn't budge, her brain didn't function. She became dimly aware that her fingers were fixed tightly round the trunk of a spindly tree which stood at the end of the kerb, as if by gripping the wood, she were keeping a grip on Emma.

She was gone. Her precious daughter, her first baby – she was gone. And Meg had no idea at all of where she was heading. Where was Matt's 'place'? She didn't even know his parents' address. Perhaps somewhere near their garage? What on earth was Matt's surname? Maybe if she could remember, it might be possible to track down a number in the book? She doubted that his parents would be any happier about this situation than she was.

Suddenly fired with a purpose, Meg flew back into the house, leaving the front door ajar as she flung herself down on the chair beside the hall phone and fumbled through the pages of the telephone directory. Bawdons – that was the name of their garage! Not a very usual surname, so perhaps she could find a private number for his family. But after minutes of scouring the list, she could only find two entries under that name, both of them with addresses some way out of town. She was almost sure that they weren't the numbers she needed. Meg slumped back in the seat, racking her brains. Someone must know where Matt lived! Who could she ask? Who COULD she ask?

She slammed down the telephone directory and raced upstairs to Emma's room. Mel, of course! Emma told her best friend everything. Frantic minutes of searching in all the obvious places for her daughter's filofax proved fruitless. Emma had obviously taken it with her. This time at least Meg knew the road in which Mel lived, and after a quick call to Directory Enquiries, she had the number safely scribbled on the pad in front of her.

It wasn't until the phone had been ringing for some time that Meg thought to glance at the clock. It was twenty-five to midnight! What a dreadful time to ring! Whatever would Mel's parents think? With a sigh, Meg realised that she didn't care what anyone thought. Her daughter's life was at stake. She had to find her.

Meg's heart fell when it was Mel's father who answered the phone, not her mother with whom she had at least a nodding acquaintance.

'Oh, I am so sorry to disturb you at this late hour, but this is an emergency.' She was aware that she was gabbling, her voice unnaturally high and nervous. 'It's Meg Barratt here, Emma's mum. I need to speak to Mel very urgently.'

'She's asleep.'

'Oh dear! Do you think you could possibly wake her?'

'I'd rather not. She has school tomorrow. Can't this wait until the morning?'

'I'm afraid not. Emma has just walked out of the house announcing that she's giving up school and university to move in with her very inappropriate boyfriend, a young man we hardly know. My husband is away in London. I'm all on my own with my young son, and I'm desperate with worry. Apparently this Matt has got some sort of flat of his own, and that's where he's taken Emma. You know what these young girls are like. If Emma has confided in anyone, it will be Mel. I'm just hoping and praying that she may know the address so that I can drive over and bring Emma back before any more damage is done.'

'Oh.' The voice at the end of the phone had softened as Mel's father recognised the plight of a fellow parent. 'Hold on. I'll go and see if I can wake her.'

Meg's fingers drummed anxiously on the table top as she waited, until she almost began to wonder if she'd been cut off. At last, she heard the sound of approaching footsteps as Mel came on the line.

'Hello Mrs Barratt.'

'Did you know about this, Mel? Did you know what Emma was planning?'

There was a hesitation as Mel considered how to answer.

'Look,' interrupted Meg, 'I'm not angry with you. I'm just worried sick, and I need help. I have no idea how to contact my own daughter, and she has her mobile switched off all the time. Have you any idea where she might be?'

'Not really.'

'Do you know where Matt lives?'

'I might know where he used to live – with his brother – but I remember Em saying something about him getting his own rooms somewhere.'

'Where? Try to remember! What exactly did Emma say?'

'I'm not sure.'

'Mel, she's handed in her notice at school. She's giving up her plans for university. She's seventeen years old and talking about getting married and having babies, for heaven's sake! She's a brilliant student, you know she is. This is a monumental mistake, you must know that. PLEASE, try to remember everything she said that might possibly be helpful.'

'I'm not sure there's anything I can tell you.'

'You mean you can't – or you won't.'

'Look, Mrs Barratt, I'm sorry you're so worried, really I am, but I don't think I should get involved in this.'

'Not get involved! You can't agree with what she's done!'

'I just know how much she cares about Matt. He's all she's talked about for months. And the fact that you've been so dead against him . . .'

'So this is MY fault, is it? I'm such a terrible mother that she would rather ruin her life completely than carry on living with me!'

'I didn't say that.'

'Mel, please, is there anything at all you can tell me? What about this brother? Where does he live? Do you know his name or phone number?'

'I'm afraid not. I think he's called Joe or John, something like that. And his flat is down by the river. Bank Road perhaps – or maybe on the other side, near the pavilion.'

'All right.' Meg's shoulders slumped. Either Mel really didn't know, or she was being deliberately vague and unhelpful. 'Look, Emma is sure to call you, isn't she? Tomorrow probably. Please, PLEASE, tell her how worried I am. Tell her to call me, or come home so that we can talk this through sensibly. If she wants to see Matt, that's fine. If she wants to bring him to our home, then I suppose that will have to be all right too. But please, just tell her to come home. Please, Mel!'

'If she calls me.'

'She will.'

'She might.'

'You won't forget. And ring me right away. Let me know what she says. Can I give you my number at school? Any time. Just ring me. Promise you will!'

'I'll try.' And with that, Mel put the phone down.

Meg stared at the receiver, unsure what to do next. Ring Alan, that was it! Alan needed to come home. He'd know how to handle Matt! With trembling fingers, she rang her husband's mobile phone number. While she waited for it to connect, she realised that she hadn't spoken to him all day. Usually when he was away during the week, he would ring her before he left work. She had been so tied up with the show that evening, she had probably missed him.

'*The Vodaphone number you are calling is unavailable. Please try later.*' Meg listened in frustration to the cold electronic voice. He'd switched his phone off! How pointless to have a mobile phone, then switch it off! He always left it on overnight when he was at home – at least she thought he did. Perhaps she'd simply never noticed.

She got up then and hurried down to the study, knowing that whenever Alan stayed up in town, he borrowed a room in the house of an old friend of his, Colin. She'd not needed to ring Colin's number for months, possibly even years, as Alan had always been easier to contact either at the office or on his own mobile phone. Now where did Alan keep the number? Would he have written it down somewhere on his desk in the study?

It was at least ten nail-biting minutes before she found it, written neatly in the back of one of Alan's old diaries. She glanced at the wall clock as she dialled. It was almost midnight. Someone else she was disturbing in the middle of the night! Gripping the wire tightly, she braced herself for a disgruntled reaction from Colin. Certainly, his voice sounded thick with sleep when he finally answered the phone.

'Colin, it's Meg here – Alan's wife. I'm so sorry to disturb you at this hour, but I need to speak to him very urgently, and I can't raise him on the mobile.'

'Alan?'

'Yes, is he asleep too?'

'He's not here, Meg. What made you think he was?'

'Not there! He's not with you?'

'He's not stayed here for ages. His job changed, didn't it, so that he could work at home more?'

'Oh!' Meg's mouth was suddenly dry. 'Um . . . well . . . there must have been some sort of misunderstanding. Perhaps I just assumed he's still staying with you. He probably did tell me about the change, and I didn't take enough notice.'

'Probably. I expect that's it.'

'Well . . .'

'Sorry I can't be more helpful.'

'Oh, that's . . . look, don't worry. It was awful of me to disturb you.'

'Hope you find him. Tell him there's always a bed for him here if he's going to be up this way a bit more now.'

'Yes. Goodbye Colin – and thank you.'

Meg blinked as she came off the phone, as if something hard had just hit her in the face. Where was he? Where was Alan? He hadn't changed the circumstances of his job, she was sure he hadn't. What had he been saying last night in the restaurant? She knew she hadn't been listening as well as she might have done because her own mind was so full of planning and preparation for the show. Her eyes narrowed as she steeled herself to think clearly for a moment. He hadn't said anything about not staying with Colin, she was sure of that. It wasn't just that she hadn't listened. He hadn't told her. Why ever not?

What should she do? Was there anyone who would know how to find him?

Mary! Of course! Alan's devoted, highly efficient secretary was sure to know what was going on. Hastily opening the family phone and address book, Meg ran her finger down the right page until she found Mary's home number. The phone was answered almost immediately.

Just hearing Mary's calm voice almost made Meg cry as she launched into a near hysterical explanation of the events of the night – the argument with Emma, the fact that she had disappeared into the night with no way to track her down – and how Meg had now lost Alan too! With occasional sympathetic clucks, Mary listened as Meg told her about the conversation with Colin.

'Well, dear,' she said at last, 'let me put your mind at rest about Alan. He's not even in London tonight. Didn't he tell you he's at a conference in Birmingham for two days this week?'

'He is?'

'And I know exactly where to find him. I dug out the number of his favourite hotel so that he could book it himself on his credit card. Hold on a moment, I've got it in my briefcase.'

'Bless you, Mary, you're an angel!'

Seconds later, Mary was back. 'The Cumberland Hotel – and here's the number. Have you got a pen handy?'

Meg hurriedly jotted down what she needed on the pad. 'Thanks, Mary! I'm so sorry about this.'

'Ask him to call me in the morning, would you? There are a few messages he should know about.'

'I will. Night!' Meg heaved a sigh of relief. It would be all right now. Alan could come home. He'd know what to do. Quickly checking the pad, she rang the hotel in Birmingham.

'The Cumberland Hotel,' said a sing-song voice at the other end. 'How can I help you?'

'Can you put me through to Alan Barratt's room please?'

'One minute please. Oh yes, here it is – Mr and Mrs A. Barratt. Putting you through!'

'No, not Mr and Mrs Barratt! Mr Alan . . .' But Meg realised from the click on the line that her call was already being connected. She was about to replace the phone and ring again, when suddenly a voice answered at the other end. A sleepy voice.

'Hello.'

Meg flung down the receiver as if it were red hot. It was a woman who answered. And in a moment of blinding clarity, Meg knew she'd rung the right room – because that was a voice she would have known anywhere . . .

Chapter Four

Val came round within minutes. When the phone rang un-expectedly just after midnight, there had been a note in Meg's voice which struck a sense of dread in her heart. Something was wrong, terribly wrong.

She found Meg standing ashen-faced in the kitchen, her eyes glistening more with shock than distress. There was something else too, evident in the rigid way in which she was holding herself, limbs stiff, fists clenched, shoulders raised. Was it anger? What on earth could have happened to bring out such a reaction in her normally easy-going, capable friend?

Gently Val led Meg through to the lounge, where she almost reluctantly allowed herself to be lowered on to the sofa. Perhaps it was the familiar comfortableness of her favourite seat which broke her, but Meg's body suddenly slumped as shining tears began to roll unchecked down her cheeks. Puzzled and feeling frustratingly helpless, Val simply put an arm around the quaking shoulders until the sobs subsided and the tightly gripping fingers relaxed as all Meg's energy seemed to drain from her.

The story came out slowly, in clipped sentences with long pauses, as though she were weighing up the relevance of each line before saying it out loud. Val listened in quiet disbelief to the events of the evening – and when the telling eventually came to an end, she didn't respond immediately, but rose instead to go to the kitchen where she boiled the kettle and collected her thoughts. Then both women sat together in the pool of light from the table lamp, neither of them touching the mugs of tea cupped in their hands.

'I have to go there, Val. See for myself.'

'How can you do that?'

'They've got to come out sometime, haven't they? And when they do, I'll be there.'

'Then what? Accuse him in the middle of the hotel foyer? Are you ready for a public scene like that? Wouldn't it be better to talk it over quietly at home?'

'He'd deny it then. He'd say I was mistaken, that it was the wrong room, the wrong hotel.'

'Well, supposing that's right? You could be putting your whole marriage at risk if you're wrong about this.'

'There's no mistake.'

'How can you be so sure?'

Meg turned to stare straight into Val's eyes. 'Because I know. I knew the moment I heard her voice.'

'But she said so little. It was the middle of the night. Perhaps it only SOUNDED like her. It could have been anyone, anyone at all.'

'It was her. And the odd thing is that now I think about it, I'm not really surprised. Shocked, of course – shattered and destroyed by the knowledge – but not surprised. Does that mean that somewhere deep within me, I knew? Were the signs there all the time, but I chose to close my eyes to them?'

'I still think you may be dreadfully wrong about this, and I worry that you might do a lot of damage by acting on impulse.' Meg shook her head. 'Listen, love, you're exhausted. It's the end of term. We've had that inspection at school, not to mention all the extra work for the Christmas show. Then there was the party to organise on Sunday, and all this fuss with Emma. You're overwrought – and who can blame you?'

'You don't believe me.'

'I don't know what to believe. You and Alan have always been such a solid couple.'

'I thought so . . .'

'Then isn't it most unlikely that he's having some kind of sordid affair? Why would he? He loves you. He adores his kids. I just think there may be an enormous misunderstanding here.'

'All the more reason for me to see for myself. What's more, I want them to see me, so that there's no possible margin for error.'

'Then I'm coming with you. If there's even a shred of truth in this, you're going to be in no fit state for the journey home again.'

'No. Thanks, Val, but I need to do this alone.'

'Meg, I really don't think . . .'

'Besides, I need your help another way. I can't leave Ben alone while I go to Birmingham. Could you possibly sleep here tonight?'

Val saw the determination in Meg's eyes. 'All right. And what about school in the morning? Do you want me to say you've gone down with flu or something?'

'I shouldn't ask you to lie for me, but I really haven't got the strength to tell the truth right now.'

'Of course not. What time do you plan to leave?'

'I'd like to be there by seven o'clock in the morning. I reckon the journey will take about two hours, and then I've got to track down the hotel. I always find that city so confusing.'

'And it's one now. How about getting a couple of hours' sleep before you leave?'

Meg nodded half-heartedly, knowing there would be no sleep for her that night. As she made her way upstairs to sort out bedding in the spare room for Val, it crossed her mind that she might never be able to sleep again. While she changed the duvet and pummelled the pillows into shape, she realised that the family photo albums were kept in the top cupboard of that room. Dragging over a chair so that she could stand on tiptoe to pull them down, she dusted them off with her dressing gown sleeve as she took them back to her own room.

She wasn't sure if she slept. Her mind wasn't clear enough to know if the images that danced before her of Ben and Emma when they were small, and of her and Alan on their wedding day, were photos from the album, or simply part of a frightening, bewildering dream. The alarm brought her round with a start. Hands cold, her body clammy, she leapt out of bed to swill cold water on her burning face and eyes. She dressed with care, choosing a trouser suit which had always made her feel good and given her confidence in the past. That morning, it seemed the magic had deserted it.

The clock read four-thirty as she turned the key in the ignition. Her elderly Fiesta was hardly built for speed or long distance, but it felt like an old friend as they travelled steadily towards the motorway. On this extraordinary mission, with her settled life so unexpectedly in tatters around her, she took comfort in the familiar squeak of the windscreen wiper, and the rattle from the boot which usually irritated her so.

In the end, the hotel wasn't that hard to find. She found it more by luck than knowledge, but by six forty-five, she was squeezing into the last remaining space in the hotel car park. It was at that moment that her stomach started to churn with apprehension, as if her arrival at the building gave substance to the reality of what she might discover there. Was she behaving foolishly? And what exactly did she plan to do? March up to their room and confront them? Wait outside the breakfast restaurant? And supposing this was all a terrible mistake? How long would she sit there before she gave up and accepted that either she had somehow missed them, or they had never actually been there at all.

Then she looked up to find herself staring at the car directly opposite her. The Volvo estate was Alan's pride and joy. He had cleaned it at the weekend. Ben had helped him. She could see still the streaks where Ben couldn't quite reach the centre of the roof on his side. The poignancy of the memory of her husband and their son working happily on the car together brought the prick of tears to the back of her eyes. Abruptly she flung open her door and climbed out. No time for tears now. No place for them either. Tears meant sadness, not the blind anger which consumed her at that moment.

If the man behind the reception desk was curious about the pale, tight-lipped woman who arrived at such an early hour to place herself straight-backed in the seat right in front of the lift, he made no comment. In fact, as the hotel came to life, and the first guests arrived in the foyer to check out, gather their luggage and order taxis, he almost forgot she was there. Some time later, as the clock hands crept round towards seven-thirty, he realised with surprise that she hadn't moved an inch.

'Can I help you, madam?' His voice made her jump as it broke into her thoughts.

'I'm fine, thank you.'

'Can I get you anything? A coffee, perhaps? As you can see, our breakfast room is open.' He gestured to the entrance of the restaurant which was only a matter of yards away from the lifts.

'No thank you.'

'Are you waiting for one of our guests?'

'Yes.'

'Why don't I ring the room for you? What's the name?'

For a moment, panic flashed in her eyes before she shook her head and looked down so that he would be in no doubt that conversation was not welcome. 'I'll wait, thank you. I'll just wait.'

✳   ✳   ✳

87

When Katherine's mobile rang, she knew straight away from the phone number which flashed up on the display that it was Robert. With a smile she put the receiver to her ear.

'Sorry to ring so early, but I'm about to go into a breakfast meeting. Just wanted to remind you about this evening. I've got the tickets.'

'I'm looking forward to it. I've been wanting to see that performance for ages. I don't seem to know anyone else who shares my passion for obscure Italian opera.'

'You do now. Do you fancy a bite to eat before the performance – or shall we have a proper supper afterwards?'

'Before, I think. Early start tomorrow.'

'Not that you need your beauty sleep. I bet you're lovely in the mornings.'

She laughed. 'Hardly. I'm a terrible grump until I've got at least two cups of coffee inside me.'

'I'll look forward to the possibility of discovering that for myself.'

'Don't hold your breath.' But he could hear the smile in her voice as she replied.

'Could you make half past six at Alfredo's? It's only five minutes from there to the theatre. I'll book a table.'

'Fine. Goodbye till then.'

She snapped the phone shut thoughtfully. Was she right to encourage him? He was alarmingly straightforward in his wish to take their friendship further. It was clear that Robert Masters was used to getting his own way. She didn't like domineering men. She never had. So why had she agreed to go to the opera with him?

Because Christmas was coming – and memory of other Christmases spent alone made her realise how much at this time of year she longed for company, especially male company, even for just a few short hours before self-inflicted loneliness claimed her again.

*　　*　　*

88

Meg jumped when her mobile rang. Fumbling to find it in her bag, she recognised Ben's voice immediately.

'Mum, where are you? And where's Emma?'

'Em's gone to stay with a friend overnight. And I needed to come to Birmingham.'

'You didn't say anything last night. Why aren't you at school today? And you never go to Birmingham.'

'I decided quite suddenly. It was a bit of an emergency.'

'Why? Where exactly are you?'

'In a hotel.'

'Whose hotel?'

'Dad's. He needed me to bring him something – so I have.' It struck Meg that she'd quickly become glib at telling lies. Hadn't she always impressed on the children the importance of being honest and truthful?

'Oh,' replied Ben. 'Val's here. It doesn't feel right without you – and Emma owes me a pound. I needed that today. When are you back?'

'Oh, before you get home from school. Tell you what, how about shepherd's pie for tea tonight? Your favourite.'

'OK. Did you fill in that form about the London exhibition trip next term?'

'Ben, I'm sorry. I'll do it tonight.'

'It was due in yesterday. Mr Elliott said anyone who didn't remember it today would get detention.'

'I can't believe I forgot. I've been so busy, although that's no excuse. I'm dreadfully sorry.'

'You'll be back tonight then. Promise?'

'Of course. Tell Mr Elliott it was all my fault. He'll have it tomorrow without fail. Right?'

Ben was plainly not convinced. 'Just come home, Mum. Val doesn't even know what to put in my packed lunch.'

'I love you, Ben. And I'll put all your favourite things in your packed lunch tomorrow.' But Ben had already put the phone down.

Meg looked again at her watch. Gone half past eight. Where on earth was he? Surely if he was going to a conference, he would be coming down to breakfast by now? Alan was always such an early riser. But then, that was when he was at home. With his wife, not his mistress. Meg settled back in the chair, and resumed her steady gaze at the lift doors.

Alan ran his hand over his chin to make sure his shave was complete. Packing away the razor, he slapped on his favourite aftershave, and slipped the bottle back into the toilet bag. He looked around the room as he put on his suit jacket. Just the last few things to pack before he left the hotel that morning.

He reached over to the bedside cabinet, noticing that it was twenty-five to nine as he folded up the alarm clock and put it in the pocket of his overnight case. Just time for a quick breakfast. For a man who only ever had a single slice of toast at home, he found he looked forward to the luxury of the full English breakfast as one of the pleasures of staying in a good hotel.

'Ready?' he asked.

'Almost.' She was sitting at the dressing table, dabbing a tiny bottle of light, flowery fragrance on her temple, wrist and throat. He found himself smiling just to watch her. He never tired of watching, loving the way she moved, the neat order in which she laid out her clothes and shoes the night before, the warmth in her eyes as she spoke to him, the memory of her arms drawing him close.

'Right!' She stood to slip her feet into elegant black court shoes, checking the line of her jacket in the mirror before she picked up the door key and handed it to him. 'Let's go!'

She spotted them the moment the lift door opened. Alan came out first, turning back to lend an arm to the woman by his side.

The intimacy of the gesture shook Meg, and perhaps it was the way in which she sprang to her feet, or the cry she didn't even know she made, which attracted his attention.

His eyes widened at the sight of her, registering first curiosity, then realisation, and finally horror, all in one split second.

'Meg! What are you doing here?' But she didn't answer him. Her eyes were fixed on the person beside him, the woman who was staring back at her in appalled disbelief.

'Hello Katherine.' Meg managed the few steps necessary to bring her face to face with her oldest friend, drawing back her hand to slap her cheek viciously. Then without another word, she turned on her heel, and ran out of the hotel as fast as her shaking legs would carry her.

Chapter Five

She didn't remember much of the next hour. She couldn't recall
finding her car, nor how she managed to navigate blindly out of
the city on to some motorway or another. It wasn't until she saw
a service area sign that she realised she was totally unaware of
everything around her with no idea exactly where she was.
Glancing down at her white fingers tightly gripping the steering
wheel, she knew she could run no further. She had to stop.

Just as she was fumbling to collect all the bits which had
fallen on to the passenger seat from her handbag, her mobile
rang. The noise startled her, and she almost answered the call
until she realised that the number which flashed up on the
display belonged to Alan. She switched the phone off and threw
it out of reach on the back seat of the car.

The drizzling rain matched her mood so she didn't hurry as
she walked from the car park to the service station entrance,
aware that without a coat she was getting soaked through, her
hair hanging in damp tendrils around her face. Seeing herself in
the expanse of mirrors in the Ladies shocked her. Her reflection
was a parody of herself – her clothes, her bag, her hands – but
the face staring back at her was both familiar and yet different,
haunted and gaunt. Her mascara had run, her lipstick gone. She
felt stripped bare and exposed, devoid of pride or control,

changed in every way from the Meg she knew. But then, after what had happened, how could that unsuspecting, trusting woman ever exist again?

She leaned forward to splash cold water over and over her face. After drying her cheeks with a tissue from her pocket, she quickly drew a comb through her lank hair and headed for the coffee shop. How long she sat there over a cold cappuccino she neither knew nor cared. It wasn't until she looked down to see the brand new eternity ring sparkling on her finger – the ring so lovingly engraved with the word *Forever* as a token of their nineteen loyal and united years – that she snapped to attention. Tugging frantically at the ring, she was on the point of deliberately dropping it into her half-empty coffee cup when she found herself almost smiling at the realisation that however much the ring offended her, she was simply too practical to make such a gesture. Instead she threw it carelessly into a dark corner at the bottom of her bag.

She couldn't think about Alan. She couldn't cope with his betrayal and disloyalty. And she couldn't begin to analyse her feelings about Katherine. Perhaps in time she would have to hear the details – how, when, and most of all, why – but for the moment, she knew she couldn't bear the answers, so preferred to avoid the questions. All that mattered to her now was her children, Ben and Emma. Where was Emma? How would she react when she heard about her beloved father and her adored godmother? She'd come home, of course. She would stand with her family, Meg was sure of that. At least, she hoped she could be sure. First of all she had to find Emma, tell her that the upset between them the night before was simply irrelevant now. Much to her surprise, Meg realised that in her misery and confusion, she longed for the company of her daughter above all else.

And then there was Ben. Poor bullied, partially deaf Ben who surely had enough problems to face without his father adding to them? And it was Ben that filled her thoughts as she made her way back to the car and found the road for home.

Chris didn't normally go back to his form room at lunch-time, as more often than not he was involved in training sessions for one of the many school sports teams at that time of day. But when the list of fixtures for the Senior Football League was in his desk rather than with him as it should have been when he had a practice session with the first team that day, he got the boys working on passing techniques, then dashed back to dig out the paper. He rushed in so quickly that he was almost on his way out again before he realised he was not alone. Sitting right in the corner of the room, tucked behind a pile of coats and PE bags was Ben Barratt.

'Ben?' The boy looked guilty, knowing that unless the weather was really bad, form rooms were out of bounds during recess. 'Shouldn't you be having your packed lunch with everyone else in the hall?'

'Yes sir.' Ben scuttled to pack his sandwiches back into the box in an attempt to escape from his form teacher's stare.

'Don't rush off. Tell me why you're here. Wouldn't it be more sociable to have lunch along with all the other lads?'

When Ben didn't answer, Chris perched himself on a nearby desk so that he was almost at the same level as the obviously embarrassed boy.

'Things a bit rough, eh?' Still no reply. 'Anyone in particular – or everything in general?'

'I'm all right, sir.'

'Then why are you hiding?' Ben shrugged. Chris leaned back slightly, eyeing him with concern. 'If certain members of the class are making life difficult for you, then as form teacher – and I don't mean just yours, but theirs too – I need to know. I will not tolerate bullying in my form, Ben. Please trust me. I can help – but you do need to tell me what's going on.'

'I can't, sir.'

'Because you think it will make things worse for you?' Ben's shoulders slumped in obvious acceptance.

Chris sighed. 'Look, I think perhaps school is the wrong place to talk about this. I know you're worried about being seen talking to me, and what loudmouths like Michael Smith will do if they think you've snitched on them. But bullies only pick on people they think can't defend themselves. It's the weakness and compliance of the victim which gives bullies their confidence and strength. The answer is for you to stop being the weak underdog. That's what I'd like to discuss with you – and with your mum too, if you'll agree to it.' Ben's eyes opened wide in horror at the suggestion.

'I've already spoken to your mum, and she's as worried about your welfare and happiness as I am. Let's put our heads together, and see if we can help you sort this out. You can beat this, you know. With a bit of support, I know you can.'

Ben stared miserably at his sandwiches. 'How could you know? How could you possibly know how it feels?'

'Because I've been in exactly your position. I was a little older than you when I went through a tough time at school. When my dad died, my mum really didn't cope at all well. Money was tight, so I never seemed to have the right kit, and my uniform was always tatty and too small for me. To make a bit of extra money, I ended up working at a local store for several hours after school every night. That made me different, because it meant I was never around to get involved in clubs or social activities with any of the other lads. There was one particular crowd who used to follow me around calling me 'Mummy's boy'. They'd make fun of what I was wearing, and steal things from me so that I'd get into trouble at school. They even used to come into the shop to wind me up until the shop owner banned them.'

'So what did you do?' There was a spark of interest in Ben's expression now.

'Well, I can't pretend there was an easy answer. There never is. But bullies get pleasure from seeing a reaction in their victim, so I decided I had to give the impression that I really didn't care what they thought of me, when in actual fact I cared very much indeed. It took a lot of courage, and they'll never know how many times I went home and bawled my eyes out – but I just wouldn't let them see they were getting to me. In the end, when I didn't react, I became a bit boring so they turned their attention to some other sucker.'

Ben nodded stiffly, plainly not convinced that finding courage in himself was an option available to him.

'Look, I must get back to football practice – but feel free to stay here and finish your lunch in peace. Term breaks up tomorrow, so we'll both have a think about this over the Christmas holiday, OK?'

But as Chris hurried back to where the first eleven were still practising their passing techniques, his heart went out to poor Ben Barratt who seemed such a misfit. How well he remembered that feeling from his own childhood. And how ironic that it's always the most deeply hurtful memories in life which reach out over the years to haunt the grown man.

Meg was lying on the bed when the phone rang. She had been home about an hour, instantly collapsing on the bed not to sleep, not to cry, but simply because she could think of nowhere else to be. She stared at the phone for a long time before she decided to answer it. If it were Alan, she knew she wasn't ready to face him yet. Her mind was too muddled, emotions raw, her body too exhausted to cope with him now. The relief when she heard Val's voice was overwhelming.

'Meg? Are you all right? What happened?'

Meg sank back into the pillow, unsure how to begin. This was the first time she had spoken since seeing Alan and

Katherine that morning, and she wasn't sure she could trust herself to mouth words that were fair and sensible. 'Well, I was right.'

'Katherine was with him? Did you speak to them?'

'Not really. I just stood and stared at them.'

'They must have been shocked to see you there.'

'I think Katherine was more shocked when I slapped her round the face in front of everyone in the hotel foyer.'

'Well, what did she expect!'

'Then I just left.'

'And you did that long drive home after an experience like that? I wish I'd gone with you.'

'I don't think the school could cope with two members of staff missing at short notice right now. What did Simon say? Did you tell him I had flu or something?'

'I was a bit vague about exactly what you were suffering from. Betrayal and heartache are hardly medical terms he'd understand.'

'How did they manage with my class?'

'I rang Simon quite early this morning so he was able to get in a supply teacher. And I gave him the impression that you might not be well enough to make tomorrow either. I hope you don't mind, but with term about to end, I thought you'd probably need this time at home.'

'Thanks, Val. And thank you for your patience and under-standing last night. I don't know how I . . .' For the first time since her meeting with Alan, Meg began to cry. Anger had been nearer than tears ever since she'd left the hotel, and the icy rage inside her had carried her home. Now, hearing the sympathetic voice of a friend was disarming, penetrating the shield of brittle self-protection she'd drawn around herself.

'Oh Meg, I'm so sorry. This should never have happened to you. I still can't believe it.'

'There is no doubt at all that it's true. My husband is having an affair with my dearest and most trusted friend — and they've

98

killed the heart of me. The two people I love most in the world apart from my children have joined forces to deceive and betray me.'

'Shall I come round? I've got half an hour before lunch-time's over.'

'No. Thanks, but I'm better on my own right now.'

'I've got a meeting straight after school, but I'll pop round when I get home.'

'I think there will need to be some painful conversations here this evening. I suppose I'll have to say something to Ben, because he'll want to know why his dad isn't living here any more.'

'Is that definite? Alan isn't coming back?'

'The decision is mine, not his. I don't even think I want to see him at the moment, let alone have him come back here as if nothing has changed.'

'You're going to have to face him soon though, aren't you? Have you any idea where he is?'

'None. And I really don't care.'

'And Emma? Have you heard from her?'

'Do you know I'd almost forgotten about all that fuss last night. We'll sort it out. She'll probably come back this evening, and I can tell her what's happened then. You know how she adores her dad – and because, in her normal efficient way, Katherine took her godmother's duties very seriously, Emma always loved and felt close to her too. I wonder how Em will react to this news. She'll probably feel as shocked and hurt as I do.'

'Well, in that case, I won't come round until you call me. Don't try and face this alone, though, Meg. I'm right here for you. Ring if you need me – promise?'

'I promise.'

The familiar sound of children shrieking during their play time moved up a decibel at Val's end of the line. 'Must go. Take care, Meg. I'm thinking of you.'

Meg leaned back against the pillows as she replaced the phone. Sleep would be welcome, but it wouldn't come. How could she possibly rest when her mind was racing, teeming with tangled images and rambling, inconclusive thoughts? She tried to focus more clearly. She needed to make plans, work out what would be best, decide what to do . . .

Because it was the end of term the following day, the regular after-school rugby practice was cancelled that Tuesday. For Chris, that was quite a relief, partly because it was Christmas Eve on Sunday and he hadn't yet done any shopping at all, and partly because he was looking forward to his session at the fitness club that evening which could not only start a bit earlier than usual, but end rather later in the company of the lads who regularly met up after training in the club bar.

He noticed from the school clock above the door that it wasn't even four o'clock as he made his way to the car. Good! He could be in the shopping arcade in ten minutes, and back home an hour later. He hated shopping, and where Christmas was concerned, the safe options were always the best – perfume for his sister, Gilly, a bottle of whisky for her partner, Colin, a pair of slippers and some continental chocolates for his mum, and a box of two hundred cigarettes for Hubert. That list shouldn't take long!

He was fiddling with the dial on the radio as he came round the corner, so nearly missed seeing the group of boys until he'd almost passed them. He was dimly aware that he recognised a few faces from his form standing in a circle on a grassy verge set some way back from the road. He idly wondered what they were doing, when in an instant he saw the menacing face of Michael Smith, and realised that almost certainly the person in the middle of that circle was Ben Barratt. Chris stamped on the brakes, failing to grab his bag on the front seat before it spilled its contents over the floor as it was propelled forward by the sharp stop. The group of boys were momentarily distracted by the screech of tyres, parting slightly as they stared curiously at the car and recognised with alarm that it was their form teacher who was climbing out and striding towards them.

What happened next stopped Chris in his tracks. One minute he was staring at the terrified face of Ben Barratt, clutching his satchel in his arms. Next, he watched from a distance as the boy's expression changed. With the attention of the group around him turned towards Chris, Ben threw down his bag – and ran! He ran like the wind, head up, shoulders back, legs thundering away in long, solid strides. Before his group of antagonists had even realised he'd gone, Ben was round the corner and almost out of sight.

Chris watched in amazement. This was the boy who had always hidden at the tail end of the crowd in sports lessons, reluctant to try anything, shrinking into the background with his reputation for clumsiness and having two left feet. And there he was – haring into the distance like a gazelle!

The boys seemed as amazed as Chris himself. He, however, was not in the mood for friendly chit-chat. Marching over to pick up Ben's bag, he turned to tower over a rather surprised Michael Smith.

'Make you feel big, does it, Smith? Having a crowd of cronies around you when you pick on someone who's all alone and unable to defend himself? I'm appalled at your behaviour – ashamed to think that most of you are in my form! Smith! You will be in school at eight-thirty in the morning, so that you and I can go to the headmaster to find out what he thinks about the fact that you're a cowardly, despicable bully. And the rest of you, I'll deal with you tomorrow. Now get off home!'

Pale-faced and silent, the group dispersed in twos and threes, heads bowed as they whispered together once they were sure they were far enough away to be out of earshot.

'Matthew!' Chris called after one of the stragglers at the back of the group. 'Do you know exactly when Ben lives?'

'Girons Avenue, sir, on the other side of the park. Not sure of the number, but I know it's the house on the corner opposite the phone box.'

'Thanks, Matthew. Get off home now.'

Chris looked towards the direction in which Ben had disappeared. If he kept going at the rate he'd started running, the boy would have reached the park by now. Best to try and head him off at the gate on the other side. Hurrying back to the car, Chris sped away round the corner. Minutes later, he ground to a halt outside the park gate nearest to Girons Avenue, quickly getting out in the hope that he could see Ben approaching. He would probably have stopped running by now, of course. A young, untrained lad couldn't keep up that pace for long. It was amazing what the body was capable of when it felt under threat.

Then Chris saw him. Some distance away, Ben rounded a small copse of trees at a speed which didn't seem to have lessened at all from the pace at which he'd started. Chris watched in stunned fascination as his pupil kept up the rhythm and momentum of a seasoned athlete. Where on earth had this come from? The boy had unbelievable talent!

When Ben became aware of Chris standing between him and the gate he needed to get through, his apprehension showed as he began to shorten his stride. He was barely running by the time he was near enough to see the delight and admiration in his teacher's face.

'What a dark horse you are, Ben Barratt – and what a lot we have to talk about! Sit on the bench and get your breath back for a while, before we go and have a chat with your mum!'

There was someone in the house! Meg sat bolt upright as she heard the familiar creak of the bottom stair. Glancing around her in panic, she realised from the dull light fringing the edge of the closed curtains that the sky had clouded over with the early dusk of the long winter evening. She must have nodded off – and now she was caught off guard and vulnerable.

'Meg?'

Alan's voice was soft, as if he were too uncertain of her reaction to dare speak louder. She backed away from him, pulling the duvet tightly up around her.

'How dare you come here! How dare you!'

'Where else could I go? We need to talk . . .'

'I have nothing to say to you!'

'But there's so much I need to explain . . .'

'I saw everything I needed to know. The shock of that is bad enough. I can't cope with more. Please, Alan, not now – not yet.'

'Meg . . .' His voice broke at the sight of her and the anguish in her expression as she stared back at him. 'Meg, I am so sorry.' The words came slowly, deliberately, as if from the very depths of him. 'So very sorry.'

'Sorry for me, or sorry you got caught?'

'For us. Because it's happened. Because it ever started at all. Because I've hurt someone I love dearly . . .'

'Because you couldn't resist loving someone else too! It is love, is it? Or was Katherine just a bit on the side? A convenient, pleasant diversion that no one was supposed to know about, least of all me and our children.'

'It's so much more complicated than that . . .'

'How long has it been going on, Alan?' He didn't answer immediately, but moved instead to perch on the end of the bed furthest away from her. 'How long? Months? Years? Nineteen years perhaps, since Katherine was matron of honour at our wedding? Has our whole marriage been a lie?'

'No! Being married to you, our family, has always meant the world to me . . .'

'But it wasn't enough, was it? You wanted Katherine! Of all

the women in the world, you chose my most loved and trusted friend. Why? Because you knew that would inflict the most pain? What did I ever do to you, Alan, that you felt the need to kick me so hard?'

'It wasn't about hurting you. That was never our intention . . .'

'So what was OUR intention then – apart, of course, from the fact that I was never supposed to find out? That we could all continue in a happy little trio with me in blissful ignorance, and the two of you having a good laugh about me when you're in bed together?'

'It wasn't like that. Both Katherine and I love you very much, you must believe that. It's just that we found we couldn't help loving each other too.'

The fight in Meg seemed to desert her then. Her face crumpled, shoulders sagged, eyes closed to shut out the painful scene she was going through. 'Of course you love her. She's beautiful, intelligent, caring, good company, a wonderful friend. I've always loved her. Why shouldn't you?'

'We really didn't mean it to happen. We fought against it.'

'It's a pity you didn't fight a bit harder for our marriage.'

'Knowing we were hurting you has been difficult for us both to bear.'

'But you were able to grin and bear it all the same.'

'Don't, Meg. Don't torture yourself by imagining that you didn't matter in all this. What's happened has got nothing to do with a lack of love for you . . .'

'It's just that you love Katherine more.'

He sighed, running his fingers through his hair as he tried to clarify his thoughts. 'Honestly,' he said at last, his eyes fixed on Meg, 'I have no idea what I feel. I find myself in the position of loving two remarkable women – loving them for different reasons, in different ways, but loving them both very deeply.'

'Fine, well, that means very little to me now. I simply have to accept that the husband I thought I could trust has deceived and betrayed not just me but this whole family. And because of that you no longer belong here, Alan, and I'd like you to go.'

'Look, I know what I've done is dreadful and probably unforgivable, but we can't leave it like this. I can't just walk away from nineteen years of all we've shared and built up together without both of us being absolutely certain that we're better off apart. What about the kids?'

'Yes, what about the kids? Did you ever think for one moment of the effect your affair would have on them? Especially on Emma? She's always been a Daddy's girl, and we both know how close she is to Katherine. What sort of example have you set her? How do you expect her to react?'

'What I mean, Meg, is that right now everything is a mess — a painful, dreadful nightmare — and I know I must take the blame. I will leave now, but only on the understanding that this is not the end. I need to know, almost as much as you do, why this happened, what it means. And if our marriage was so idyllic and perfect, how did it come to this?'

'It was probably my fault, is that what you're saying? You have an affair with my best friend, but it's my fault! Oh, I know, you can tell everyone that your wife doesn't understand you. Well, let me spell it out to you, Alan. I understand all too well — and I'd like you to leave now, PLEASE!'

For a moment, it looked as if he were going to speak again, but one look at the determination and distress in Meg's face made him think better of it. Reluctantly he rose to his feet and started towards the door.

'How long, Alan? I need to know. How long has this been going on?'

He didn't even look back when he spoke, shame and defeat etched into the line of his shoulders as he stood in the doorway. 'About a year.'

'A year,' she repeated tonelessly. 'A whole year – and I never had the slightest idea. How stupid can you get?'

She heard the door bang behind him. She wanted to move, then somehow she didn't. Instead she stayed huddled in the bed, duvet pulled up to her chin, staring at the bedroom door as though any second Alan may reappear. It was several minutes before she allowed both the taut muscles in her shoulders and her vice-like grip on the duvet to slacken a little.

It was then that she realised she hadn't told him. The whole business had started with the shock of Emma leaving home. Alan had always adored his beautiful, strong-willed daughter, his 'Goose'. Meg should have told him – and she'd forgotten.

At that thought, she swivelled round to pick up the phone, thumping in the number of Emma's mobile. It was switched off – ironically for a girl who seemed to have the phone permanently glued to her ear. Should she leave a message? Meg tried to decide whether to speak as she heard Emma's bright voice on the answerphone. What could she say? After last night. After this morning. What could she say in twenty seconds that might suggest to Emma that there was a great deal she needed to know?

'Speak after the tone!' invited Emma's voice.

Still uncertain, Meg began. 'Em, something's happened. It's about Dad and – well, just about Dad. I need to talk to you. You must come home really urgently. Forget about last night. This is important, really important. Ring me. Phone as soon as you can, Em, please . . .'

Damn! Meg was aware that her message ended on a note of pleading and the start of tears. Emma would hear she was crying. Em hated tears unless they were her own.

Meg caught sight of herself in the wardrobe mirror. She looked dreadful, her pale face puffy, hair like a scarecrow's. Half-heartedly she dragged herself to her feet. She didn't have the energy to take a shower. A swill of cold water over her face revived her enough, plus a few brutal strokes with a hairbrush, a clean pair of trousers and sweatshirt.

The phone was ringing. Her hand hovered over the receiver for a moment while she tried to decide who it was. Alan? Val? Emma? It could be Emma! She snatched the phone to her ear.

'Mum?'

It WAS Emma! Thank God! 'Em, where are you? Are you all right?'

'Is that what you want to talk about, because in that case we have nothing to say.'

'No! No, there's something else – something that happened last night.'

'Well?'

'I can't tell you on the phone, Emma. I really can't.'

'And I'm not prepared to step into that house again unless I know what I'm in for. I don't live there any more, Mum. That's not my home.'

'For God's sake, Emma, why does everything have to revolve around you? This isn't a trick! I simply can't speak about this on the phone because it's too shocking for ME, not you! We need to talk face to face.'

There was silence at the other end of the line. 'What do you mean, it's about Dad? Is he all right? He's not ill or anything.'

Meg drew breath before answering. 'No, he's definitely not ill. Sick, maybe. But something has happened, something which will change our family for ever.'

'Is Dad home this evening?'

'No.'

Emma considered this reply. In the end, curiosity got the better of her. 'I'll come over soon then.'

'Oh, Emma, it will be so good to see you . . .'

'But I'm not staying!'

'Just come home,' begged her mother wearily. 'Please, just come.' But the line had already clicked dead.

She didn't expect Emma to arrive so quickly. It was barely ten minutes before the bell rang. Meg flew down the stairs to fling open the door. A complete stranger stood there.

'Mrs Barratt? Chris Elliott, Ben's form master. Do you remember we spoke on the phone the other evening? I hope you don't mind, but I've brought Ben back tonight. He had a rather frightening encounter with a group of lads while he was walking home.'

Chris watched in alarm as the blood drained from the face of the woman in front of him. 'Is he all right? Where is he? Ben!'

Chris turned towards the gate where Ben was just ambling up from the car. 'Oh, he's fine. Just collecting his things together . . .'

But as Chris turned round to smile reassuringly at Ben's mother, he was just in time to see the glassy veil that came across her eyes before she fell to the floor like a lifeless doll.

'Robert?'

'Katherine! I hardly recognised you. You sound dreadful!'

'Yes, well, I just wanted to let you know that I won't be able to manage our visit to the opera tonight after all.'

'Are you all right? There are one or two really nasty bugs doing the rounds at the moment.'

'So I hear.'

'Come on quite suddenly, has it?'

'I'm not sure that I can explain right now how I feel. I just need a bit of time to get myself together.'

'Heavens, you do sound down. Should you be alone? Would you like me to drop around with a strictly medicinal bottle of dry white wine?'

'No, Robert. And I have to be honest enough to tell you that I'm not really ill. There's been a bit of upset, something very distressing. I suppose you'll hear about it soon enough — and when you do, I don't expect you'll think much of me.'

His voice was concerned and curious. 'I pride myself, Katherine, on being a good judge of character. And I don't think there's anything you could do which would change my opinion of you.'

She didn't answer immediately. 'Well, that's it. I just wanted to let you know.'

'Then I just want to let you know that I'm only ever a phone call away. If you need a friend — and I AM your friend — I'm here.'

'I'm not worth your friendship, Robert. I'm not fit to be anyone's friend, believe me. Goodbye.'

When he realised that she had put the phone down, Robert rang her back immediately. The line was engaged — and she had obviously taken the phone off the hook, because that was the way it remained all evening.

'That's right, just keep your head between your legs for a while. I know it's not very comfortable, but it will get the blood back in the right place.'

Meg stared groggily at her feet, dimly aware that she didn't recognise the voice above her. She could see Ben's scuffed school shoes across on the other side of the room. Slowly, through the fog in her mind came the memory of the stranger at the door. Ben's school teacher! That was it. Imagine what he must think of her now.

She struggled to sit up in an effort to stop the world being on such a tilt. As her head sank back into the softness of the sofa, she tried to focus her eyes on the man beside her.

He had a nice face, long, angular and slightly tanned as if he were used to an outdoor life. That face was very close to hers as he studied her with concern. 'Water?'

'Just a little.'

He cupped the back of her head while he held the cup to her lips. At the oddly intimate gesture, she felt herself redden with embarrassment. 'Good, the colour's definitely returning to your cheeks now.'

'I can't apologise enough. That was so stupid of me.'

He grinned. 'Well, I have to say I don't usually have that effect on women! I can't ever remember anyone swooning at my feet before.'

'I don't know quite what happened . . .'

'Well, it was certainly very dramatic. Good job my teacher training includes first aid!'

She managed a watery smile. 'Head between the legs, eh?'

'Works a treat when boys get knocked out on the rugby field. I never tried it on a lady before.'

'Inelegant – but effective . . .'

'Thank goodness for that. And the text book says that a warm cup of sugary tea is supposed to do the business too, once you've recovered a bit. Ben, nip out and put the kettle on, there's a good lad.'

'She doesn't take sugar, sir. She hates sugar.'

'I'll have the sugary one then, seeing as I've had a shock too. Just make a cup of tea for your mum exactly as she likes it.'

'Tell me about Ben. What happened to him?'

'He's been having trouble with a particular group of lads for some time. Did you know?'

'Not until your call the other night. I thought there must be something wrong, although he simply wouldn't talk about it. I've tried to draw him out, but he always just clams up.'

'I had the same experience when I tried to get him to tell me what's been going on. Tonight, though, I just happened to be driving not far from the school when I saw that group of boys, and knew they were up to something. When I stopped to take a closer look, I realised that Ben was in the middle of them all, plainly scared out of his wits.'

'Oh no . . .'

'But this is the interesting part. Something really very remarkable happened. Did you know that Ben is an absolutely outstanding runner?'

She looked at him in surprise. 'I know he used to love running when he was younger. On summer holidays over the years, we often go to relatives of ours in East Anglia. The first thing Ben always wanted to do when he got to the farm was to start running – as if he couldn't wait to get out and explore every corner of the place. He just keeps going, sometimes for hours. Never seems to run out of energy for it.'

'Well, that's just it. When I came on that rather nasty scene this evening, Ben started running. Now, Physical Education is my subject at school – and honestly, I've never seen anything like it. He must have run at top speed for at least ten minutes, and covered the distance between where I first saw him and the end of the park every bit as fast as I could myself. And what struck me most was that when I eventually caught up with him, it wasn't exhaustion he was feeling, but exhilaration. It was written all over him. He obviously has tremendous stamina and strength. I believe that your son has an extraordinary talent.'

'He does?'

'But how come he never revealed his interest and ability in class? I've been teaching him sport for more than a year now, and I would have rated him as a no-hoper – always at the back of the line, shrinking behind the other boys rather than be picked out to do anything.'

Meg nodded in amazement. 'He didn't want to be noticed, I suppose. If he was being consistently bullied, he'd hardly want to draw attention to himself, would he?'

'Well, maybe it's time he did. He should take a pride in his talent, because I have a feeling that it could be the key to the confidence he needs to cope better at school. If you agree, I'd like to work with him out of school hours, just to see exactly what we're dealing with here. What do you think?'

'I think that's an extremely kind offer — but why should you? I'm a teacher too. I know how long the hours are. This is going to mean extra work for you, so why should you do all this for us?'

Chris's expression was serious as he replied. 'Because I remember feeling the same exhilaration in running that I saw this evening in Ben. Because I was the butt of bullies at school too, and I don't like to see any other kid going through that sort of treatment. Because it would be my pleasure. Honestly.'

Meg looked at him incredulously before a slow smile spread across her face. 'In that case, we have many reasons to thank you. You care for your pupils, you put yourself out to help other people, you rescue damsels in distress . . .'

Chris laughed out loud. 'That's agreed then? Give me a chance to work with Ben away from school for a month or two — then we'll see where it takes him.'

'That would be wonderful!' And she stretched out to take his hand, shaking it to seal the deal.

'Look, I'll move some of my stuff into the other room, then you can unpack your things into this side of the wardrobe.'

'I don't want to put you out.'

'Alan, how could you possibly do that? I love you being here, you know I do.'

He didn't answer, apparently concentrating on finding a corner for his suitcase to one side of the cupboard rather than actually placing anything inside. Katherine noticed it all — saw his awkwardness, his reticence to move in with any sense of permanence — and her heart lurched with dread. This was the man she loved, the person who for so long had filled her thoughts and claimed her complete devotion. He had been in this room a thousand times. They had fallen together in a tousled heap at the end of the day, and woken up in each other's arms. He was used to being in her home.

But suddenly, unexpectedly, this was to be his home too — something they had spoken of wanting for so long. How come, then, that two people who knew each other that well, longed for one another so intimately, should feel like awkward strangers now?

She reached out and gently pulled him towards her so that for a moment, they leaned against each other, heads touching, fingers entwined. Words hung in the air between them, yet neither spoke. They were both too wounded, too exhausted by the events of the day to know where to begin.

'I'm sorry,' he said at last.

She pulled him closer. 'Don't. Neither of us could have know it would happen like this.'

'I feel so guilty.'

'I know. I do too.'

'It's all such a mess.'

'It was bound to come out come time. You always said that you wanted us to be together.'

'But not like this. You should have seen Meg's face today. I couldn't believe I had done that to her.'

'Not only you. Me as well.'

'She trusted us. She loved us.'

'And we love each other.'

His shoulders fell, and gently he set her away from him. 'I wonder if I should stay here now?'

'Staying here is what you've always said you wanted.'

'Yes, but this feels too soon, as if we're just rubbing salt in the wounds.'

Katherine reached out to take his face in both of her hands, her eyes level with his. 'Alan, do you love me?'

'Yes.'

'Do you still want us to spend our future together?'

'Of course, but . . .'

'Then that is what we must do. Otherwise, all of this – the pain, the upset, the trauma – will have been for nothing.'

'If you'd seen her today . . .'

'I know, my love, I know. The way this has happened is too awful for words. But it's behind us now. We have to deal with a new situation. We all have to move on – not just us, but Meg too.'

He stared at her for a few seconds before she realised he was crying.

'Oh, Alan . . .'

And as he allowed her to draw him into her arms, he knew that his cheeks were damp with her tears as well as his own.

Chapter Six

When Meg heard the sound of a motorbike outside, she thought for one dreadful moment that Matt was coming into the house with Emma. He didn't. She listened as his bike drove off again seconds before the bell rang, and she rushed to open the door.

'Oh, Emma, it's so good to see you! Why didn't you use your key? Have you forgotten it again?'

Emma's face was blank. 'I keep telling you, Mum, I no longer live here. I have no right just to walk in.'

'Of course you do!'

Emma shrugged her shoulders impatiently. 'Look, this is no good. I knew I shouldn't have come until Dad was here. When is he back?'

'He isn't coming back.'

'What's that supposed to mean?'

'Come inside, Em. I think you'd better sit down.'

Emma allowed herself to be shown into the lounge, where she chose to sit as far away from her mother as possible before demanding, 'Well?'

Meg's good intentions about staying calm, not breaking down, fell away from her at that moment. She clasped her hands tightly in her lap to stop them visibly shaking as she looked at the challenging expression on her daughter's face.

'I'm afraid I've had to ask Dad to leave the house.'

'Huh! So you've driven him away too! Good work, Mum!'

'I've asked him to leave,' continued Meg, now perilously near to tears, 'because I discovered last night that he's been having an affair with Katherine.'

'Don't be stupid. Katherine? Of course he's not!'

'I find it hard to believe too – but it's true.'

'How do you know? What did he say?'

'I know because I met them this morning in the hotel in Birmingham where they were staying. And he's saying very little. What is there to say?'

'How long has it been going on?'

'About a year, so he tells me.'

'But why? I mean, they've known each other for ages. Why now?'

Meg's hands opened in a gesture of helplessness. 'I don't know.'

'This doesn't make sense. Where is he?'

'I don't know that either, and honestly I don't care.'

'Have you tried his mobile?'

'No.'

Emma leapt to her feet. 'I'll ring him. I'll ring him now! You've got this wrong, I know you have.'

Meg looked at her daughter incredulously. There was no sympathy for her in Emma's reaction, just a blind belief in her father, and a wish to be there for him in his time of need. While Emma dialled Alan's number, Meg quietly rose and left the room, unable to bear a conversation between her husband and her daughter, both of whom seemed to care so little for the effect of their actions on her. In the whole of her life, Meg had never felt so utterly alone as she closed the door behind her, sitting on the stairs because she simply had no idea where else to go, what else to do.

Emma was noticeably pale when she finally opened the door,

leaning against the frame as she stared at her mother. 'I'm seeing him tomorrow. He's at Katherine's.'

That news was like a knife in Meg's heart, but she said nothing. 'He's going to collect me so that I can go and talk to them both.' Emma's finger drew a line around a silver ornament on the hallstand beside her. 'I'm surprised,' she said at last. 'I didn't think Dad would do that, especially not with Katherine.'

From outside came the unmistakable sound of a motorbike pulling up at the gate. 'I rang Matt. He's come to take me home.'

'This is your home, Emma, OUR home. This is where our family lives — you and Ben, Dad and me.' Meg's voice was low and broken as she looked up at her daughter. 'Please don't go. Don't leave again, not now. Please.'

For just a second, Emma's expression softened. 'I must. Matt's waiting, and he doesn't know anything about this. Don't worry, Mum. I'll talk to Dad. It will work out.'

Meg nodded dumbly, as Emma picked up her bag and opened the front door.

'Will you be all right?' When Meg didn't answer, Emma turned on impulse and came across to give her mum a quick hug. Then she was gone.

Meg sat where she was, staring at the closed door, listening as the motorbike roared off. And then she buried her face in her hands, letting grief and shock and anger wash over her as she wept and wept.

Sleep didn't come for Meg that night. She paced the floor. She made tea and didn't drink it. She stared unseeing at the television. She cried a lot, swore a bit, and battered her pillow to a pulp. But still sleep didn't come.

At half-past seven the next morning, she knelt beside Ben's bed looking down at him as he slept. What thoughts haunted his dreams? Being bullied? Running away from faces filled with venom and hatred? If so, none of that showed now as he lay relaxed and half smiling in slumber. She ran her fingers through his hair, calling his name softly until his eyes opened, and he managed a sleepy grin.

'It's Wednesday, the last day of term! I bet you don't do any work at school today.'

'Cool.'

'Are you OK? After that business last night, I mean? You aren't worried about going to school this morning?'

He shook his head, plainly not keen to talk about it. 'Where's Dad?' he asked instead. 'Is he coming back today?'

'Probably not, love.'

'Only he said he'd take me down the town. We've got plans . . .' His eyes shone mischievously as he spoke. 'You know, Christmas plans that you're not allowed to know about.'

'Oh, I see. Well, I'm not sure what he's doing. It's possible that things aren't working out quite as he thought they would.'

'When does he finish work? He said he was going to take some time off at the end of this week, otherwise we'll only have Saturday before Christmas Eve, and that might be too late to get all our shopping.'

'Ben, it's just possible that Dad won't be with us after all this Christmas.'

'Not with us?' Ben's eyes were like saucers in the semi-darkness. 'Dad wouldn't miss Christmas! He loves it. He's really into the crackers and the lights and everything. You remember last year how he went through all that business of putting out a carrot for Rudolph and a glass of his best port for Santa – and he knew that I hadn't believed in all that for ages!'

'Well, this year may be rather different.'

'What do you mean?'

'I'm not sure what I mean just yet. I really don't know exactly what will happen.'

'He's not working, is he? I know he's always going on about

how much he's got to do, and he's away most of the time these days. But we can't have Christmas without him. He's got to be here!'

Meg stroked her hand across his forehead, pushing back a soft lock of hair. 'When you come home tonight, let's have a proper natter, shall we? You and I?'

'I don't want to talk about school.'

'Understood. But I still need a quiet chat with you. Is that OK?'

'Are you all right?'

'Not really.'

'Are you ill? Have you got one of your headaches?'

'I'm not ill.' He eyed her suspiciously. Reluctant to say more, Meg got to her feet. 'Come on, into the bathroom with you, and get dressed. Do you fancy eggs and bacon as a special treat this morning?'

'Is Em having some?'

'Em's not here either, Ben. Don't you remember? She's gone to Matt's.'

'But she's coming back. You've told her to come back, haven't you?'

'I've asked her, but she's a bit mixed up at the moment.'

'Oh.' Ben digested this information, before suddenly flinging back his duvet and jumping out of bed. 'Do I get her bacon then?'

Meg smiled. 'Seems only fair to me.'

And in a gesture which was totally out of character these days, Ben slipped his arms around his mother's waist to give her an affectionate squeeze before skipping out of the room and into the bathroom.

After the events of the evening before, Meg gave Ben a lift to school that morning, arranging to pick him up again at the end of the day. Alone after he'd got out of the car, Meg knew that she couldn't face a moment more in the house. There was so much she should be doing there – Christmas shopping to be organised, presents wrapped, last-minute cards to be written and delivered – but she had neither the heart nor the energy to think about any of it. Christmas was a family time. Overnight, her family had disintegrated. Their tight little unit which had always seemed so solid and loving had fallen apart. First Emma had gone. Now Alan.

For as long as she could remember, whenever she had a problem, she had talked to Katherine. She shuddered now to think of the secrets they had shared in the past – little tiffs she'd had with Alan, complaints about what he had or hadn't done. How Katherine must have laughed, when all along she had known more about Alan than Meg could ever have guessed. And to think of the times when Meg had pushed eligible men in Katherine's direction. No wonder she was never interested. She didn't need a man. She had one. Hers.

Suddenly Meg felt an overwhelming need to feel breeze on her face and fresh air in her lungs. Turning the car away from the centre of town, she thought longingly of the hill where she and Alan often walked on Sunday afternoons. She could be alone there, with a sharp wind to clear her mind and clarify her thoughts. That's where she'd go!

'I'm sorry. She's not here this morning.'

Robert didn't recognise the voice answering Katherine's office phone. 'I'll give her a ring on the mobile then.'

'I don't think she's got that with her. I've already tried it.'

'She is all right, is she? Not under the weather or anything?'

'I'm not sure. All she said was that she won't be in today, and in fact, may not be back in the office until after Christmas.'

'Oh.'

'I can take a message for you. Perhaps she'll ring you back.'

Robert considered that option for a second or two. 'Thank you, but no. I'm sure I'll be able to track her down myself.'

He stared at the phone thoughtfully after that call, wondering why he felt so disturbed firstly by Katherine's odd conversation the previous afternoon when she'd cancelled their date at such short notice, and then by her non-appearance in the office that morning. Something was wrong, he was sure of it. He recognised the professional workaholic in Katherine, because he was aware of the same qualities, or perhaps failings, in himself. If she wasn't at work, then something was definitely awry. Who would know? Who could tell him?

Alan, of course. He dialled Alan's office number immediately, and was pleasantly surprised when the phone was picked up straight away.

'Alan? Good to speak to you. Robert here. I wonder if you can throw any light on something that's puzzling me a bit.'

'I'll try.'

'It's about your friend, Katherine. We've seen each other a couple of times, you know?'

'How can I help you, Robert?'

'Well, she seems to have disappeared. All very mysterious really. Is this usual? Have I missed something here?'

He heard Alan take a deep breath at the other end of the phone before he replied. 'Robert, I don't know quite how to tell you this — but, yes, there is something you probably should know.'

Meg spotted her immediately. As she swung her old car around the corner, she almost ran into the back of the distinctive Saab simply because she was so shocked to see it there. It was a deep blue colour, stylish and elegant just like its owner. And Katherine was still sitting in the driving seat.

For a split second, Meg considered simply driving on. Then in a flush of anger, she made the decision that she would not be stopped from entering her own home. If anyone had to go away, it was Katherine. That woman had no place here.

Stepping out of her car, she slammed the door loudly behind her, deliberately not looking in Katherine's direction as she marched purposefully up the drive.

'Meg! Meg, please! I must talk to you.'

'There's nothing to say. Go away, Katherine.' Meg's fingers fumbled to get the key in the door. It wouldn't go in. It WOULDN'T go in!

'Please, I need to explain. I'm sorry, Meg. I'm so, so sorry . . .'

Still the key was refusing to slide neatly into the hole. No wonder when her hand was shaking uncontrollably.

'I'm not asking for your forgiveness. I don't deserve that. But there are things you have to know . . . Please, Meg, you never need set eyes on me again after today, if you don't want to. But after all these years, all we've been through – please, I beg you, give me a few minutes now!'

The key went in! Meg didn't look back as she walked through – but with relief Katherine realised that she had left the door slightly ajar behind her.

She found Meg backed into the far corner of the kitchen clutching the work surface, her stance and expression under careful control. Katherine hardly stepped over the threshold of the kitchen door, so that a decent distance could be kept between them. She sensed that Meg would bolt immediately if the intervening space was invaded by someone she now clearly looked upon as an enemy.

Katherine was uncertain how to start. She had been practising various lines over and over in her head on the drive down from London, but all coherent thought seemed to drain from her as she looked into the challenging stare of this woman who had been her dearest friend for years. To her horror, her eyes began to prick with tears. Abruptly, she turned to go. 'You're right. I shouldn't have come.'

'Just tell me why, Katherine. Was it because of Alan, because he was the only man in a world half full of men that you wanted? Or was it because of me? Had I hurt you? Did you despise me? I just don't understand.'

Katherine slowly stepped back into the kitchen, her face wretched. 'You have always been the best friend I could possibly have. I'd have given anything not to have hurt you in this way. I love and admire everything about you, all that you are . . .'

'Was it jealousy then? Is that it?'

'If I'm honest, I have to say I have always been envious of you, but only in the right kind of way. You've created a wonderful home for a family who are as dear to me as if they were my own . . .'

'And so you set about destroying that family by taking my husband? You were jealous of me, so you wanted him.'

'It wasn't like that. I didn't set out to destroy anything, and I certainly didn't imagine Alan would ever be remotely interested in me . . .'

'You had to do a lot of persuading, did you?'

Katherine sighed heavily. 'Meg, for me, this wasn't a sudden thing. I've always loved Alan. From the moment you first introduced me to him, I remember thinking how special he was. He hardly noticed me, of course, because he was so besotted with you – but from then on, I found myself measuring every other man against him.'

'I don't believe you. I'd have known if you felt that way. Are you asking me to imagine that you have been nursing a passion for my own husband all these years, and I never had the slightest inkling of how you felt? That's ridiculous, Katherine – and it's a lie, a lie to cover up what is really a brief, sordid affair.'

'You have the right to call it sordid, but is "short" the word to describe a deep and committed love which has already lasted nine years?'

Meg's knees seemed to buckle as Katherine stared at her with a mixture of shock and compassion.

'I thought you knew. I thought Alan told you yesterday afternoon . . .'

'A year. He said a year.'

'Then he probably didn't have the heart to tell you the truth. I'm so sorry, Meg, but you have to know that what's happening here isn't just a bit of sex on the side. Alan and I discovered what we felt for each other more than nine years ago . . .'

'That was when Ben was ill. He had meningitis that year. He nearly died.'

'And you were so incredibly distraught, which was completely understandable in the circumstances – but you grieved alone, Meg. You were so focused on Ben and his needs that you overlooked how your husband was grieving too.'

Meg stared at her. 'For heaven's sake, I had a small boy who was desperately ill. Of course he needed all my attention. He was my son, OUR son. Alan knew I had no choice but to be with him.'

'You shut Alan out, Meg, and in his loneliness and worry, he turned to me. I wanted to be there for you both, but even I found it difficult to reach you during that awful time. Alan rang and asked me to meet him one evening when he was up in London, and I agreed immediately. It was obvious he just needed someone to listen, someone it was safe to pour out his fears and frustrations to . . .'

'And you were there – just waiting for a chance to pounce on the man you had coveted for so long.'

'Yes, I admit I loved him. Just as my love and commitment for you had grown over the years, so my feelings for him had grown too. But I harboured no hopes at all, never even considered the possibility because Alan was YOUR husband. It didn't occur to me for one moment that he might have feelings towards me as well.'

'Oh, how convenient. His wife was almost out of her mind with worry because their small son was at death's door – and he discovered he had FEELINGS for the one woman I thought I could trust above anyone in the world!'

'We just realised how easy it was to talk together, how comfortable we felt in each other's company . . .'

'. . . so you decided to continue the chat in bed!'

'It took a very long time before anything like that happened. At first, even though we both realised something important was developing between us, we tried to ignore it.'

'Until you simply couldn't resist, is that it? Never mind our friendship! Never mind the years of marriage Alan and I had behind us, the home we'd built, the life we shared, or the children we'd brought into the world! Why didn't you just find your own man, Katherine? Why steal mine? How could you have done that to me, to US?'

Katherine's voice was wretched as she stared miserably at Meg. 'It was selfish. It was disloyal and unforgivable. But I loved him, Meg. Alan is the love of my life, it's as simple as that. Having met him, and become close to him, there was never anyone to match Alan. I don't believe there ever could be.'

'So what happens now? I hear he's already moved in with you. That didn't take long, did it?'

'He was in such a state after yesterday morning. Where else could he go?'

'Because I threw him out, is that what you mean? Did either of you really think he could go on living here after all this?'

'No.'

'No, of course not.'

Both women fell silent then, Katherine squirming under the steady scrutiny of Meg's stare. Then suddenly Meg's shoulders dropped as if all the fight had gone out of her. 'Katherine, you have behaved despicably – but I do realise that you are a single woman with no one to answer to but yourself. Alan, on the other hand, is a husband and a father, and it is not just me, but our children he's betrayed. You have wrecked our friendship. He has wrecked our family – and he's the love of my life too, at least he was.'

'Meg, I'm . . .'

But Meg wasn't listening as she swung round to delve into her handbag which was sitting on the work surface behind her. Katherine watched with a mixture of fear and curiosity as Meg walked over to face her. 'I have nothing more to say to you, nothing ever. And I sincerely hope that I won't have to set eyes on you again.'

Katherine started in surprise as Meg reached out to place something hard and cold into the palm of her hand. She looked down to see the sparkle of diamonds as she recognised the eternity ring which Alan had given his wife on their wedding anniversary just a few days earlier.

'Alan said this ring came with his love forever. If it did, then he obviously gave it to the wrong person. You should wear it, Katherine. Goodbye.'

When the bell rang that afternoon to announce not just the end of school but the end of term, the boys needed no encouragement to grab their bulging bags full of screwed-up PE kit dirtied by thirteen weeks of winter sports as they headed for home – and Christmas. As the last few stragglers wandered out of the form room, Chris called over to Ben that he'd like a word.

'Are we agreed then? You'll put in a regular commitment to training for the next few weeks, and I'll work with you to develop your running skills.'

'OK, sir,' agreed Ben, although from his expression it was clear that he wasn't totally sure what he was letting himself in for.

'It'll be hard work. A half-hour run before school every

morning, and circuit training at least three times a week. Are you up for that?'

'Circuit training? Will anyone else be there?'

'Well, I suggest that rather than going to the county circuit, or even using the school field here, we start off by working at the comprehensive school in Barford. I know how excellent their track facilities are because I regularly teach sessions there.'

'You teach at Barford Comprehensive?'

'Yes, but not for the pupils of that school. I'm one of the team of trainers for the county athletics squad.'

Ben digested this information in awed silence.

'Look, Ben, I recognise real potential in you. Heaven only knows how you've managed to hide your running ability so successfully for so long, but your talent is something you should accept with pride. Give it a few months. Put your heart into this. See where it might take you.'

'I just like running, sir, but only for myself. I never wanted to compete with anyone else.'

'That's the trouble though, isn't it? It's mostly because you keep yourself so completely apart from everyone else that you're having these problems with mixing at school.'

'I don't want anyone here to know.'

'I realise that, and I don't see why they should, initially at least. But we need to make a deal. I suspect that with proper training and encouragement you could be an outstanding asset not just to the lads in this form, but to the school itself. If at the end of, say, three months, it's clear that you have a natural talent for running, then you must repay my time and commitment by agreeing to join the school team here. That's only fair, now isn't it?'

Ben almost grinned as he nodded in agreement.

'Right, we start tomorrow.'

'But it's Christmas.'

'So? We'll try an initial session at Barford just to see how you get on. OK?'

'Shall I meet you at school?'

'No, it will be closed. I'll pick you up at home. Will you check with your mum that that's convenient. Ask her to give me a ring on this number if it isn't, but as I discussed all this with her yesterday evening, I think she'll be happy for you to start training immediately. Eleven o'clock all right with you?'

Ben thought for a moment about his dad, and whether he would actually arrive home for their planned shopping session. Somehow he thought that was unlikely.

'OK, sir. See you.'

And as Chris watched Ben amble off, he wondered yet again at how practised the boy had become in appearing to be average at everything, so that no one noticed him, nothing challenged him, and he could fade into the obscurity of the shadows.

But not for long!

As her father got out of his car to greet her, Emma was shocked at his appearance. His pallid face matched almost exactly the grey of his hair. From the glassiness of his eyes, and the dark shadows smudged beneath them, she could see he was in dire need of sleep. Her dad had always been a smart man, tailored and neatly groomed. Tonight he looked crumpled and exhausted, not himself at all.

And he had always been uncomfortable about emotion aired in public, with Emma herself being the only chink in his armour as far as any display of affection was concerned. But now there was despair in his embrace as he clasped Emma tightly to him. 'Oh, Goose, it's so good to see you.'

His desperation was almost frightening. To Emma, her father had always been privately loving, but in control with an air of authority too. To see him like this unnerved her. She pulled herself away from his arms so that she could stare closely at him. 'You look awful. What are you doing, Dad? What's all this rubbish about you and Katherine?'

'It's not rubbish, I'm afraid. There's a lot to tell you. Climb in, and we'll find somewhere to talk.' Ten minutes later they were seated opposite each other in a quiet booth in a small pub.

'Mum's in a real state,' said Emma at last.

Alan's face clouded with concern. 'Oh, I know. I feel so bad about it. You will look after her, won't you Em? She won't let me anywhere near her, and who can blame her for that – but she'll rely on you a lot right now.'

'I don't think so . . .'

'Goose, you must promise me. I know you've not always seen eye to eye, but your mum really needs your support right now.'

'I'll do my best, but things have changed quite a bit at our end too . . .'

'Well, obviously Katherine and I never meant our relationship to come out under circumstances like these.'

'But you must have known it would come out at some point? Did you always plan to leave Mum for Katherine?'

Alan sat back in his seat to consider the question. 'Honestly, I'm not sure. I love Katherine, I openly admit that – and the spark went out of my marriage with Mum years ago. It became mundane, as I suppose all marriages do.'

'So when were you planning to go?'

'I don't know. Katherine never put any pressure on me – she wouldn't, would she, bearing in mind that she's known and loved our whole family for years?'

'That's what I can't understand. She DOES love us. And she especially loves Mum. They've always been so close. How could she do this to her best friend?'

'It's hard for you to understand, Goose. Katherine and I have recognised our love for each other for a very long time, but we agreed that until you two kids were safely off our hands and settled in your own lives that we should leave things as they are.'

'Just have an affair behind Mum's back, is that what you mean?'

'Would it have helped if she'd known? Look at the devastation it's caused now. Wasn't it better to remain discreet — not just for you and Ben, but for Mum too, to let the family remain intact.'

'And Katherine accepted that? Didn't she want a husband and children of her own?'

'Yes, that's something we've talked about too. But she agreed with me that in a way you and Ben have been almost like her own children. She's been part of our lives and our family for so many years.'

'Poor Mum.'

'I love your Mum, Em, I need you to understand that. In fact, I realise just how much I love her now all this has happened. Ours may not be the most sparkling of marriages after all these years, but we rub along together all right. I can't help but wonder now if I'd ever actually have found the courage to leave her. Somehow when Katherine and I talked about the possibility in the past, it didn't seem real. I suppose as long as you and Ben were living at home, then it was not a decision Katherine expected me to make.'

'But now it's all out in the open.'

'And Mum's thrown me out. Who can blame her?'

'Is it true you've moved in with Katherine?'

'Honestly, Em, I was so shell-shocked yesterday, I simply didn't know where else to go. Probably I should have booked into a hotel or somewhere else that was neutral — but Katherine and I were both in such a state, we just needed somewhere safe and private.'

'So what happens now?'

'I suppose that's up to your mum. Perhaps we need to get Christmas out of the way . . .'

'Christmas! You won't be around for Christmas?'

'How can I, Goose?'

'You may not be the only one missing from the Christmas lunch table. I don't think I'll be there either. What you don't know is that you're not the first member of the family to leave home this week.'

Alan's face clouded with concern as he listened to the events which led to Emma's stormy parting from Meg on the night of the school concert. 'So that's why Mum tried to make contact with me that night.'

'Suppose so.'

'But, Em, she's right. This is your "A" level year. Whatever you feel for Matt, couldn't you just give your studies the next few months, so that you've at least got them under your belt?'

'I knew you'd say that. I knew you'd side with her.'

'It's not a case of siding with anyone. It's simply good sense.'

Emma rose from her seat. 'Look, I only came to make sure you're all right. I don't agree with what you've done. I think you're a shit actually, but I can hardly criticise you for leaving, now can I?'

'Whatever happens between Mum and me is a completely different matter to our joint concern over your welfare and future. Where are you living? Can this Matt support you? Couldn't he come and talk to us properly about what you were planning?'

'How could he talk to you when you wouldn't even let him in the house?'

Alan ran his hand through his hair with an air of frustration. 'Look, Em, I don't want to belittle you. I know you're nearly eighteen . . .'

'Old enough to marry without your permission in just a few months.'

'. . . and I know I've probably been as guilty as any loving parent in trying to keep you safely in our protection until you leave us for university . . .'

'Smothering, you mean.'

'. . . but Mum and I have only had your best interest at heart. We were your age once, you know?'

Emma gave an exaggerated sigh. 'Dad, spare me this. You don't understand. You've never understood.'

'I just know that you change a lot as you mature from being a teenager to become an independent twenty-something. You don't want to limit your options at this stage.'

'I think my options have always been limited because my life has been completely mapped out for me by you and Mum, and by school.'

'Goose, you'll love university. I know you will.'

'Well, I love Matt. He means more to me than university ever could.'

'Can't you do both? If whatever it is between you is really strong enough, it will last through your years at university – and without a doubt, a degree would give you much better prospects for a career later in life.'

'I won't need much of a career while our kids are small.'

'Kids! You're barely more than a kid yourself!'

'Goodbye, Dad.'

'Em, wait! I don't mean to be insensitive. I'm hardly in a position to criticise, am I?' She shrugged, eyeing him suspiciously as she settled once more into her seat. 'Do you mean what you say about not being at home for Christmas?'

'I can't, Dad. I do feel very sorry for Mum, but I don't want what's happening between the two of you to get in the way of what's going on between Matt and me. If I go home, it will be like admitting Mum was right all along. I've told her I no longer live at home, and I have to mean it.'

'Are you absolutely sure that what you're doing is right for you?'

'Honestly, Dad, I don't know. I just think that we've come this far, and it would be pointless just to scuttle back at the first hurdle.'

'So where are you planning to spend Christmas?'

'With Matt, I suppose. His flat's not much, but we'll work on it.'

'Won't he want to be with his own parents?'

'He's not a parent-person really. He works with his dad at the garage, and I know they get on each other's nerves a bit. He doesn't seem to want to spend his spare time with his family too.'

'So how about coming to join Katherine and me?'

Emma's eyes widened with surprise. 'Really? In London, do you mean?'

'You know her flat in Hampstead? That's where we'll be. Fancy coming to spend the day with us?'

She considered the possibility for a second or two. 'Mum will hate it. She'll think I'm in cahoots with the enemy.'

'She might, but I hope she'll realise that if the family isn't going to be together as usual this year, then it's better that it's split into two locations rather than three.'

'When would we come?'

'I could collect you on Sunday, Christmas Eve. Then you could stay the night so that you're there for present opening in the morning.'

A slow smile spread across Emma's face. 'Sounds nice.'

'It would be nice.'

'I'd have to ask Matt.'

'Can you ring him?'

'No. I'll talk it over with him tonight, and ring you in the office tomorrow. And talking about the office, have you been in today? Aren't you supposed to be really busy at the moment?'

'Yes, I'm putting in the hours as usual, but my heart isn't in it. Can't seem to clear my head to think coherently right now.'

'What's going to happen, Dad? Is this the end of our family? Are you and Mum going to divorce, just like so many of the kids' parents at school — because I have to tell you I don't like that idea at all.'

'I don't know, Em. It all feels so raw and hopeless at the moment.'

'Do you think you'd be happier living with Katherine?'

'In some ways, without a doubt, the answer is yes. But then there's you and Ben, and our home together, and your mum, of course, who's been part of my life for so long that I can't quite imagine things without her.'

'Are you going to talk to her? Really talk to her, I mean. Try and sort it out?'

'She won't even see me. Perhaps we've just got to let the dust settle for a few days, put Christmas behind us — and then, well, who knows?'

'How's Katherine?'

'Shattered. Stoic. Supportive. Heartbroken. As confused as I am — and yet still so confident of her love for me.'

'She thinks you should make a go of this then?'

'I suppose that's what she's always wanted.'

'So in the end, it's what you want that will decide it all.'

'Well, I think your mum's reaction is the most crucial in all this. I recognise that I've taken a sledgehammer to our marriage, and even though it may be possible to glue all the pieces back together, it will never be quite as good, as convincing or as strong again.'

'You've made a right mess, haven't you?'

'Umm, and I've hurt the people I love most in the process.'

'I'm still here, Dad.'

'Thanks, Goose. You've no idea how much that means to me.'

Meg's quiet chat with Val that evening was interrupted by the arrival of Sandy, bristling with indignation, flushed with the scent of gossip and tragedy.

'It's true then. He's gone — and with HER!'

'Hello Sandy.'

'I knew it! I thought as much at the party. The way they never look at each other, have you noticed that? I suspected something all along.'

'Well,' replied Meg wearily, 'I can't say I noticed anything at all.'

Sandy plonked herself down on the sofa beside Meg, throwing a comforting arm around her friend's shoulder. 'Of course you didn't. You weren't meant to. He wanted it all, didn't he! His bit on the side, and his adoring wife and family at home! Of course you weren't meant to know!'

'I just feel so stupid. The signs must have been there, but I just didn't think about him being interested in anyone else. Actually, if I'm honest, I don't think I imagined anyone would be interested in HIM! He's just comfy, familiar, lovable old Alan — my husband. I didn't imagine he'd have the energy, let alone the inclination to be comfy and lovable with someone else as well.'

'You see, you can never trust them. They're all the same. Can't resist the opportunity to play away from home. It's just Alan's bad luck that he got caught out!'

'More like Meg's bad luck,' interrupted Val, throwing Sandy a look which was supposed to warn her of Meg's brittle vulnerability. The gesture was totally lost on Sandy as she launched into her next onslaught on men in general, and Alan in particular.

'So he'd been telling you that he was staying with his work colleague, and he's been staying at Katherine's flat all the time? The audacity of it! Suppose you'd dropped in on Katherine one evening unexpectedly?'

'I was hardly likely to do that, was I? She lives in London. We live in Hampshire. We speak on the phone every couple of days, and see each other often when she pops down here. Why would I need to drop in during the week? No, they knew they were quite safe.'

'And just exactly how long has this been going on?'

Meg swallowed hard and stared down at her hands as she answered. 'Nine years. Katherine said they got together nine years ago.'

'Nine years!' Sandy's brow furrowed as she puzzled over the significance of the number. 'Why then? What happened nine years ago?'

'Ben had meningitis.'

'That's right! Ben was so dreadfully ill that year. You nearly lost him. I remember that nightmare time so well.'

'Katherine said that I shut Alan out, that we were grieving in our own different ways, and because I was so preoccupied with Ben, Alan felt I excluded him.'

'Oh, the poor neglected baby! You were out of your mind with worry about your little boy – and Alan felt neglected – so neglected that he jumped into bed with your best friend! Ooh, I'd like to punch that man on the nose very, very hard!'

'The thing is, Sandy,' Val interjected firmly, 'Meg's finding it very difficult to deal with the way she's obviously been betrayed in the past – but she knows that she needs to concentrate in the present and future right now.'

Sandy's eyes widened like huge saucers. 'Well, you'll throw him out, of course! And if he doesn't want to go, you pack his bags and dump them unceremoniously in the street outside Katherine's flat, so that all their neighbours know how disgracefully they've behaved. And then you get your hair cut, buy a complete new wardrobe, push back your shoulders and get on with your life without him. That's what you'll do – and Val and I will be right here to help you do it!'

Meg sighed heavily. 'I can't imagine any life without him, that's the trouble. We've been a couple for ever. I'm not sure I can operate on my own any more. Alan and I have always been a *we*. It's always been the two of *us* making plans, sharing memories, building a life together. Until yesterday, we were such a tight little family, at least I thought so. Now Alan's gone, Emma's run off with her awful boyfriend, Ben is being bullied at school and I've lost my best friend.'

'And it's all his fault. I hope his conscience never gives him a moment's peace after this!'

Meg stared at her. 'Peace. Yes, that's what I've lost. I've always taken peace of mind for granted, complete confidence in our family's ability to weather any storm – and suddenly, I realise it was all built on lies. Our family life is wrecked, and the hurts are just too deep to heal, too shocking to forgive.'

'It's early days yet, love,' said Val in her common-sense, practical way. 'It doesn't help that Christmas is right on top of us, because there's no routine to help you get your thoughts straight. But I think you can safely assume that everyone – Alan, Katherine and Emma too – are just as bewildered and unhappy as you feel right now.'

'Hardly. Alan has Katherine to share his "unhappiness", and I can only assume that having him move in with her is what she's hoped for all along. And I feel really helpless where Emma is concerned. She flatly refuses to come home, and was only too anxious to rush to talk to her dad to make sure she got his point of view before she'd listen to anything I have to say.'

Val covered Meg's hand with her own. 'I wouldn't assume anything just yet. Emotions are running high. You may all still have a very bumpy ride ahead before things settle down.'

'And then,' said Sandy, patting Meg's knee emphatically as she spoke, 'straight after Christmas, you must go and see a solicitor, just to protect yourself! Men can be very demanding when it comes to the division of property, even if it is all their fault!'

Noticing that Meg was perilously near to breaking, Val thought it best to change the subject. 'What about Christmas, Meg? I don't like the thought of you and Ben being on your own.

I'd invite you to join me, but I'm going to spend a few days with my mum, as you know.'

'That's settled then!' said Sandy triumphantly. 'The two of you will spend the day with us. It will be good for Ben to have young company around him – and Jason, Darren and Joely will be so excited to share Christmas with the two of you. No, Meg, I won't take no for an answer! That's absolutely settled!'

Only Val caught the despair in Meg's expression as suddenly the future seemed bleaker than ever.

Chapter Seven

When he realised the door was slowly being pushed ajar, Ben squeezed his eyes tightly shut, and lay as still as he could. It was gone eleven o'clock on Christmas Eve. Soft light spilled into his room from the landing as he realised his mum was tiptoeing cautiously towards the bottom of his bed. Even with one deaf ear, Ben could just catch the exciting, unique rustle of the filled stocking as Mum laid it gently to one side of his feet. He sensed her shadow on his face as she stood for a moment to look down at him, then felt her fingers softly touch his hair before she moved away again.

But he wasn't asleep – and the second the door closed behind her, he crawled across the duvet to investigate the intriguing shapes and textures in the stocking. Of all the traditions of Christmas he loved, the feel and sound of his stocking had always been the most exciting. It heralded a whole day of presents, games and endless eating, when normal household rules were dropped and an atmosphere of good fun prevailed. At least, that was how it had always been. Never again though. Not without Dad and Emma.

The last few days had been so confusing. Mum was different, not just in the way she looked, so pale and worn out – but in the way she was. She had always been a smiley mum. Everyone liked her. All the children she taught adored her. Their parents loved chatting to her. She was constantly doing things for people – producing shows, organising jumble sales, taking the Brownies, cooking suppers, popping round to help a neighbour, welcoming friends to the house. Best of all, when the visitors had gone and their phone had finally stopped ringing at the end of another busy day, Mum was all his. For as long as he could remember, they would make time for a chat over a cup of hot chocolate before he went to bed. She might help him with his homework. He might tell her about a new computer game, or an interesting insect he'd found on the way to school.

Of course, there were some things they never mentioned. He didn't feel the need to tell her about Michael Smith, and that was why when Mr Elliott arrived to explain what had been happening at school, it had been a real shock for her. And she had never mentioned to him that she wanted to divorce Dad so that he could live with Aunty Katherine. She had obviously been aware of it for ages, because something like that could never have happened without her knowing. So she must have chosen not to tell him – and that had been a real shock for him too.

More than a shock. It was devastating news. He loved Aunty Katherine. She always smelt nice, and looked as smart as a newsreader off the television. Sometimes she played rounders with him, even if it was raining. She always bought him the biggest Easter egg. She would come up to his room and lie on the floor cushion with him to watch *The Simpsons*, even though he suspected she didn't really like them at all. And before she left, she never failed to slip a shiny pound coin into his coat pocket, which Mum and Dad were to know nothing about. Yes, Aunty Katherine was all right. More than all right.

But she lived in London – and Dad lived here in Hampshire with him and Mum and Emma. Except that now Dad lived in London too. He had left Mum and left him, and gone to live with Aunty Katherine.

The whole thing was so odd. Ben had always thought that Aunty Katherine came mostly to see Mum. He remembered how they used to talk all the time, and how Mum would get a bit annoyed if he tried to interrupt their conversation in the hope that one or other of them might like a game of rounders. But it seemed that the games Aunty Katherine played with his dad must have been the ones she enjoyed most — so now Dad had left them and gone to live with her.

Often this week he had heard Mum crying. Last night when he went downstairs for their usual cup of chocolate together, he had found her sobbing as if her heart would break. Her anguish horrified him. This was his mum — and Mum was always smiley and sensible and comforting. To see her in such a state made him feel scared and uncertain, and she must have known that because suddenly she reached out to draw him to her, hugging him so close that he couldn't breathe and he wondered if his neck might break.

He supposed he must be the man of the house now. He would have to look after Mum. Dad had said as much to him when he left last night. He had brought armfuls of brightly wrapped presents, mostly for him but a few for Mum too. She had stood stiffly to one side as Dad put the parcels under the tree, then packed the presents waiting for Emma into a carrier bag so that Dad could give them to her in the morning. Emma was going to be with Dad and Katherine for Christmas. That was odd too, very odd indeed.

He missed Emma. He missed the way she bossed him about. He missed how she nagged him to get things for her, or told him to buzz off when she was sharing secrets with someone or other on the phone. He missed the way she slammed her bedroom door whenever he walked past, and the rough and tumbles they'd sometimes have in his room when she was in a good mood.

And now she was gone too. Sadly, he pushed the stocking to the far corner of the bed, then huddled down inside the duvet until he disappeared beneath it.

If he hadn't been just thirteen and beyond these things, he might have cried. As it was, he stretched out to grab his CD player, and plugged the earpiece into his good ear, something the consultant had told him never to do. He thumped the pillow a few times, then laid it right across his head so that he could turn his favourite track up to full volume and no one would know if he was singing – or screaming.

Meg pulled Ben's door shut behind her, then made her way out of the front door and into the garage where she reached up to pull down the black bag full of Ben's presents which had been hidden behind the toolbox on the top shelf.

Alan and she had always loved the family tradition of laying out a separate pile of presents for Ben and Emma on opposite sides of the Christmas tree. Last year, Alan had spent ages writing cryptic messages around the house which Ben had had to follow until he found his new bike next door in Val's garage. And there was the time when they had bought Ben an electric train set which Alan decided to set up for him. He had begun at half past ten on Christmas Eve, and finally fallen into bed exhausted at quarter to two! It wouldn't have been so bad if their darling son hadn't bounced on top of them barely an hour later to show them what Santa had left in his stocking, and to demand they all go downstairs to start the day!

Meg laid out Ben's presents in a minute or two, then as she got off her knees to give a final check around the room, her eyes fell on the tattered but glittering figure on the top of the tree. That fairy had graced their family tree when she had been a child herself. She had looked down benignly on countless happy Christmases. A few years ago, Alan had placed a piece of mistletoe in her outstretched china hand – and on the stroke of midnight, had drawn Meg to him and kissed her passionately as the first faint sound of bells drifted across from the parish church.

Of course, now she knew that by last Christmas he was also kissing Katherine. He was probably kissing her now. And Meg found herself sinking to her knees again as she mourned Christmas past, love lost and trust betrayed.

He was asleep. She could hear how his breath had become slower, deeper, more even. She gazed through the darkness to make out his face in slumber, less strained, more peaceful now than ever when he was awake.

His body felt hard and warm beside hers. Katherine moved her leg slightly so that she was closer to him, near enough to feel the bone of his hip, the hair on his calf. She loved his body, the feel and smell of him. She loved his hands, and the hazel flecks in his green eyes. She loved the way his hair had become more grey than brown in recent years so that he seemed both distinguished and kindly. She loved his smart dress sense, except for his favourite old brown suede shoes which she always laughingly said made him look like her granddad. She thought of the way his lips twitched to one side when he flirted with her, and how his face suddenly became serious as he looked into her eyes. He had filled her world with love. She simply adored him.

And now he was here. Not just visiting for a night or two in the week. Not living out of a suitcase at the bottom of the bed which was always packed and ready to leave the next morning. Now his suits hung round her picture rail, his shoes were stacked beneath the bed and his laptop was on her dressing table. When the dust settled and he had more time, his clothes would join hers in the wardrobe because this was no longer simply her home. It was theirs.

Perhaps they would need to move? Maybe a different place, something larger that they could choose and plan together, would be the best idea. Then he might find it easier to relax, and perhaps, the guilt that haunted his eyes and had him calling out in his fitful sleep, would be replaced by real contentment. He loved her. She didn't doubt that for a moment. But the change from being Meg's husband to her own full-time lover and live-in partner had been sudden and traumatic. Of course there would be a time of adjustment. Naturally it was a painful process for them all. But this phase would pass. They would come through this.

In the meantime, she just had to love him through it – surround him with so much care and affection that he would never question that they were destined to be together. They belonged to one another, that was so clear. And however bumpy the road or devastating the journey, she knew she had enough love to carry them both through, a love to last a lifetime.

As she snuggled in closer to him, he began to stir in his sleep. He was turning over to find a more comfortable position when his arm swung across and caught Katherine's face. Giggling, she dug him in the ribs. 'Hey, you bully, pick on someone your own size!'

She sensed his smile as he sleepily replied, 'Sorry Meg!' Then within seconds, he was sound asleep again.

'What do you think, Ben? Is that the one you wanted?' Meg's expression was anxious as she watched her son opening the computer game.

'Brill!'

'The man in the shop said it's the hot favourite at the moment. Everyone's after it. I think I must have got practically the last copy. I hope you like it. You do, don't you?' Ben was too busy peeling off the cellophane to feel her question merited an answer. 'Have you opened Dad's present yet? What did he get you?'

'Which one is it?'

'I think he brought a couple of them, in that red shiny paper over there by the settee.'

Seconds later, Ben's eyes widened with surprise and delight as he pulled a DVD player out of its box.

'Wicked! Dad KNEW I wanted one of these. Everyone's got one now! Cool!'

Meg fell silent as she recognised that Alan had not only chosen the perfect gift for his son, but had also spent so much money on him that she could never have bought something like that for Ben herself. This extravagant present represented a huge burden of guilt, of course – but nevertheless, a knot of resentment tightened its grip in the pit of her stomach. 'That's great, Ben. You'll have to show me how to use it.'

Ben's nose instantly disappeared into the instruction manual as he pulled out various accessories. Meg glanced down to see there was a message on the label stuck on to the red paper. 'To Ben,' it read, 'Love, Dad.' And the handwriting was Katherine's.

'Don't you need special disks for a DVD?' she asked stiffly. 'Not much point buying you all this without the right disks!'

Ben was already reaching towards a smaller package wrapped in the same elegant paper. Inside were three DVD films, all Ben's favourites. Meg turned the paper over to check the label. 'Merry Christmas, Ben,' it said. 'Hope you enjoy these! Aunty Katherine.' Meg screwed the paper up into the smallest ball she could manage, then threw it on to the open fire to enjoy the pleasure of seeing it go up in smoke.

'You've not opened your presents, Mum. Look, here are the ones Dad left last night.'

There were three parcels, all small and discreet – probably some perfume, perhaps some stationery, and another which looked suspiciously like a CD. Alan had always been very predictable in his choice of gifts.

But perhaps this year he had been more imaginative? Maybe

when he did his Christmas shopping this time, he had Katherine at his side. She would know what perfume Meg liked best. She would instantly guess her taste in music.

At that thought, Meg pushed the pile of presents behind her, knowing that at the earliest opportunity, she would throw them straight in the bin. Better not in front of Ben though. He would never understand.

Ben's face was suddenly concerned. 'I'm sorry my present for you wasn't much. I meant to get you something else, but then Dad didn't manage our shopping trip . . .'

She smiled warmly at him. 'How clever of you to notice how much I like plants, Ben. Your poinsettia was just perfect.'

At that moment, the phone rang. Meg sank on to the settee with relief at the sound of her daughter's voice. 'Em, it's so good to hear from you! Merry Christmas, darling!'

'And you, Mum. Are you all right?'

'Of course,' replied Meg brightly. 'We're having a great time, Ben and I. We're still surrounded by piles of wrapping paper. You know what it's like here on Christmas morning!'

'Yeah.' Was that a wistful note in Emma's voice? Meg hoped so. 'You know we're at Dad's. Well, WITH Dad, that's what I mean. You know we're here though, don't you?'

'Uh-huh.' Even Meg could hear the brittleness in her reply. Don't break down, Meg! Don't let them see how much this is hurting you . . .

'Do you want to speak to him?'

'I don't think so, Em . . .'

'Hang on, he's just coming.'

There was no time to pass the phone over to Ben. Before she knew it, Alan's voice was in her ear. He sounded hesitant, unsure of his ground, neither of which she would ever associate with her husband. This was a stranger.

'Merry Christmas, Meg.' She couldn't answer. 'How's it going? Has Ben finished opening his presents yet?'

LETTING GO

There was something wrong with her throat. Her voice sounded small and unfamiliar. 'Almost.'

'It feels strange – to be here on Christmas morning.' There was simply no reply she could make to that. 'Em and Matt seem to be having a good time. She liked the top you bought her, and the perfume. She said that was her favourite present. You always have the knack of knowing exactly what people really want.'

The small talk was as much as Meg could bear. 'I'll pass you over to Ben.'

'Are you all right, Meg?' The trace of concern in his question both relieved and sickened her.

'Here he is.' And handing the phone over to her son, Meg rose and left the room so that she didn't have to listen to the conversation between them.

Damn him! Damn the man! Damn his selfishness and insensitivity! Damn his attempt to be concerned and friendly, when he had crushed her heart and trust and confidence under his heel as he walked away! Damn, damn, DAMN!

The cat shot out of the kitchen in alarm as she thumped her fists down on the work surface. How strange that her kitchen should be so orderly on Christmas morning. They had always spent the day at home, when one of the greatest pleasures for her had been producing a lavish turkey lunch with all the trimmings. Today there was no turkey. This Christmas she hadn't got round to honey-roasted ham spiked with cloves, or golden mince pies made from her own highly secret recipe.

This year Ben and she would be spending the day with Sandy and her family. And as she buried her head in her arms against the door frame, Meg knew that she had never viewed any prospect with less enthusiasm or more misery.

✤   ✤   ✤

'She's upset, isn't she? I could tell. Just imagine what it must be like for Ben and her being there all on their own today.' Emma stared accusingly at her dad and Katherine as she spoke.

In a familiar gesture of helplessness, Alan ran his fingers through his hair. 'I know, Goose. This is really hard on your mum. It's hard on all of us.'

'Why should it be hard on you? You've got exactly what you want!'

'I'd never WANT to hurt your mum.'

'Well, of course you hurt Mum if you have an affair with her best friend! And you, Katherine? How do you think Mum must be feeling about you, bearing in mind all the years you've been the best of friends?'

Katherine's face was pale, her gaze steady on Emma. 'I think it must have been a nightmare for her. I wish she'd never found out this way. I wish so much that we could have kept this from her a bit longer, until there was a kinder way to tell her . . .'

'. . . that you're her husband's bedmate?'

Katherine reached across to feel for Alan's hand. 'To tell her that your father and I regret so much the hurt and anguish this has caused her, and brought to you all. To tell her we never chose for this to happen . . .'

'Oh, please!' Emma snorted with disapproval.

'We didn't, Emma. When you're older you'll understand . . . you'll realise that in the span of many years, people change. Things change around you. Sometimes partners in marriage grow closer, but often they grow apart.'

'Dad and Mum were always close. You know they were.'

'It might have seemed that way, Goose,' interrupted Alan, 'but the truth is that your mum was so involved in her school work, and I was so tied up in my business, that we ended up not having much in common. We couldn't talk to each other about the things that filled our week, because honestly we weren't interested enough in what the other was thinking and feeling. I know I'm every bit as much to blame as your mum . . .'

'She didn't have an affair! She didn't walk out and leave you to cope on your own! You did!'

'Em, you must understand that what Katherine and I feel for each other is not just an affair. We're in love, very much in love. We've known for a long time that we have to be together. We just intended it to happen later when it would cause less distress not just for Mum, but for you and Ben too.'

'Well, bully for you! You're in love, are you! I'm sure Mum will feel that makes everything all right.'

'But haven't you left home for just the same reason? You say you love Matt, and because of that, you can no longer live at home?'

'But I'm seventeen. I'm supposed to be in love at seventeen! You're old. You're married to someone already. And you're a dad, MY dad! What right have you got to be in LOVE now?'

'The same right as you!' It was Katherine who broke across the raised voices. 'You never lose the ability to love, Emma, just as life never fails to surprise you with the situations it throws your way. Your father is the last man I would have chosen to fall in love with, but it happened. For a long time, we fought against it – but our love is simply a fact. We could have chosen to reveal how we felt years ago, and really wrecked your lives. But we didn't. And we both really regret the way it's all come out now. We're hurting about it, just as you are. And yes, I do love your mum, and of course she's the last person in the world I'd ever mean to hurt. But we didn't INTEND this. We didn't plan to cause pain and damage. It just happened – and now we've all got to deal with it, and move on to the next stage of our lives with dignity and compassion.'

Just as Emma was about to respond, Matt moved across to take her hand. 'Come on, Em. No need to get upset about this. It's Christmas. Let's go into the other room and listen to that new CD you bought me.'

For a moment, it seemed she might argue. And then without a backward glance, she allowed Matt to lead her out of the room.

'Darren! If I have to tell you one more time to stop doing that, I'll take that contraption away and put it in the dustbin! Do you hear me?'

Apparently he didn't, or perhaps couldn't over the high-pitched electronic screech and flashing lights of the Star Wars gun.

'The Force is with him!' grinned Dave.

'There'll be a force with him in a moment – the back of my hand!'

Dave stood behind Sandy and put his arms around her waist. 'Calm down, sweetie. You always get uptight when you're cooking Christmas dinner.'

'I do not!' she retorted sharply. 'But getting the timing right when you're cooking a complicated meal like this not just for the five of us but for visitors as well, is very difficult if you're under my feet all the time.'

'Can I help?'

'Yes. Get out of my kitchen!'

'I'd rather be in here with you than in there with Meg. She's plain hard work. Why on earth did you invite her?'

'Dave, I had to. She's wretched, poor love. Can you imagine how she must feel with everything that's happened, especially right on top of Christmas?'

He nodded. 'She looks as if she's about to burst into tears any minute. And Ben's not much better. He's a funny little kid, isn't he?'

'He does have a lot of problems, and I think he misses quite a bit because of his deafness. He's getting on all right with our kids though, isn't he? Is Jason letting him have a go on the computer?'

'I get the impression that Ben thinks Super Mario is beneath him . . .'

'Tough, that's all we've got. Isn't there anything on telly? A Walt Disney or something?'

Dave grinned. 'I have a feeling that might be a bit below the dignity of our lot too. If it's not at least a fifteen certificate, Darren simply isn't interested.'

Sandy looked at him with an expression of fondness and exasperation. 'Have we failed as parents?'

'Probably. Do you need a sherry?'

'At eleven o'clock in the morning, of course not!'

'Fancy a Turkish Delight then?'

Sandy's face softened. 'Heavens, I couldn't possibly! How anyone could be insensitive enough to buy me something as debauched as a box of those sugary, calorie-stuffed, melt-in-your-mouth sweets is quite beyond me!'

'I'll bring them through then, shall I?'

'I'd only have to look at them to put on pounds. And then you'll go off me, I know you will!'

A slow smile spread across her husband's face. 'Sweetheart, you never listen. I LIKE my women to have a bit of meat on them . . .'

'Women! I knew it! I KNEW it!'

But the sliding door into the kitchen was abruptly shut as with a chuckle, Dave disappeared from view.

Robert switched off the television with a grunt. If he heard one more Christmas carol, he thought he might throw something – and that would never do, not in his mother's pristine, neat-as-a-pin bungalow.

He thought longingly of Jonathan and Naomi, who would have opened their presents by now, judging by all the Christmases he remembered while the family had been together. Jonathan would probably have disappeared back up to his room with the typical secretiveness of a sixteen-year-old. Naomi, at six, with gaps in her teeth and excitement in every fibre of her small body, would be noisy and chatty, wanting to share the wonder of each and every present with her mum. With her dad too, if only he'd been allowed to be there. Would it have hurt Wendy to have relented on just that one special morning, so that they could both savour the pleasure of being with their children on Christmas Day?

It was hard now to recall a time when he and Wendy had been truly happy. Had they ever really been suited? In that heady time when they first married, was it possible that their romance and undoubted physical attraction had masked the difference in their needs and approach to life which had become a gulf between them in recent years. He hardly recognised her these days, her face either stiff with indifference or flaming with righteous indignation. Where had that vitriol come from? Had he put it there? Had the long hours he'd devoted to work, ostensibly to provide a good standard of living for them all, actually destroyed the family he thought he was working to support?

'Won't be a minute, dear! Just need to find my gloves . . .' His mother's voice rang through from the other room. She was always losing things, and rarely found them. He sat down heavily in one of her frilly, comfy armchairs knowing he could be in for a long wait. He hoped that his brother's wife who was cooking Christmas lunch for them all, knew her mother-in-law well enough to understand.

And then there was Katherine. Alan's revelation about their relationship had been such a bombshell. Even Robert, who was a veteran at keeping an extra-marital affair strictly secret, was shocked at the news. Who would ever have guessed it of steady old Alan, happily married family man? And more to the point, who would ever have imagined that Katherine, with her sleek, elegant looks and lifestyle, her quick brain and sophisticated sense of humour, could ever be guilty of anything as common as deceit, not just for a few days or weeks or months, but for year upon year?

He wondered how she was feeling now. He knew her friendship with Meg had meant a great deal to her, but he also recognised that any tittle-tattle which spilled over into her professional life would be an embarrassment for her. Would her love for Alan help her through that? Was she feeling triumphant to have got her man at last – or was she, as he suspected, a mixed-up bundle of excitement, remorse, guilt and trepidation? They were all emotions he knew so well.

He lay his head back against the soft cushions of the seat, closing his eyes as he thought of her. She was lovely. From the very start, he'd been drawn to her. And in her own quiet way, he knew that she had responded to him, even though he now knew that her passion for Alan had probably always stood between them.

So he had a choice. He could either write her off as a mistake, and keep his distance from both her and Alan – or he could be the caring, experienced friend she probably needed during this unsettled time. Whether she would want his friendship was another consideration, of course – but as he pictured her face framed by that shiny bob of dark hair, and those huge brown eyes which perhaps even now were brimming with tears, he made a decision. He would make contact with her. Not immediately – but he would make sure he saw her again.

'Oh, there you are, dear!' His mother bustled into the room, smelling of Evening in Paris, and wearing her treasured fur coat that for years she'd kept for best. 'Come on, we'll be late!'

'What do you mean, duck? We always have turkey for Christmas.'

Katherine didn't look at Emma as she leant over the beautifully laid table with its soft candlelight glowing in the cut crystal glasses, and placed the duck on the heated tray in the centre.

'I thought it would make a nice change.'

'Who wants a change? At Christmas everyone has turkey.'

'Well, we're not,' replied Katherine firmly. 'Do me a favour, Emma, and bring in the vegetables, will you?'

'I will,' volunteered Matt.

'I don't like duck. It's too fatty.'

'Have you ever tried it?'

'No, but I've read about it.'

'It's delicious. You might be pleasantly surprised.'

'Mum would never do anything as crass as duck on Christmas Day.'

A reply was on Katherine's lips, but she plainly thought better of it. At that moment, Alan came into the room carrying a plate of roast potatoes and the gravy boat, followed by Matt who was concentrating on not dropping the delicate antique serving platter which contained a variety of vegetables.

'What's that?' Emma's finger pointed at a pale vegetable in white sauce.

'Fennel. Very sweet, unusual flavour. You might like it.'

'What's wrong with Brussels sprouts?'

'Come on, Goose,' interrupted her father. 'Sit down and try it. Katherine's produced a wonderful spread, don't you think?'

Plainly Emma didn't think much at all as she stared at Matt hoping for his support. He was too busy tucking in his serviette to notice.

'Wine, Matt? Emma?'

'Matt would rather have a beer, and so would I.'

'We haven't got beer,' said Alan, 'so the choice is red or white. We've even got some champagne, if you fancy a glass.'

'Champagne gives me a headache.'

'Actually, Emma,' replied her father, 'it's you who's the headache. You've done nothing except moan and whinge about everything from the moment you got here.'

'Take me home then!'

'Alan . . .' But Katherine was ignored as Alan was too angry to stop.

'We've tried really hard to make you welcome here. It meant a lot that you chose to spend the day with us. But you try the patience of a saint, Emma, you really do.'

'This isn't your home! Home is where you SHOULD be on Christmas Day – and Mum is the person you should be with, not Katherine with her fancy glasses and her duck and her fennel. This isn't like Christmas at all. You've ruined it! Wrecked it completely!'

Katherine stood stock still, her eyes glued to the table for fear of what she might see in Alan's reaction to this tirade. In fact, he didn't reply immediately. He simply stared at his daughter as if unable to believe she could behave this way.

'Right,' he declared at last. 'Get your things. I'll take you both home.'

'Couldn't we have lunch first?' suggested Matt hopefully.

'No.' Emma was on her feet, red-faced as she faced Matt. 'Do you know, you can be completely useless at times!' She stormed towards the door. 'Especially when we both know this whole scene stinks!'

'Jason, how many times have I told you? Guests first! Pass the plate to Ben before you serve yourself.'

'It's all right,' said Ben. 'I'm not really hungry.'

'Don't worry, love.' Meg eyed her son anxiously as plates piled high with potatoes, Brussels, carrots, turkey and Yorkshire puddings were handed around. 'Just eat what you feel you can manage. He has a very small appetite,' she explained, although no one really was listening.

'Roast potatoes, babe?' asked Dave, offering the dish to Sandy.

'I can't. I'd love to, you know I would – but really I can't!'

'It's Christmas!' he announced, placing two particularly large potatoes on her plate. 'Calories don't count at Christmas.'

'Darren!' shrieked Joely. 'That was mine! I only asked you to pull my cracker, not KEEP it!'

'Give it back, Darren.'

'But Mum, why would she want a pack of cards? Joely, I'll swop you those cards for this keyring thing. Right?'

Joely's bottom lip was wobbling dramatically. 'Mum, make him give me my cards back. Make him, please . . .'

Dave suddenly leant across the table, grabbed the offending pack of miniature cards, and thumped them down in front of Joely. 'There! Satisfied now?'

Joely wailed. Darren slumped down in his chair and sulked. Jason helped himself to another three slices of turkey.

And Meg felt more alone than she had ever been in the whole of her life.

Meg and Ben escaped as fast as they decently could. By the time the washing up was done, the Queen's speech watched and the two adults in Sandy's household had fallen asleep in front of the James Bond movie, they felt they could make their excuses without anyone minding too much. With relief, mother and son shut their own front door behind them, pausing for a few seconds as they stood opposite each other in the hall to grin with relief that they were back on home territory. Then, of an accord, they fell together in a hug which told, without a word being spoken, of love and sadness and feeling dreadfully alone in a crowd.

Ben wanted to play his new computer game, and Meg longed to sink her shoulders into the comfort of a warm, soothing bath – so they agreed that they would meet up later in the lounge, where Ben would try and decipher the intricacies of the new DVD player in the hope that they could watch a film together with chocolates on their laps and favourite drinks to hand.

An hour later, with Meg in her dressing gown and her hair newly washed, the two of them curled up in companionable silence to watch the movie. It was then, just as the titles filled the screen, that the doorbell rang. With a groan, she dragged herself to her feet, wondering who on earth would be calling at that time on Christmas night.

Emma stood on the doorstep — but there was none of the belligerent, argumentative girl who stormed out of the house — was it really only a matter of days ago? At the sight of her mother, her face crumpled. 'I'm coming home, Mum. All right?'

There was no need to answer. Meg simply opened her arms, and Emma fell into them.

A movement just outside the gate made Meg look up to see that someone was standing there. For a second, as she glimpsed the raw pain and wretchedness in Alan's face, she thought of following her instinct to run to him and hug away all the hurt and nightmare of the past week.

But only for a second — before she drew her daughter into the hallway, and shut the door firmly behind them.

Chapter Eight

Chris looked down at the speedometer on his bike with a sense of satisfaction. Even in the failing winter light, he could see that they were making terrific time. Ben had just covered the distance of a mile in a little over seven minutes. That alone was surprising enough, but this was the second mile he'd covered at more or less the same speed. And if Chris was honest, he'd be hard pushed to match that pace himself – and he wasn't a twelve-year-old novice with no formal experience of running at all.

That February afternoon, they had decided to abandon the track facilities at Barford School, and head for the Valley Park just off the centre of the town. Any previous doubts that Ben was simply a natural talent at cross-country running were swept away as his circuit of the valley cycle paths confirmed his ability once and for all. Chris cycled alongside him, noticing that the boy was not only completely calm and focused, but that his breathing was far from laboured, and he didn't even seem to have broken out in a sweat. He was like a powerhouse of determination and stamina – not over-excited, not straining, simply steady, strong and inwardly resolute.

Finally, they swung round the slow bend which took them back to the car park where they'd begun.

'That was a good time, Ben.' Chris kept his voice matter-of-fact. He knew that over-enthusiasm from him would put unbearable pressure on the boy who would undoubtedly recoil if too much was expected of him. For the time being, running must remain a hobby, a personal challenge. Once the training had paid off, his strength was achieving its potential, and good technique had become second nature, then Ben would hopefully find the confidence to display his skill. At the moment, any public attention would frighten and embarrass him. Chris knew that in the future the boy's talent was likely to draw a great deal of positive attention and praise in his direction, but Ben would have to be emotionally as well as physically prepared for that.

Ben nodded without comment. He never said much, but somehow he didn't need to when the pleasure he obviously found in running was written all over his face – a very different expression from the apprehension Chris remembered seeing on the first day they had begun his training. Over the two months since, there had been a subtle shift in the relationship between them. They had started out as teacher and pupil, one knowledgeable and in control, the other nervous, almost as if he thought of the sessions as a form of punishment. But before long, Ben's enthusiasm grew to match his achievements. With Chris's experience and encouragement to spur him on, he found himself reaching his accepted limits, then going further to overcome them. He began to take a pride not just in doing what was asked of him, but a little bit more, and then more again.

As the two of them watched his stamina grow, the distance he covered lengthen and his times shorten, they both felt a glow of anticipation and accomplishment. More than that, a respect and genuine liking had filtered its way into their teacher-pupil relationship. Chris discovered that Ben combined a very pragmatic understanding of his own strengths and shortcomings with a quirky sense of humour. He was able to laugh at himself, quipping about his deafness, the size of his ears slowing him down when he was running at speed, and the beloved old knitted hat he insisted on wearing on cold days.

In Ben, Chris saw so many traces of himself as a boy – introverted, shy, different from all the rest. His own memory of how that felt guided him in the way he reacted to Ben – and gradually over the weeks, their initial distance and formality mellowed to become an easy companionship born from shared interest.

They avoided discussion about goals. Ben never asked why he should be learning the skills of running, and Chris never mentioned how those skills might be used. Certainly they both tacitly accepted that for the time being Ben's training sessions should remain private knowledge. There was no need for other members of the school to know about Ben's coaching, not because there was anything to hide, but because there was nothing to tell.

Chris glanced at his watch. 'Come on, we'll call it a day. It's starting to drizzle anyway. Hop in!'

With their bags and the bike safely installed in the back of Chris's elderly Mondeo Estate, it took them little more than ten minutes to arrive back at Ben's house – and as they pulled up outside, it was clear that Ben's mum had just returned from a trip to the supermarket judging by the heavy carrier bags she was struggling to pull out of the boot. While Ben hared from the car towards the house, Chris followed more slowly, meeting her eyes as he reached down to pick up the carrier bags.

'Don't worry, I can manage.'

'It's no trouble. Let me help.'

Gesturing to Ben to pick up the remaining bags, he followed Meg through to the kitchen before turning immediately to leave.

'Got time for a cup of tea?' she asked.

The suggestion surprised him. Since the first evening he'd met her when she had fainted so dramatically at the sight of him, he had never been invited over the threshold. He guessed that the family had been going through some sort of trauma. He didn't know exactly what had happened, and he would never ask, but he was aware that although Ben spoke often of his dad, there seemed to be no sign of his father living at home. Perhaps he worked away? Or perhaps, as was so often the case these days, he had left his wife and children. That would account for the unfathomable sadness he occasionally glimpsed in Ben's mother's eyes. It didn't take in-depth conversation or even much intuition to see that she was unhappy. But it was not his place to pry, so he didn't. He kept his distance and she kept hers. Until now.

'Well, if you're sure . . .?'

She didn't answer, stretching out instead to fill the kettle and pull two bone china mugs down from their hooks above the work surface. With sudden insight, Chris realised from the slight tremble of her hands that she was nervous. What had happened to this woman – a teacher well used to company and responsibility – that she was now so anxious and uncertain?

'Ben's doing really well.' When Chris opened the conversation with what he hoped was a safe topic, he was relieved to see her face light up with interest.

'I thought he must be. He doesn't say a great deal, but I know he loves the training sessions.'

'He's regularly running the distance of a mile in just over seven minutes. For a youngster of his age, that's a remarkable achievement.'

'Is it?'

'Actually I think your son has great potential.'

'You do?'

'Absolutely. And the most surprising thing is that I'd been teaching him games and PE for more than a year, and had no idea at all of his ability. He certainly kept it well hidden.'

'Didn't want to draw attention to himself, I suppose.'

'I'm sure you're right, Mrs Barratt, but it's a pity he felt that way. He really does have an outstanding talent.'

He held her gaze for a while, watching in fascination as his words brought a glow of pride and pleasure to her face.

'Meg,' she said with a smile. 'Please call me Meg.'

He nodded acknowledgement of the shift in their friendship. 'Thank you. And I'm Chris.'

The kettle belched out a jet of steam, then rattled to a stop. He watched as she filled the pot, then placed it on a tray along with their mugs and a half-eaten packet of biscuits. Minutes later, mug in hand, he settled back against the cushions at the opposite end of the sofa from Meg.

'Did you always want to be a teacher?' she asked.

'I always wanted to be involved in sport. Teaching seemed like a viable way to do that. But I love passing on my own enthusiasm for games and movement. I can honestly say that I've never regretted my decision to teach — apart from the money, of course . . .'

She grinned. 'Oh yes, we teachers do it all for love . . .'

'I could have been a David Beckham!'

'And just think of all the pleasures you'd have missed . . .'

'Surly fifteen-year-olds who are more interested in girls and alcohol, probably in that order, than kicking a ball around a field . . .'

'Working lunch times . . .'

'Late sessions after school hours . . .'

'Saturday morning matches . . .'

'The Sunday mornings are even worse . . .'

'Keeping the kit clean . . .'

He threw his head back and laughed. 'I'm talking to a fellow sufferer, aren't I? Do you teach sport too?'

'Drama is my speciality, and of course I work with a younger age group, infants and juniors. I've always got the Drama Club on the go though, and we do productions at the end of every term.'

'That must be hard work.'

'Yes, but I love it.'

A look of mutual understanding passed between them. 'Of course you do, and so do I. And you'll know it's especially encouraging when you come across a pupil who has real potential – like Ben.'

'But I'm very aware that you are using your own spare time to fit in all these extra sessions. Why should you bother?'

He shrugged. 'One bright spark like him makes all the effort worthwhile.'

'How much do the other boys at school know about the way he's training?'

'Nothing at all. Ben is anxious that they're told as little as possible.'

'It will have to come out eventually though.'

'Yes, and I've been thinking about the best way to do that.'

'Oh?'

'Have you heard of the Midsummer Run?'

She frowned, nodding her head.

'Well, it's been going for years. It's a challenge to all the senior schools in the area to compete in a cross-country run around the Valley Park. Some philanthropist set it up about thirty years ago in memory of his son who died very tragically just after his fourteenth birthday. Because of his age, the race is just for under-fourteens, so only the first two years at senior school are eligible to compete. Not only is it quite prestigious for the school that wins, but there's a rather magnificent trophy awarded to the winner.'

'And you think Ben should take part?'

'Most definitely.'

'Have you told him about this?'

'Not yet. We never really talk about his future in running.'

'I can understand that. Ben likes to feel safe in whatever he does. He's not keen on change. He's happy with the situation as it is, but I expect he'll get anxious if he thinks his running might make him the focus of attention at school.'

'Is that mostly because of his deafness?'

'Yes. He had meningitis when he was just five years old. We very nearly lost him. Somehow the fact that he's now stone deaf in one ear seemed a small price to pay when he might not have been here at all.'

'Would a hearing aid help? I notice he doesn't wear one.'

'He is profoundly deaf in that ear, so no, it wouldn't help at all. There's some talk of an operation which may provide hope in the future, but Ben isn't all that keen.'

'How much is he able to hear? He seems to cope quite well in class.'

'Well, he's become very practised at lip-reading over the years. He has problems when people turn their faces away from him, or when he's in a crowd. He just hears a jumble of sounds, and can only make out what an individual is saying if he's able to watch their lips.'

'But if he's managed with his deafness for so many years, why has it become so traumatic for him now?'

'It's the old problem of having to cope with change. Going to senior school was a real challenge for him.'

'And because he's covered his nerves by keeping himself to himself, he's become a target for the bullies.'

She sighed. 'There are always bullies in any school, just as there are people in every walk of life who love to feel big by belittling those who are unable to cope. He's been on the receiving end of bouts of bullying throughout all his school life. I suppose, though, because I taught at his junior school so could keep an eye on him, that he's got away fairly lightly until now.'

'Until Michael Smith.'

'Is that his name?'

'Oh, I'm keeping a very tight rein on young Michael Smith. Actually he's a lad I know quite well because he's a pretty good runner himself. I've got no illusions about him though. He can be a nasty piece of work, as Ben is learning the hard way.'

'And he has so much on his mind at the moment. I expect he's told you about all the changes we've been going through here . . .'

Chris's voice softened as he answered. 'I thought there was something, but he's not said a word.'

Meg studied her hands as she spoke. 'His dad . . . my husband . . . has moved to London. He's not living here any more.'

'When did he go?'

'The night I first met you. It had all happened that day. It was such a shock, a bolt out of the blue. I've been meaning to explain to you ever since. You must have thought my behaviour very odd . . .'

'Not at all. I realised you were going through a tough time. My only concern was that I was intruding . . .'

'Actually, your offer to befriend Ben has been the only bright spot in a pretty dismal couple of months.'

'Does Ben still see his dad?'

'Yes, but because Alan's now living so far away, it's not as often as he'd like.'

'And is his father – Alan – good with Ben? Do they get on well?'

Meg considered the question for a moment. 'It's difficult. Ben has always idolised his dad, and wanted to be like him in so many ways. Then Alan not only chose to leave, but has set up home with a woman who has been a really close friend of the family for years.'

'A close friend – of yours?' He watched closely as she

swallowed hard, unable to answer. 'Then in time he'll regret it — leaving a son like Ben, a home like this, a woman like you . . .'

'You don't know us. You don't know me. In the end, we didn't matter enough for him to stay. And I suppose it was me he really left, not the children. She meant more to him than I did. He preferred her. Perhaps he always did, and I was the only one who didn't realise it.'

'But that says more about him than it does about any of you.'

'I only know that he has been the centre of my life since I met him more than twenty years ago — and now he's gone, and so has Katherine. I'm left with a broken family, a broken home and a broken heart.'

'But you're coping. Your home looks wonderful. Ben is a credit to you. If there's any failure here, it seems to me it lies with your husband, not with you.'

She stared up at him then, as if looking closely at him for the first time. 'It doesn't feel like that.'

'Just because someone treats you as if you're worth nothing, you mustn't make the mistake of believing it's true. Isn't that exactly the lesson you want your son to learn? Ben is overcoming the odds to win through — and he will. You will too. Don't doubt that for a moment.'

'I haven't got the energy to think about winning anything. It's hard enough just getting through every hour of each day at the moment.' She got up suddenly, her arms folded tightly across her chest. 'I'm sorry. I can't believe I'm telling you all this.'

'I'm glad you did.'

'I just feel a bit raw about it all right now . . .'

'I'm not surprised.'

'It was unforgivable to burden you this way . . .'

'Don't worry about it.'

'I'm sorry, I'm holding you up. You must want to get home.'

'I'm fine.'

She held his gaze. 'You're very kind. Kind to Ben — and very patient with me too. We appreciate it. Thank you.'

'It's a pleasure.' They almost smiled at each other across the room, before he dug into his pocket for the car keys. 'Well, I'd better be on my way.'

'Of course.'

'I'll call for Ben again on Wednesday — about five o'clock, if that's all right with you.'

'Of course. Thank you again, Mr Elliott.'

'No thanks needed. And the name's Chris.'

'Chris.'

'I'm a good listener, Meg.'

'Look, you must understand I don't make a habit of pouring my heart out to someone I hardly know . . .'

'I'm sure you don't, which is why I consider it an honour. Sometimes it's easier to talk to a stranger. And the listening service is always on offer. Any time. Please remember that.'

For a moment, he thought she was going to cry as she bit down on her lower lip to stop it trembling. To his surprise, it was all he could do to stop himself crossing the room to put his arms around her, to try and take her pain away.

But he didn't. And she didn't speak as he inclined his head in a gesture of farewell, then left closing the front door quietly behind him.

'This is delicious.'

Katherine beamed at Alan across the softly lit table. 'Good. I'm glad you like it.'

'I worry about you organising special dinners like this every night when I know you're so busy at work yourself.'

'It's no trouble. I enjoy it, honestly.'

He stretched out across the table to touch her fingers. 'You're beautiful.'

'I love you.'

He withdrew his hand and carried on eating. 'I saw Robert Masters today,' he said.

'Oh?'

'He asked after you. He always asks after you.'

'He must think very badly of me.'

'If he does, it doesn't show. We have to work together, of course, because of the software systems I'm introducing for him – but I get the feeling he'd like to punch me hard on the nose for stealing you from him.'

'You didn't steal me from anyone. I was always yours.'

'But he didn't know that.'

'Well, he does now. Everyone does.'

'How do you feel about it?'

'About our love being common knowledge? I'm relieved of course.'

'You don't feel embarrassed – don't feel that people are judging you, condemning what we've done?'

Katherine laid down her fork and stared steadily across at him. 'No. But you plainly do.'

He shrugged. 'I suppose I can't help thinking about what people must be saying. I've left the wife I've been married to for nineteen years. I've walked out on my children . . .'

'But you've always said you wanted it to happen one day. It was only a matter of time.'

'I know, but I still feel guilty. I can't help it.'

She sat back in her seat. 'Are you having second thoughts then? Do you miss Meg?'

'Don't you? She was your friend as much as she was mine.'

'Are you saying you want to go home?'

'I couldn't even if I wanted to. That door is definitely shut.'

'That's not what I asked. Do you WANT to go home, Alan – because you can leave any time, you know that.'

'I do – and no, I don't want to leave. I'm happy here. I am happy with you.'

She looked at him thoughtfully for a few moments, before picking up her fork again. Apart from the Celine Dion CD playing softly in the background, there was silence between them.

Much later, while Katherine busied herself with loading the dishwasher and making freshly ground coffee for them both, Alan stretched out on her elegant sofa, his hands clasped behind his head, his feet resting on of the business papers he had spread out right across the nearby coffee table. How different life was here. At home, meals were always rushed affairs, with each member of the family working to a different timetable, and sometimes, especially in Emma's case, a completely different diet. Over the years, it had become the habit that if Meg cooked supper, then Alan would wash up while his wife marked books, then organised Ben's bed-time by sharing a cup of hot chocolate with their son. Life with the family was disorganised, irregular and often downright chaotic. How he loved the peace and orderliness of life with Katherine . . .

She came into the room at that moment, placing a cafetière of coffee on the low table in front of him. He looked up at her, taking in the smile which flicked across her mouth as she leaned forward to kiss him. Pulling her roughly down towards him, he lost himself in the feel of her, the softness of her body, the smell of her hair as it draped across him.

'I do love you, you know.' His voice was muffled as he buried his face against her shoulder, her arms tight around him.

'But do you really want to be here? Do I make you happy?'

He tilted her head back gently so that he could look straight into her eyes. 'More than you'll ever know.'

'I'm so scared I'll lose you – that you'll change your mind, choose to go back.'

'Katherine, I love you. And I'm here to stay . . .'

Her lips silenced him then. With a sigh, he drew her closer, coffee forgotten, all thought postponed by the familiar comfort as their bodies entwined.

Emma dragged on her cigarette as she sat cross-legged in Matt's bedsit, watching him pull out the last two lagers from the cupboard under the sink. He gulped down half a can before handing her the other, then laid down beside her on the battered old futon.

'I need to go.'

Matt's shrug was noncommittal. 'Your decision.'

'She's still in such a state. She'll only worry.'

'You should never have gone back home at Christmas. When you made the break, you should have stuck by it.'

She pivoted round so that her knees were touching him. 'I wanted to, Matt. You know that.'

'Do I?'

'Christmas was horrendous. You thought so too. I just couldn't leave Mum facing all that on her own.'

'Easier to leave me, was it?'

She knelt forward so that her arms encircled his chest. 'I'm here, aren't I?'

'But you're back in little girl mode, having to get home because Mummy expects you.'

'You always said that what you liked most about me was my heart. Caring, that's what you said. Well, I am – and you can sulk all you like, but I think that's how you really want me.'

His only answer was to pull her head down towards him, kissing her soundly before reaching out again for the can. 'You haven't stayed for a whole night since Christmas. I miss you, that's all.'

She smiled. 'Good!'

'It's not.'

'Well, at least she doesn't try to stop me being here. And now you can come to the house whenever you want, it's not so bad, is it?'

'I just feel her watching me, as if she thinks I'm going to pinch the silver or something.'

'Actually, she quite likes you.' Matt gave a snort of disbelief. 'She does. I think she's just so relieved that I came home, she'd forgive anything.'

'Even me?'

'You getting her car started the other evening probably helped. She'd be lost without that old Fiesta of hers.'

'I have my uses then, do I?'

She slipped her fingers inside the buttons of his shirt. 'You certainly do.'

'Will your dad come back, do you think?'

'I've wondered about that. He misses us, I know he does. I think he misses Mum too.'

'That Katherine is real classy though. He's landed on his feet there.'

'But it's not where he belongs.'

'He seemed pretty settled with her at Christmas.'

'Do you think so?'

'Well, he's been there for a while now, hasn't he, so he probably hasn't got a choice any more. Your mum would never have him back, would she?'

Emma considered the question for a while. 'I'm not sure. They've been together for so long. Mum's not very good on her own.'

'She's not on her own though, is she? She's got you back at home again.'

'Yeah, and that's where I'm going right now.' Her hair fell on either side of his face as her lips brushed his. 'Ring you later.'

'From under the duvet.'

'The best sort of goodnight.'

'Except when you're under the duvet here.'

'Love you.'

'Sure?'

'Sure.'

'That's all right then.'

The three women sat round the scrubbed wooden table in Val's kitchen, which they had long acknowledged as the very best place for heart to hearts, especially when the subject was as important as the one under discussion that day. Sandy was almost red-faced with determination to get her point across.

'You must, Meg, you simply must. You have to protect yourself, and the children too.'

'But I don't believe Alan would ever do anything to jeopardise our security . . .'

'Like going off with your best friend, do you mean? Of course he'll jeopardise your security if it suits him!'

'But it's sure to get bloody once solicitors get involved. Everyone says that. I just don't think I'm ready to do anything official yet.'

Val pushed the biscuit barrel in Meg's direction. 'Well, I think you're right. Talk to him about terms of separation, by all means. See what you can agree amicably between you – but that might be all that's needed right now.'

'Oh, for heaven's sake!' Sandy looked as if she might explode with frustration. 'Don't you see? He won't want to live in Katherine's place for long. It's too small for a start. Besides, he's a money man, isn't he! He's not going to leave his share of your equity sitting in a house in which he no longer lives. He's going to want to take what he feels is rightfully his so that he can set up on his own. He's far too much of a business man to do anything else!'

'Look, I do know that Alan feels really guilty about what he's done, so why should he choose to hurt us even more? He knows I don't earn a lot. He knows how expensive it is to live with two teenagers. I honestly don't think he'd mean to harm us any more than he has already.'

Sandy snorted. 'He's a man, isn't he? When it comes to a choice between loyalty and money, money will win hands down. He's moved on, Meg. He's not your reliable old Alan any more. In fact, he never was, was he? Wake up and see things as they really are.'

'Perhaps it's too soon,' said Val soothingly. 'Starting divorce proceedings is an emotional decision. I'm not sure Meg's up for that yet.'

'But emotion can get in the way of good old-fashioned common sense. Don't forget he'll have Katherine in his ear encouraging him to get things settled . . .'

'I don't think she'd be like that, really I don't.' Meg leaned forward on the table cupping her forehead in her hand. 'She's got what she wants now. Alan has left me, and is living with her. What could be more settled than that?'

'But you can't move on, can you? You're still married to a man who is sharing his life with another woman. You are living in a house that is as much his as yours – but he still holds the purse strings, so if he decides to stop paying the mortgage and the other bills, you'll be in trouble but he can walk away. You're still in his power. You can't get on with anything without his permission.'

'I don't feel strong enough to cope with any more change. As long as Emma, Ben and I can carry on living at home, and Alan keeps up maintenance, then he and Katherine are welcome to each other. I have very little interest in them.'

'Ah, but you must have, especially if Alan decides he needs money to sort out his life with her. Really, Meg, I speak as your friend. You have to give this serious thought.'

Meg stared at Sandy blankly. 'OK, but no promises.'

'Good! And just to help you focus your thoughts, I've booked an appointment for you with David Salmon, the solicitor on the High Street.'

'You what!'

'He's a friend. You can trust him. Just go and have a chat, Meg, please.'

'I can't afford fancy solicitor's fees.'

'The first consultation of twenty minutes is free. You've got nothing to lose. Look, here's his card. Your appointment is after school on Thursday.'

'Do you want me to come with you?' asked Val.

'No.' Meg drew back her shoulders and took a deep breath. 'It can't do any harm just to talk. I can do that.'

'Good girl!' beamed Sandy. 'You show him!'

It was a letter that arrived first, and the request it contained took Katherine by surprise.

Dear Miss Blake, it began.

Your name has been suggested to me with very high recommendation. I know we need help, and I think you may be exactly the right person to assist us. I am aware that you already have an extremely busy workload, but I hope and pray that you might feel able to consider our request.

I belong to a small order of nuns based at the Convent of Mercy just off Commercial Road in East London. In fact, we are only a mile or two away from your own office, but life for residents in this area couldn't possibly be more different from the big business world with which you are familiar in the City of London. Part of the richness of this old dockland area is the great diversity of nationalities and traditions to be found here, from true cockneys to families from the Caribbean, India, Pakistan, Ireland and a very established Jewish presence. On the whole, they are a hardworking, fairly harmonious community, but there is a great deal of poverty here, not just of the body but of the soul too.

For more than eighty years, the sisters of the Convent of Mercy have worked in a small, independent hospital, St Mary's, which has provided a very personal service for the community around it. We have time for our patients. We recognise the cultural elements which may mean they need a particular approach or special understanding. Because of this, the hospital is held in very real affection by this community, so you can understand how much shock and resistance there is to the fact that it may soon have to close its doors for ever. We know the building is old and in desperate need of renovation, as the authorities are constantly pointing out to us. In fairness, they have supported us very generously in the past, but our facilities have reached the stage where they feel it would be bad financial practice to pour more money into what they see as our dilapidated facility, when there are so many other calls on their limited resources. Our community is appalled at the thought of losing the hospital they love and trust, and we are mounting a campaign to save St Mary's. We need two million pounds at least; a daunting amount, I know, but we are determined to find it. After all, we stand just a couple of miles away from a square mile of London in which millions of pounds change hands each day. It MUST be possible for us to touch the hearts of our neighbours in the world of high finance, and enlist their help so that St Mary's can continue its unique work in the community.

And that is where you come in. Your name was mentioned very warmly at our Trustees' Meeting the other evening, and I was delegated the task of making contact with you. We need to get our message across to the men with money in the City of London. You, I understand, run a public relations company which deals specifically with just the people we need to meet. Could you be our go-between? Could you help us with some public relations work which might save the life of St Mary's?

Of course, you must feel free to refuse at once, because I recognise how busy you certainly are, but I hope that before you make a decision, you will allow yourself the opportunity to come and see for yourself just how much our work means to the people in this area.

I will wait anxiously to hear from you. My very warm wishes to you until then.

Yours in Him,
Sister Mary Lawrence

Katherine sat back in her chair and read the letter again. 'Mentioned warmly'? 'Suggested with very high recommendation'? That was nice to know, but she simply couldn't think who would have described her in that way.

There were two very good reasons why she should say no. Firstly, she had more work than she could comfortably manage at present. Secondly, her company was still young enough to suffer from cash-flow problems. This work would undoubtedly be done for love not money. On a personal level, she was quite happy about that. Her bank manager, however, would probably not agree.

That was settled then. She would simply write Sister Mary Lawrence a friendly but definite refusal.

So it came as rather a surprise to her when without another thought, she picked up the phone and dialled the number of the Convent of Mercy.

A letter was waiting on the doormat when Katherine walked through her front door that evening. It was long, white, obviously formal – and surprisingly it had been sent to Alan at this address. When he left, Meg had immediately arranged for his mail to be re-directed to his office, so in fact this was the very first letter to be sent to him here. Intrigued and curious, Katherine decided to put the envelope on the mantelpiece where he would be sure to see it as soon as he got in.

Stepping into the lounge, she was greeted by a sight which was equally unusual. Having been used to living alone for so many years, her home had always been scrupulously tidy. There was a place for everything, and everything had its place. Cushions once plumped and shaped remained plump and in shape. The pile on the carefully vacuumed carpet stayed upright and fluff-free. Dust was never allowed to settle or flowers fade. Newspapers were whisked into the bin immediately they stopped being current. Any work brought home was filed away in the cabinet or back in her briefcase without delay so that nothing could be lost or fall into confusion.

Until Alan came. She looked around her cherished room with dismay. His shoes were lying at the side of the sofa, beside his jacket which had been thrown across the arm of the chair. One silk cushion was on the floor, the other had been squashed awkwardly into the corner of the seat by the weight of his body as he had stretched out the night before. On the coffee table among an array of his work papers was a wineglass, still half full. When she picked up the uncorked bottle beside it, she frowned at the sight of the ring of red wine left behind on the polished surface.

She doggedly ignored the bubble of annoyance within her, putting on one of her favourite CDs before starting to clear, polish and make good again. At last, with her arms full of his jacket, papers and shoes, she made her way through to the bedroom, where she picked her way across his bags and suitcase which were piled up between the foot of their bed and the stylish old stripped-pine wardrobe which she had been so pleased to find for her room. Even though she had cleared hanging and drawer space for him, he seemed reluctant to unpack his bags and move in properly. He plainly wasn't ready to settle yet, and that thought depressed her – but then so did the state of the flat since his arrival.

When the time was right, she would have to say something. It wasn't that she was unwilling to compromise. They both understood how thrilled she was to have the man she adored living with her at last. In so many ways, their contentment together was almost too good to believe. But his untidiness, learned from years of family life with Meg and the children, was not appropriate in such a small flat. He would understand that. He would have to.

She smiled as she heard his key in the door. Within seconds

she was in his arms, as eager as she had always been to be close to him, taste his lips, feel his body moulding itself against her. Sighing deeply, she relaxed into the pleasure and security of his embrace. 'You look tired,' she said, touching his face.

'Umm. Tough day.'

'Me too. Are you hungry?'

'Quite.'

'I'll get supper started then.'

He leaned down to kiss her. 'You're lovely.'

'You're not so bad yourself . . .'

'I think I'll have a shower.'

'Right. Oh, and there's a letter for you – on the mantel-piece.'

It was some time later, once Katherine had cooked the fresh pasta, tossed it in pesto sauce and prepared a crisp green salad, that she joined Alan in the lounge, where she was shocked to see that the blood seemed to have drained from his face.

'Darling, whatever's wrong?'

He looked down at the letter in his hand. 'Meg is divorcing me.'

'Is that such a surprise?'

'It is to me.'

'But you've left her. You're living here now. In her position, what else could she possibly do?'

'But I'm still paying the mortgage and all the bills. She and the kids are lacking for nothing – so why the hurry? Why does she have to do this?'

'Because what she hasn't got is a husband. She obviously wants to get on with life as a single woman again.'

'What do you mean? She can't do that. She's a mother.'

'Well, I suppose she just wants to get the financial arrange-ments settled so that she can move on.'

'The financial arrangements are fine as they are. I'm happy to keep supporting my family as I always have done. I simply don't see what difference a divorce would make at the moment. It's too soon.'

'It would make a difference to me, for a start.' He stared at her as she continued. 'Don't look so surprised. Of course the details of your separation must be discussed and agreed before too long, so that Meg knows where she stands, and we do too. This flat is too small for us now, we both know that. You need space of your own — a study perhaps, and a workshop for all that carpentry you enjoy so much. How can we possibly do that unless you take your fair share out of the house?'

'Meg loves that house. So do the kids. I couldn't possibly ask them to leave.'

'Then perhaps Meg will have to buy you out? You'll have to come to some compromise which is best for all of you. But it has got to be done, Alan, and probably the sooner the better. Your solicitor will tell you that.'

'Don't you think, Katherine, that I've caused them enough upset already? I don't want to be responsible for them losing their home too.'

She looked as if she were about to say more, but changed her mind. 'Supper's ready. Come and eat.'

'I'll have to talk to Meg about this.'

'Can you? I thought she was refusing to talk to you about anything.'

'And that really upsets me. After all our years together, Meg and I must be able to discuss things like this which matter so much to us both.'

'To all of us, I think you mean.'

He looked across at her as she began to dish out the pasta. 'Yes, you're right. But you must understand, Katherine, that Meg and the children are the priority here.'

She handed him his plate. 'Of course they are. Now eat this while it's hot. And I've got a bottle of chilled Chardonnay in the fridge.'

The pasta was delicious, and the salad crisp and fragrant with herbs. But each of them was plainly so preoccupied with their own thoughts that for the first time since their relationship had begun, they ate almost in silence.

Chapter Nine

Emma had been reluctant to return to school after Christmas, determined as she had been to go through with her declaration to the head teacher at the end of term that she intended to give up her 'A' level studies and get a job (and as it was a rather strict all-girls school, she thought better of mentioning her intention of living with Matt in case they either chose to patronise her or not take her decision seriously at all).

However, after the shock of her father's defection with Katherine, followed by the Christmas fiasco at the London flat, Emma had found herself unexpectedly longing for the familiar comfort of home. On Christmas evening when her dad had gone along with her request that he first dropped off Matt, then took her home, she had been overwhelmingly grateful to sink into her mother's arms. Since then, for two women who had always found the mother–daughter relationship surprisingly strained, they had discovered an element of respite in each other's company. To see her mum obviously heartbroken, when she was usually so busy, organised and detached from the everyday ups and downs of her teenage daughter's life, made Emma feel valued and vital to the remaining trio of their family.

The three of them, Meg, Ben and Emma, drew strength from each other as they struggled to come to terms with their change of situation. Hearing her mother sob herself to sleep at night, noticing how she went quiet whenever Alan or Katherine's name were mentioned, seeing how she struggled to sort out bills, repairs and other decisions around the house that had previously been the domain of her father, added to Emma's own deep sense of loss. Both Meg and Emma were aware of a subtle re-aligning of their relationship, from mother and daughter who actually didn't know each other very well, to two women who needed each other's love, understanding and friendship. It was a fragile truce for which each in their own way was very grateful.

The turning point for Emma was her mum's change of heart about Matt. She seemed so thankful that her daughter was home that she was prepared to accept anything in order to keep her there. When first invited in, Matt had been reserved and awkward, but increasingly Mum was getting used to seeing him at their home, even making him cups of tea when he arrived, or inviting him to stay for a meal. More than that, Ben liked him – and if ever anyone needed a friend, it was Ben. He had taken his father's leaving as a personal rejection. Apart from occasional flashes of genuine enthusiasm for his new hobby of running, he cut a rather forlorn, solitary figure.

When Matt first started standing behind Ben's shoulder as he played the advance levels of a particularly challenging game on the computer, Ben had felt irritation and a sense of intrusion. It wasn't until Matt quietly suggested a move which gave his game the advantage he needed that Ben decided discussion with Matt would be all right providing it was confined to computer talk. Even now their conversations covered little more than that, but Matt had developed the knack of very gently teasing Ben, not offensively, but with good humour to which the younger boy responded.

Emma knew that her mum probably still thought Matt wasn't anywhere good enough for her only daughter – and perhaps in the long term she may be proved right – but for the time being, as weeks went by, attitudes adjusted, and emotional wounds, although still raw and throbbing with confusion, were kept for private moments rather than public perusal, Matt was accepted as a regular and welcome visitor.

And so, in this new climate of understanding and need for each other, Emma had gone back to school. She didn't mention her decision to her mother in advance, and when she returned home at the end of the first day of term, Meg made no comment beyond a silent hug.

Now, almost three months later, the workload on Emma as her 'A' levels approached was heavy and challenging. Her mother tentatively suggested that perhaps she was seeing too much of Matt, because plainly more study time was needed. Emma curtly responded that faced with the burden of work ahead of her, her time with Matt was more precious than ever. If there was anyone she would happily give up seeing, it wasn't Matt, but her father.

In spite of herself, Meg couldn't help taking comfort in the fact that her daughter felt a sense of rejection by Alan almost as keenly as she did herself – but remembering the former closeness between her husband and their daughter brought sadness too. To be fair, although she hadn't spoken directly to Alan since his visit on the day it all happened, she recognised how painful Emma's distance would be for him. It was undoubtedly a loss for them both.

Alan made a point of coming down from London each Sunday afternoon to see Ben and Emma. Meg could avoid him because he didn't come to the door, but when Ben heard the toot of his dad's car horn, he would sidle reluctantly away from the computer to join him for a couple of hours. Emma, on the other hand, ignored the fact that he was there, just as she refused to take his calls. And when Ben returned, Meg was aware that he was often quiet or even tearful enough to scuttle straight back to his room where he firmly locked the door to all intruders.

One Sunday in March when Alan and Ben returned from

wherever they'd been that afternoon, Meg was sitting at the table marking books. To her surprise, instead of heading straight upstairs, Ben poked his head around the lounge door.

'Dad wants a word.' Meg froze. 'He's waiting at the front door. Shall I tell him to come in?'

Her mind was racing. What should she do? This was no longer his home. He didn't belong here. Her thoughts were too muddled for conversation, and there was the humiliating danger that just seeing him face to face would make her want to cry again, perhaps with anger, perhaps regret. No, she couldn't see him. It was out of the question. Besides, she looked a mess.

She started as she heard him knock on the open front door. 'Meg? Meg, I just need a short chat. I'll understand if you feel you'd rather not – but please, I would appreciate a few minutes of your time.'

This was an Alan she didn't recognise. This man sounded uncertain, contrite, conciliatory – and she knew instinctively that she couldn't trust him, or herself in his company. Then, perhaps because she KNEW that, or maybe because just the sound of his voice, familiar and yet unheard for so long, touched a chord deep within her, she realised she was walking zombie-like towards the door.

A jolt shot through her as she saw him. He looked thinner, greyer both in his appearance and attitude. The man she saw before her was hesitant and unsure of his ground, as if he expected the door to slam immediately in his face. Endless seconds passed as they stared at each other. For twenty years, they had been intimate partners. Now they stood on opposite sides of the threshold: defensive, curious, hearts thumping with fear.

At last she stood back to let him come in, leading him through to the kitchen where she could remain standing and in control with the front door only yards away so that if necessary, she could simply ask him to leave.

Neither knew quite how to start. At last, Alan broke the

awkward silence. 'It's good to see you, Meg.' She could hardly say the same of him, so she said nothing. 'How have you been?' he continued.

'What do you want, Alan?' Her heart lurched as he ran his fingers through his hair, knowing that had always been a sign that he was anxious or apprehensive.

'I got a letter – from your solicitor.'

'Yes.'

'I didn't know you'd done that. I never imagined you'd go to a solicitor straight away . . .'

'Why not? You must agree we need to sort things out. Seeing a solicitor is the first step.'

'Can't we just discuss things between us? You're happy with the financial arrangements at the moment, aren't you?'

'Yes, but that can't continue, can it? You left me for my best friend. Your actions have torn the heart out of our family, and this home which we've all loved for years is full of painful memories now. The children and I need to move on, just as you and Katherine have.'

'But I didn't think you'd divorce me – not yet.'

'I don't understand, Alan. What are you trying to say?'

'That it's all so recent. Why the hurry? If in the future, divorce seems the only answer, then why can't we wait two years or however long it is, and do it quietly then?'

'Oh no, I don't think so. Have you any idea how I'd feel for the next two years to be married to a man who is living openly with another woman?'

'I don't want a divorce yet, Meg.'

'So you say.'

'And I don't want you to sell this house. It's the kids' home. It would be unfair to uproot them now.'

Meg's eyes narrowed as she stared at him. 'So you don't want a divorce, and you don't want Ben, Emma and me to leave this house. Why not, Alan?'

'Surely there's been enough upheaval already?'

'Of your choosing. You've made your decision and acted on it. Now it's time for us to make ours.'

'Please, Meg . . .'

'And I'll tell you why you don't want me to sell this house. Because you think you may want to come back here. That's it, isn't it?'

He swallowed hard before he answered, his eyes fixed on hers. 'Yes.'

'You're not sure that things are going to work out with Katherine?'

'I'm not sure of anything at the moment. I have no idea how I feel, where I am, what to do . . . Meg, I'm just lost, floundering . . .'

She watched almost in horror as he seemed to crumple before her, arms clasped around his chest, despair contorting his face until he looked almost in physical pain. Shocked at the sight of him, Meg was rooted to the ground for some seconds before she felt herself moving towards him, covering the distance between them to draw him into her arms. For minutes they stayed there, damaged and distraught, soaking up the familiar comfort, smell and feel of their bodies as they clung together. Then, as she felt his lips on her hair and the shift of his arms as he tightened their hold around her, she pulled back abruptly.

The wretchedness in his face appalled her. Did Katherine know he felt like this? Did he allow her to glimpse the despair Meg was seeing in him now? Was it for this that he had wrecked their marriage and family? If, after everything that had happened, after all the shock, the heartbreak, the humiliation, he wasn't happy, then what on earth was it all for?

'I'm sorry, Meg,' he managed to say at last. 'Sorry I hurt you. And the kids — I can't bear to think how I've let them down. Ben looks at me as if I'm the enemy. Emma can't even stand to be in my company . . .'

'What did you expect? You're their father. They've grown up secure in the knowledge that you'd always be central to their lives – and then you made a choice that excluded them. By choosing to make a home with Katherine, you are no longer here for them. Is it surprising that they are making choices too – to get on with their own lives without you? Isn't that exactly the same decision that you've made?'

'I don't remember making a decision. I only remember making a mistake.'

'Getting caught, you mean – and how much of a mistake could it have been if it's already lasted more than nine years?'

'Meg, I accept it all. I've behaved in the most appalling way. I have hurt and betrayed you when all you've ever given me was your love and trust. I've wrecked the children's lives by robbing them of their sense of security, and their instinct of what is right and wrong. I've been selfish, arrogant, deceitful . . .'

'And all because you love Katherine?'

'Do I? It doesn't feel that simple. I look at you and feel overwhelming love for you. Oh, I know you could never trust me again, and I don't know what I'm trying to say really. I'm just not sure of anything any more.'

There was a mix of hardness and pity in her eyes as she looked at him. 'Are you going to continue living with Katherine?'

'I don't know.'

'Then I don't know that there is anything more to say. Go please, Alan. Just go.'

He didn't argue. The fight was gone out of him. Without a word, he slowly backed out of the kitchen, pulling the front door closed behind him.

Meg remained perfectly still, her fingers gripping the work surface, until she felt the trembling begin in the pit of her stomach, spreading until her whole body was shaking beyond control, and her mind blissfully, thankfully cleared of all coherent thought.

Katherine had grown to dread Sunday afternoons. Weekends in Alan's company were always so wonderfully special, and yet without any question of discussion, at noon each Sunday he would get in the car and go. What hurt her most was the fact that he always talked about going 'home' to see Ben and Emma, as if the flat they now shared had no role in his mind as 'home'. Whether or not he also saw Meg, she didn't know because she couldn't bring herself to ask. In fact, she thought of Meg often, missing the ease and comfort of their long friendship. Her betrayal of the trust between them laid heavy on her conscience. Whatever Meg thought of her now – and she deserved every ounce of vitriol and blame that came her way – Katherine had always really cared for Meg. Falling in love with her husband had been a dreadful, unplanned, shocking revelation.

For years, Katherine had kept her fondness in check to the extent that no one, particularly not Alan himself, would ever have guessed how she felt. His despair during Ben's illness, and his need for a sympathetic and understanding listener, had awakened emotions within her that she'd thought had been buried for good. In the end, it had been Alan who had made the first move – but once made, Katherine couldn't help but respond. Months passed after that in which they deliberately made sure they were never alone, each of them appalled at the implications of their attraction to one another. Whenever Katherine visited Meg and the children, which was often, Alan kept his distance – and if Meg noticed his new detachment towards Katherine, it was never mentioned.

It had been Alan's move to work in London that had changed their relationship from old friends to lovers. Once he started basing himself in the City throughout the week, they found it impossible to resist the temptation to meet first for a coffee during the day, then a drink after work one evening. Later, lunches when they met very respectably during daylight hours became candlelit dinners, initially in restaurants, eventually at her flat. From there, it was only a matter of time before Alan arrived (for supper) one evening not leaving again until after breakfast the next morning.

Katherine knew that within their small circle, she was now reviled and blamed for stealing the husband of her very dearest friend, but nothing anyone else said or thought could be worse than her own guilt and remorse at hurting the woman who had always felt close enough to be a sister rather than just a friend. So many times over the years, Katherine had tried to put an end to their affair, but Alan wouldn't hear of it. They loved one another, of that there was no doubt. Perhaps it sounded trite to say that they both loved Meg too – but they did.

The passion between them felt too strong, too important, too overwhelming to be abandoned – and although for all those years neither of them had ever seriously voiced the suggestion that he should leave his family, they both acknowledged that one day they would be together. That day had always seemed far off, at an unspecified time when the children would be independent, and Meg perhaps in the position of wanting more of a life of her own.

They had never intended their feelings to cause hurt for the people they loved. They had never planned for their relationship to become public in a way which made it seem sordid and tacky. But it had happened – and in the depths of her, Katherine was pleased. Except on Sunday afternoons, which always stretched ahead of her as times of loneliness and remorse.

That day, after she'd tried to do a bit of work, read the paper from cover to cover, then made three abortive phone calls to old friends none of whom were in, she made a decision. A phone call to Sister Mary Lawrence, then she was in the car and heading through the City of London towards St Mary's Hospital.

There was a smile on Katherine's lips as she turned the key in the flat door at gone seven that evening. The experience of being at St Mary's had got her buzzing. From the moment she'd picked her way up the steps of the once grand old building, she had been engulfed in scenes which challenged her senses and touched emotions in the very heart of her.

It had started the moment she pushed open the creaking swing doors to find herself walking into the open arms of Peter. At least that's how he introduced himself after he allowed her up for air, and she looked into a face fringed by tufts of greying hair, clear blue eyes, and a lop-sided grin in which the lack of an occasional tooth only added to its unique charm.

'Hello!' he bellowed. 'I've been waiting for you.'

'For me?'

'I'm Peter.'

'Peter.'

'I wait for people. I was waiting for you.'

'Well, hello Peter. I wonder if you can tell me where I might find Sister Mary Lawrence?'

'I wait for her too.'

'I bet she likes that. Do you know where she is now?'

'She told me to stand here and wait.'

'So she's coming back? Should I wait for her here?'

'I'm Peter.'

'And I'm Katherine Blake. Is it me you've been sent to meet?'

Leaning forward close enough for her to feel his hot breath on her cheek, she almost jumped when he grabbed her hand. 'You come! You come!' For a big man, he was surprisingly light on his feet, and Katherine was propelled at speed along first a wide corridor, then through what appeared to be a ward for mostly elderly people, and finally up some stairs to an area which seemed to be a mixture of private rooms and offices.

'Sister Mary Lawrence!' boomed Peter as he ran. 'Sister Mary Lawrence, she's here!'

To her great relief at that moment Katherine saw a head peer around one of the doors ahead of them.

'For heaven's sake, Peter,' said a soft Irish voice, 'you'll be frightening poor Miss Blake if you drag her around like that! I'm so sorry, my dear. Our Peter takes his doorman duties very seriously.'

Released from his grasp, Katherine smiled up at her guide. 'Thank you, Peter. It was kind of you to show me the way.'

'Fine!' His face lit up with a sunny smile. 'Fine! Bye!' And at a much slower pace, he shuffled back down the corridor to resume his guard on the front door.

Katherine turned her attention then to the small, wiry figure beside her. Sister Mary Lawrence's small, pale face, framed by its black and white hood, looked at her with warm curiosity.

'You're younger than I imagined you would be. What a wise head you must have on your young shoulders, my dear, that you should succeed in such a challenging profession.'

'I think the work you do here is far more challenging than anything. I ever have to face.'

'Well, come and see. Let's start upstairs. The children's ward is such a favourite of mine.'

Two hours later, her mind was alive with countless images of all she'd seen, the people she'd met, the hands she'd held. Some encounters would stay with her always – like Mitesh, the little Asian boy who had lost his hair because of the chemotherapy treatment they were using to try and control the cancerous tumour in his brain. But it wasn't the sight of his bald head that touched her, nor the end of a tube which remained embedded in his arm – it was his giggle. Not being a mother herself she had forgotten songs and games from her own childhood – but because Meg was an infant teacher, she had learned so much from being at her side when Emma and Ben were little. Suddenly she remembered the game which both her godchildren had loved so much. She asked Mitesh to close his eyes tight, then she knocked her fist gently on his forehead.

'Knock at the door. Peep in.' She pulled open one reluctant eyelid which immediately closed again. 'Press the buzzer.' Her finger pushed on the tip of Mitesh's nose.

'Oh dear,' she said, 'there's no one in! I'll just walk round the side and take a look in the window!' Her fingers walked their way across his cheek until she had reached his ear, where she peered closely inside. 'Definitely nothing to see in there, I wonder about the other side.' Again her fingers walked several times round the top of his head until they reached his other ear, where she peered inside once more. 'I know, I'll try the front door again!' Back the fingers marched until they reached his top lip. 'Wipe my feet on the mat!' She prised open his mouth with one finger so that she could look into his mouth.

'Hello!' she called, 'Is there anyone home? Oh, there is!' Then she gripped his chin as if it were a hand, and shook his head up and down.

'How do you do, Mr Jones!'

At that point, Mitesh began to giggle, and once started, didn't stop until Katherine promised to do it again and again. At last Sister Mary Lawrence gently pulled her away, taking her next to the bedside of an elderly lady who told Katherine of her longing to go back to Jamaica.

'Thirty-seven years I've been here, and I still miss home. Came here with my husband, but he's long gone. But I'm going home soon. Gonna be buried alongside my mother. Won't be long now . . .'

'And your husband? Is he buried in Jamaica too?'

Her eyes widened. 'Buried under a pile of lager cans just down the road, more likely. No, I might be going in a box, but home is where I'm heading. Should never have followed that darn man here in the first place.'

'Miss! Miss!' Katherine turned to see that the tiny, white-haired lady in the next bed was anxious to attract her attention. The moment Katherine moved over to stand at the woman's bedside, her hand was gripped tightly by two small hands on which deep blue veins stood out from paper-thin skin. 'Is the doctor coming?'

'I'm not sure. Would you like me to ask?'

'He said he'd come. He's very worried about me.'

'Then I expect he'll be in to see you soon.'

'It's my waterworks, you see.'

'Oh.'

The vice-like grip tightened as Katherine felt herself pulled closer. 'Doctor's very concerned . . .'

'Really?'

One bony finger beckoned Katherine to bring her ear closer. 'He says that if I don't improve soon, he'll have to put in a cafetière . . .'

By the end of her visit, Katherine was left in no doubt of the affection in which this little hospital was held, nor its value to the most vulnerable members of the community who surrounded it. Without any hesitation, she told a delighted Sister Mary Lawrence that she would be glad to help in any way she possibly could.

'That's wonderful, just wonderful,' the little nun enthused, 'and I don't want to hurry you, but decisions may be taken in the corridors of power within the next few weeks which could spell the end of our little facility here. Would you mind if I arranged a meeting for you with the Chairman of our Trustees?'

'An excellent idea.'

'Well, I happen to know that he plans to be here next Thursday evening. Would that be too soon for you? About seven o'clock?'

Later, with a spring in her step, and a very positive instinct about the good to which she could contribute here, Katherine made her way to the car.

At just gone seven when she put her key in the door of the flat, she was surprised to discover that Alan was already back from his visit to see Ben and Emma. But he wasn't watching television or hard at work on his computer as usual. Instead she found him sitting in the dark on the edge of the bed, leaning into his cupped hands.

'Alan? Are you all right?' When he lifted his head, it was clear he'd been crying probably for some time. 'Darling, whatever's happened?'

But he didn't answer as he clutched her to him, burying his head in her shoulder while he allowed her to rock him back and forth as though he were a small child.

It was the second week of the Easter holidays when Meg answered the door to find Chris Elliott standing there. 'Is Ben ready?' he asked.

'Heavens, was he supposed to be? He didn't mention it to me, and I'm afraid he's playing a computer battle over at his friend Daniel's house this afternoon.'

Chris frowned. 'Well, perhaps I've got it wrong?'

Meg grinned. 'I doubt it. Chris, I am sorry. Can I get you a cup of tea to make your visit worthwhile?'

He eyed her with a smile. 'Tell you what I'd prefer. It's a lovely day, and I do feel like some fresh air. How about you? Fancy a walk round the Valley Park?'

'As long as you promise not to put a clock on me, and make me run!'

It was one of those bright, golden spring afternoons when everything around them seemed to be bursting into colour. The grass was a vibrant, fresh green, and patches of daffodils swayed in perfect unison beneath trees decked in creamy white and soft pink blossom.

She breathed in deeply. 'The air smells so sweet.'

'I love this time of year when everything comes to life again. It's as if all the troubles of the dark winter days are behind us, and we can look forward to a new start.'

She sighed. 'A new start. Well, this year has certainly brought that.'

'How's it going? Still pretty rough?'

'Very. It took a while for me to cope even with the most basic things. I suppose that's what shock does to you. But because of Ben and Emma, I've had to keep going. It's a bit like bereavement really – except it's a double-whammy because there was no love in Alan's leaving – and the body keeps coming back to haunt me! I remember someone telling me right at the beginning, "if you can't make it, fake it, and before long you'll find that you aren't faking it at all". And that's true. I already feel it. Mostly the pain of what's happened is like a dull ache nagging away inside me whatever I'm doing, wherever I am – but recently I've noticed that I've got through whole minutes without thinking about Alan at all. Moments like this – times when just for a blissful while, I don't think about how I've been hurt. I just AM. It's not as if I can feel pleasure yet. To be honest, at the moment I don't think I'll ever be truly happy again – and yet, every now and then I realise that I've managed to get through a minute or two feeling something akin to contentment. You've no idea what a relief that is when the only emotions of which I seem capable these days are grief and the most dreadful fear.'

'Well, it must be frightening, to face the future alone when you've been part of a couple for so many years.'

'That's it. I was hardly the little woman at home, but it wasn't until he left that I realised just how much Alan looked after – paying the bills, sorting out problems around the house, making decisions about all kinds of things that I've never needed to think about before.'

'But you're managing. It may have been a steep learning curve, but you are coming through, I can tell.'

'I've started divorce proceedings.'

'Was that hard?'

'I didn't want to. It was my friend, Sandy, who insisted I went to see the solicitor, and he convinced me that the children and I would be much more secure if everything was settled in a divorce.'

'No chance of a reconciliation between you and Alan?'

'He's living with my best friend.'

'I guess that's a no.'

She smiled. 'I guess it is.'

'Do you still love him?'

She hesitated, as if she were considering the possibility for the first time. 'Yes, I suppose I do. Old habits die hard, don't they? I still feel a tremendous depth of love for him, even after all we've been through. I loved him from the moment I first met him, and although I suppose the years have knocked the romance and freshness out of our relationship, I never doubted my love for him – nor his for me. Perhaps I should have done.'

'Let me ask another question then. Do you like him?'

Her expression was hard and certain as she answered. 'No.'

'Meg, just because someone treats you without love doesn't mean that you are unlovable. You're a delightful person.'

'You hardly know me.'

'But I do know Ben. I know how much strength he gathers from you. There's a lot of love in your house, that's plain to see.'

'I don't feel that.'

'Not yet. But you're doing fine, believe me.'

It was at that point that she realised that he was very loosely holding her hand, and that he had probably been doing that for some time while they walked. She thought of pulling away from him, then didn't. This was OK. Chris was her friend. 'Have you ever been married?' she asked.

'No.'

'No inclination?'

'No real opportunity. Oh, there've been women I've been fond of – one in particular I really loved – but nothing has ever lasted. Must be me. Women don't seem to think of me as marriage material.'

'Well, after nineteen years of being a wife, I obviously wasn't marriage material either.'

'Two misfits then?'

'Out in the cold together.'

'Do we care?'

Her pace slackened slightly as she turned her face towards him. 'Not really. Not any more.'

'That's all right then.' And hands still linked, they chose a bending path which stretched away in the direction of the setting sun.

'Here, Barratt!' Ben's blood froze as he recognised Michael Smith's voice. 'Barratt, I'm talking to you!'

Ben's heart started to pound as adrenalin pumped through him. Breathing deeply he turned round to see his protagonist and a handful of cronies just a few yards behind him.

'Becoming a teacher's pet, are you, Barratt? Too scared to fight your own battles?'

Ben didn't know how to answer.

'Creeping up to Mr Elliott, like the fat slug you are?'

Ben glanced frantically around him, wondering about the possibility of escape. No chance. He was cornered.

'What's going on then, Barratt?' Smith was nearer now, until his face towered just inches away from Ben's eyes. 'Telling a few porkies, are you? Blubbing to that nice Mr Elliott how no one likes you and how mean we all are?'

'No.' Ben's voice was barely more than a mumble.

Suddenly Smith's huge hand shot out to pin Ben against the wall. 'That's not the way to make friends, Slug. If slugs like you want to stay alive, they have to learn a few basic lessons.'

Ben's breath came in painful gasps as the older boy's hand grasped his throat. He and Smith were practically nose to nose now.

Creepy crawlies get trodden on. They get squashed. Do you understand me, Slug?'

Ben was too terrified even to nod.

'So what were you doing in Mr Elliott's car? Over half-term, not even school time – and you're seen large as life in a teacher's car? That's not natural, Creep – so what's going on?'

'I'm running . . .'

Smith's eyes widened suspiciously. 'Running away? Running to tell Mummy? What do you mean?'

'Just running. Mr Elliott is coaching me.'

For several endless seconds Smith stared straight into Ben's face, as if he were considering the possibility of truth in this reply. Then with a glance to the admiring crowd around him, he threw back his head and laughed loudly.

'Running? Slugs don't have legs, Creep – especially a weedy, insignificant little worm like you! I run. I win races. You simply creep and crawl, do you hear me?'

Even if Ben could have come up with a response, he thought better of opening his mouth at all at that moment.

Abruptly, Smith's laughter stopped as he glared menacingly down at the terrified boy. 'Well, you may need to run, Worm. You may need to run very fast if I hear that you've been whispering into the wrong ear. Do I make myself clear?'

Ben managed the slightest nod of the head in agreement, then his body slumped as the vice-like grip on his neck was suddenly released. Satisfied, the small group looked at him with pity and disdain, then sauntered off down the corridor leaving Ben to slide down the wall into a crumpled heap on the floor.

'Mum, I'm only eighteen once. Everyone has a party for their eighteenth!'

Meg was rather proud of herself when the smile on her face didn't drop at all. Even though organising a party was the very last thing she needed, Emma was right. Every girl needed a party on their coming of age.

'Well, having a May birthday has its advantages. Perhaps we could have a barbecue in the garden?'

'You're joking!'

'No, we can manage, if that's what you'd like. And if we use the garden, we can invite a lot more people than we usually fit into the house.'

'Mum, I can't have it here!'

'Why not?'

'Because nobody has their eighteenth at home. We have to hire a hall.'

'We do?'

'Or preferably a hotel where we can have music till really late at night.'

'And how many people are you thinking of inviting?'

'I don't know. A hundred or so.'

Meg sighed. 'I don't know, Em. With everything that's going on with your father at the moment, money is pretty tight, you know.'

'Look, he may have left us, but I'm still his only daughter, and this is my only eighteenth birthday. He'll just have to help with this.'

'I'm not sure he can. Don't forget he has to pay for two homes right now.'

'That's his fault. Besides, I don't suppose he has to pay Katherine for staying there, do you?' Meg didn't feel that merited a reply. 'I'm going to ring him!'

'Not while he's at work. He may be busy . . .'

'He'll speak to me.'

'But you've not said a word to him for months. Wouldn't it be better to break the ice more privately by ringing him this evening?'

But Emma already had the receiver to her ear as she punched in her father's office number. Preferring not to hear the conversation, Meg closed the lounge door behind her as she went out to do the washing up.

'Mum!' yelled Emma, 'Dad needs to speak to you.' Meg leant back slowly, her hands dripping over the sink. 'Mum! He needs to speak to you now!'

Reluctantly Meg dried her hands and made her way back to where Emma was waiting for her with the receiver in her outstretched hand.

'Meg? Can you hear me?'

'Yes.'

'What do you think of this idea?'

'I'm not sure really. I'd like her to have a party, but I worry about the expense . . .'

'Well, I think it's a marvellous idea.' There was a lightness to Alan's voice, and Meg knew why. His beloved Goose was speaking to him again. Her distant silence must have hurt him deeply. Even if it cost the earth, he wouldn't let this chance to make amends to his daughter slip through his fingers. 'But I do think you and I need to plan it together.'

Meg hadn't thought of that.

'How about I pop down after work tomorrow night?' She hesitated. 'Come on, Meg, I promise not to outstay my welcome. This is for Emma.'

She was beaten. With Emma at her elbow and Alan in her ear, all she could do was give in graciously. 'Tomorrow will be fine. Perhaps you'd like to come to tea so that you can spend time with both the children.'

The pleasure in his voice was unmistakable. 'That would be wonderful.'

'See you tomorrow then.'

Katherine felt a chill slide down her backbone when she heard about Alan's plans to spend the evening with Meg, Ben and Emma. It wasn't that she meant to keep him from his family, especially when she was well aware of his distress at being estranged, particularly from Emma.

It was just that after all these months, this was the first time such an invitation had been offered. He would be welcomed into the home he had shared with his family for so many years. She knew how much he missed the house. In truth, she suspected he was missing Meg too, more than he ever dared reveal. But seeing the excitement on his face as he spoke of his visit, she smiled encouragingly. Of course he must go, and she hoped he'd have a truly wonderful time!

Besides, she thought, after he'd kissed her goodbye and left the flat, she was busy herself that night. Meeting the Chairman of the Trustees of St Mary's to discuss a fund-raising campaign for the hospital should keep her mind occupied. At least, she sincerely hoped so.

'Hello Goose.'

Emma simply held open her arms to him as she stood in the doorway, and they clung together for several moments. 'Welcome home, Dad,' she whispered, 'Welcome home.'

Seconds later Ben was bounding down the stairs, demanding that his father might like to try his latest computer game. With a laughing, half-exasperated glance in Meg's direction, Alan allowed himself to be pulled upstairs.

Meg kept her distance, even closing the kitchen door – which was totally unheard of – rather than risk overhearing conversations from upstairs. As she chopped up the iceberg lettuce, she suddenly laid down the knife and stretched out her fingers to see they were trembling.

How ridiculous to be this nervous of a man with whom she'd spent nineteen years of her life! She had no further interest in him now. Tonight was only happening because of the need to talk about their daughter's birthday. He'd come not as her husband, but as Emma's father.

The cooker pinged. The moussaka was ready. Calling up to the others, Meg carried the loaded tray through to the dining table.

'Miss Blake! I've been waiting for you!' Katherine smiled broadly as she allowed herself to be enveloped in Peter's huge hug. 'Come, come, come!'

And before she had time to say a word, he'd grabbed her hand to whisk her at top speed towards the offices where she had met Sister Mary Lawrence on her previous visit. The little nun looked up with a smile as she saw them approach.

'Perfect timing. Our chairman has just arrived himself, and I know he's anxious to meet you. He's popped up to the orthopaedic ward at the moment. Let's go and find him there.'

Peter refused to relinquish her hand as the three of them made their way up the wide, echoing flight of steps to the ward on the third floor. Once they had pushed through the swing doors, Sister Mary Lawrence spotted the chairman immediately.

'Oh, there he is. Let me introduce you.'

But in fact, he needed no introduction as Katherine looked into the smiling face of Robert Masters.

✳   ✳   ✳

It's funny how easily you can slip back into well-worn habits. Meg looked around the table; at Ben, with his mouth full, talking animatedly to Alan about the latest cheat he'd discovered on a computer game; at Emma, a typically tetchy teenager most of the time, but who'd had a broad smile on her face ever since the arrival of her father; and at Alan, who was sitting in his usual place at the table looking for all the world as if he'd never been away. Every now and then, he would glance across at Meg, holding her gaze for just a moment before she turned away. It all felt so normal, comfortable and ordinary as if it had always been.

Am I the only one who wants to scream out loud about this, she wondered. Am I alone in remembering the betrayal, the deceit, the pain his actions brought to our family? Does he think we can just turn back the clock, be polite and civilised, as we chat over tea and moussaka?

Across the table, Alan laughed. Ben and Emma joined in. They're happy, Meg thought. They've missed each other. And the children would realise after this evening that whatever the circumstances they needed to see their father regularly again. Of course they did. It was only her pure selfishness which wanted them to continue punishing him, to withhold their company from him until he realised exactly how much damage he'd caused, and what he'd lost. She was appalled at her thoughts, shocked at the depth of her bitterness and pain.

She pushed back her chair and began to clear the plates away from the table. The three of them hardly seemed to notice her leave. Why should they? It was clear that they were only interested in each other.

After that, she tried to keep out of their way. She heard Alan go upstairs again to spend time with Ben — then she was aware that when he came down again, he sat for some time in the lounge talking to Emma. Eventually it was she who came into the dining room to find Meg sitting at the table surrounded by school paperwork.

'Come on, Mum. You need to be in on this!'

Meg watched the matching excitement in both Emma and Alan's faces as they mapped out their plans for her party – a mixed group of around one hundred people, some of Emma's own friends plus other family acquaintances, who would all enjoy a buffet meal and disco in a specially adapted barn at the back of a nearby country pub. Meg nodded and agreed in what she hoped were all the right places, because although her smile stayed in place, inside she felt completely numb. On the face of it, this party would be a happy family affair, an occasion when old hurts and grievances would be laid aside for Emma's sake. Alan and she would appear to be united in love for their daughter when for her united was the last thing she felt.

Emma's mobile rang. Predictably it was Matt. 'Got to go! Bye, Dad – and thanks!'

As the door slammed behind Emma, silence seemed to close in on Alan and Meg. Irritated that she should feel so ill at ease in her own home, Meg turned away from him to go back to her paperwork. She felt his eyes following her, heard his soft step as he came to stand behind her.

'I've missed this, Meg; the family, this home of ours. I've missed Ben and Emma so much, missed being a dad – and a husband. I've missed you – your friendship, your love. Oh, how I've missed you . . .'

She didn't answer him. She couldn't. And eventually she heard him move away until once again the house was silent, except for the sob which escaped her as tears of anger and regret began to slide down her cheeks.

When Alan walked into the flat that night to find it empty, he felt a surprising sense of relief. He was restless, unable to settle as he prowled around the small apartment which bore the same elegance as Katherine herself. He decided a shower might help, but when he couldn't find his dressing gown, which for years he'd always kept thrown over the end of his bed, he felt a twinge of irritation to find that Katherine had put it away tidily in the wardrobe. Music would make him feel better, especially the CD which was his current favourite that he'd left in the player after he'd been listening to it the previous evening. But it was no longer there. Katherine had tidied that too, and it took him several minutes to track it down in the rack in the far corner of the room, where a hundred or more CDs were neatly arranged in alphabetical order. With music blasting loud around him, he poured himself a generous helping of whisky, then sat down heavily on the sofa.

He didn't belong here. He didn't fit among the embroidered cushions, the silk bed linen, the immaculate deep pile carpet which never dirtied or flattened. He missed his own haphazard collection of CDs, and the desk in his study where their cat always curled up on his lap as soon as he took a seat there. He missed the garden he never got round to weeding, and the workbench in the garage where at least three half-finished woodwork projects were waiting for him to complete them. He missed the pink-blossomed cherry tree which bloomed outside his study window in April, the old welly boots which had been part of his life for perhaps twenty years, and the big enamel bath in which he could stretch out his frame without touching the end. He missed kicking a ball about with Ben in the back garden, and the late-night drives to pick up Emma from some event or another.

Why had he let it all slip away? How had this madness begun? It wasn't that he didn't love Katherine, because he had honestly never felt a depth of emotion to match what he had discovered over the years with her. It was just that what had been a wonderful and passionate affair had not settled comfortably into an everyday relationship. Their life together seemed to fluctuate between moments of great drama followed by times of silence and uncertainty. In giving up his past, he seemed to have lost the future he'd always imagined he would have, leaving him rootless, without direction or purpose. Now, nearer fifty than forty, he was paying for a home he loved but in which he was no longer truly welcome, sharing his life with a woman who starched his shirts, used slimline spread rather than butter on his toast and insisted on putting down the loo seat after him – all of which he hated but didn't dare mention.

He shifted position in an attempt to alleviate the heaviness in his chest. When it wouldn't budge, he got up hoping that movement would help him breathe and ease the pain.

But the pain wasn't physical, that he knew. It was the hurt of guilt and regret deep within him which no pill nor whisky nor any woman who wasn't his own dear Meg could ever take away.

Chapter Ten

Thinking she'd never sleep after the evening in Alan's company, Meg took a pill that night, so when the phone rang shrilly on the bedside table, it took her some time not just to register what the noise was, but to fumble in the darkness for the receiver.

'Meg?' Suddenly she was wide awake. It was Katherine. 'I'm sorry to disturb you like this, but I thought you should know . . .'

'Alan? What's happened to Alan?'

'They thought he'd had a heart attack.' Katherine heard Meg's sharp intake of breath. 'He's all right. They're still not sure exactly what's happened, but it seems he may be suffering from angina . . .'

'Where is he? In hospital?'

'At the Royal Free, you know, just down from the flat?'

'I'll be right there.'

'Meg, listen, he's resting now, but they say he'll be in for a few days at least while they do ECG's and blood tests on him. But he'd like to see you, I know that. Could you come in the morning?'

Meg's mouth was dry, her throat tight, the shock like a physical blow which winded and flattened her. 'Is he conscious?'

'Yes, he was, although he's sleeping now.'

'And you're still at the hospital?'

'Yes.' Meg heard the catch in Katherine's voice. 'I didn't know what to do. I don't want to go home, but I'm not really helping him now by being here. I just didn't want him to wake up and be alone . . .'

'Go home, Katherine. Get some sleep.'

'Yes.'

Meg's voice softened. 'You won't help him much if you're exhausted.'

'No.'

'Come back in the morning.'

'Right.'

'Thank you for letting me know.'

There was a pause before Katherine spoke again. 'It's good to hear your voice, Meg . . .'

'Go home, Katherine.' And very deliberately, Meg put the phone back on the hook.

Katherine didn't go home. The nurses told her she should, but they turned a blind eye as she chose instead to curl up in the hard, torn, plastic-seated, wooden-armed, bright orange chair beside his bed. Light was just beginning to stream through the blinds when she became aware of the sound of the tea trolley making its early morning way down the corridor.

Alan began to stir. Almost falling off the chair in her hurry, she knelt down beside him so that her face was close to his.

His eyes only opened a fraction as if the daylight hurt him, then he ran his tongue across dry lips as he reached out to touch her hand. 'Hello Meg,' he whispered. 'Hello.'

For a boy who'd never liked early mornings, Ben adapted very well to getting out of bed once he got the paper round. That morning he walked out of the newsagent's with the canvas bag heavy on his shoulder, then looked at his watch as he usually did.

He had to cover three streets and almost one hundred and twenty houses. Yesterday he had done the round in less than three-quarters of an hour. It was now five past seven, and his aim today was to trim five minutes off that time. He glanced into the bag to make a final check that he had everything he needed – then started running. He would run down streets and up garden paths, dodging cars and pedestrians, leaping over cats, dogs and gates. And because there was no question of him failing, he would be back at the shop at precisely fifteen minutes to eight.

Two women stood at the side of Alan's bed. As the duty nurse arrived to check Mr Barratt's pressure and take him off for blood tests, she was curious about the obvious tension between her patient and his visitors. Realising that her arrival had hardly broken up their conversation because she'd already been aware of the rather unnatural silence between them, she turned to smile at the woman who had spent all night curled up beside him.

'I'm just going to take your husband down to Pathology now, Mrs Barratt. Shouldn't be more than half an hour or so.'

At her elbow, it was the other woman who answered. 'Thank you. Would it be best if I went with him, or would you like me to wait for my husband here?'

They watched without comment as Alan was led away in a wheelchair, then suddenly they were alone.

'Would you like me to find us a cup of tea?' Katherine was plainly nervous, uncertain what to say, how to behave when alone in the company of this woman she knew so well but had hurt so badly.

'I'm fine, thank you.'

'Meg, I . . .'

She was cut short as Meg turned away. 'I think I should find someone who can tell me about Alan's condition.'

'Can't we even speak? When we're both worried about him, can't we even share what we know, how we feel?'

'Years ago you decided I should share my husband with you, Katherine. Isn't that enough?'

Katherine looked as if she had been slapped in the face. Then, pale and plainly shaken, she picked up her bag and set off briskly down the corridor.

For several moments, Meg stood rooted to the spot before her shoulders dropped as she let out a long slow breath. Finally pulling herself together, she started a search for someone who might know how Alan was doing. It took several enquiries to harassed nurses, many minutes of waiting for other telephone conversations and discussions between professionals to be completed, then more patience still while Alan's notes were unearthed and deciphered before she was finally introduced to the junior doctor who had taken over Alan's treatment that morning.

'How old is he?' the young woman doctor asked, scanning through his notes.

'Forty-six.'

'That's quite young to be in this condition.'

'Condition? What do you think is wrong with him?'

'Almost certainly he had an angina attack last night, which must be considered as a warning shot across the bow for a future heart attack. Has he been under a lot of stress recently?'

'He's certainly had to cope with a great deal of change.'

'Well, that won't have helped – and of course, he's rather overweight for a man of his age and height. We're checking his cholesterol levels this morning, but I think this is a classic case of a man who works too hard, tries to fit in too much, doesn't exercise, has a lousy diet, and thinks he's invincible.'

'He doesn't think that now.'

'Then perhaps this attack has scared him enough to change his lifestyle. We can help him plan a new diet not just to control his cholesterol levels but his waistline too. He'll need a regular exercise regime, plus the right medication.'

'Then he should be fine?'

'He might be. We'll need to keep him in for monitoring for about three days so that we can be sure of his condition, but then it's up to him. We can't do anything about the stress that's probably set this off – but perhaps you can?'

Meg nodded. 'I understand, doctor. Thank you.' She was deep in thought as she made her way back down the corridor to the side ward where Alan had his bed. To her surprise, she saw the porter leaving with his wheelchair, and realised that they must have brought him back. With a smile, she turned the corner to greet him.

But Alan didn't see her. Katherine was sitting beside him, clutching his hand – and the expression in his eyes as he looked at her was so tender and intimate that Meg exclaimed in shock.

Alan looked up immediately, and the delight at seeing her which first crossed his face was quickly followed by obvious regret that she should have witnessed his closeness to Katherine.

Meg didn't stay to see more, and by the time Katherine had turned to follow Alan's gaze, the doorway was already empty.

'I really think I'm losing it!'

'Your spare tyre?'

Sandy grimaced. 'Oh, wouldn't that be nice! No, it's my mind I'm talking about.'

Meg grinned as she carried on chopping onions. 'Oh, that!'

'You know how disorganised I am about shopping.' Sandy perched on a kitchen stool as she spoke. 'Hate it. Always have. All the family pounce like vultures on anything they find the moment I get back from a big shop, but are they there to help me buy it? Not likely! All that wandering round the aisles, packing the trolley so that the lettuce and bananas don't end up under a pile of tins, then unloading at the checkout so that it all comes through in the right order to go into bags in a way which will be logical when I get it home. Then piling up the trolley again, pushing it out to the car, unloading into the boot, unloading from the boot and getting it into the house – and then I've got to unpack again and put it all away! And you can bet your bottom dollar that the moment the crisps are in the cupboard, the two-legged mice in my family will have devoured the lot within the hour!'

Meg chuckled. 'Sounds familiar.'

'Well, about three months ago I did all the unpacking bit, you know, found a place for everything when I got back home. And the one thing I bought for myself was a pack of tampons – and could I find them when I'd finished? Could I heck! Well, guess what? I came across them in the freezer this morning when I was looking for the garden peas!'

Meg laughed out loud. 'You need a coffee. Put the kettle on.'

'I won't stay if you're busy. What are you cooking?'

'Spaghetti Bolognese. The kids always love that. And Ben will be ravenous when he and Chris get back.'

'Chris? He eats with you now?'

'Hmm. Quite often. Saves him cooking at home. I get the impression he lives on the rather limited menu of a bachelor.'

Sandy pulled up her chair to look closely at Meg. 'It all sounds very cosy.'

'Hardly. It's just a way of saying thank you.'

'How often does he join you for meals?'

'A couple of times a week. Sometimes more.'

'That's a lot of thank yous.'

Meg put down her knife. 'Sandy, I can't thank him enough. He's done wonders for Ben. You remember what he was like, jumping at his own shadow. I've watched that boy's confidence grow not just in his physical ability but in his attitude to himself. Chris has helped Ben recognise his potential at a time when Alan's leaving had really undermined and confused him.'

'And what does Alan think of Chris having his feet under your table?'

'What's it got to do with him?'

'Absolutely right – but that won't stop him being a dog in a manger. He may not want you, but I bet he won't like the idea of you getting close to someone else.'

'I'm not getting close to Chris. He's a friend, just a kind friend.'

'Yes, he is, Meg. And as a man, he'll have noticed that you're a pretty lovely woman.'

Meg smiled as she shook her head. 'It's not like that.'

'Of course it is. It always is.'

'The trouble with you, Sandy, is that you're an old romantic.'

'Nothing wrong with that. And a bit of romance would do you a power of good too.'

'No chance!'

'Because you won't let yourself.'

'I'm still married to Alan.'

'Not for much longer, and he's hardly playing the role of husband, is he, at least not to you!'

'Perhaps I'm a bit old fashioned, but . . .'

'But you're scared. After twenty years of devotion to just one man, you're terrified at the thought of giving your heart again. Being single is pretty scary, especially after you've been a couple for so long.'

'I'm not even thinking about that.'

'You should ask my Dave about all this. He acts like a single man the moment he's out of my sight, I know it!'

'Oh, Sandy, he doesn't. He adores you.'

'Then why does he keep mentioning the new woman PC who's just been posted to his station?'

'Because she's a colleague, and she needs to be made welcome. And you're paranoid.'

'I'm practical.'

At that moment, the doorbell went. 'Heavens, they're back. Is it that time already?'

Sandy headed immediately for the door, anxious to get a good look at Chris, then introductions were made as he and Ben came in and she left. On the garden path, Sandy stood on tiptoes to peer over Chris's shoulder and give Meg an enormous thumbs up before waving and disappearing in the direction of her own house.

Much later, when Ben was once again in his room supposedly doing homework but more likely on his beloved computer, Chris and Meg shared a pot of tea as they both stretched out on the settee, their feet on the pouffe in front of them.

'He's running brilliantly. We did three kilometres today. The brightest of our lads running at regional level would be covering that distance in about a minute less than Ben, so he's doing really well.'

'So what now?'

'I had a long talk to him today. He's been adamant up to now that his training be kept completely separate from school, but I think now's the time for him to come out.'

Meg chuckled. 'Sounds dramatic.'

'I think it will be, when not just the school but Ben's own form-mates realise they have a potential champion in their midst.'

'What was Ben's reaction today? Was he nervous?'

'A bit, but I detect excitement there too. I've encouraged him to feel proud of his achievements, and some of that is plainly rubbing off. He's always been worried about standing out in a crowd, then failing – but at running, he's a winner, and he's finally beginning to accept that for himself.'

'So how are you going to introduce his running at school?'

'Well, our own school distance trials are coming up, and as head of PE, I'll use them to select two runners from each year to take part in the Midsummer Run. I've already put Ben's name down on the list for the Year Eight trials, and once that goes on the board tomorrow morning, everyone will know.'

'And when are the trials? When will they finally realise he CAN run?'

'Friday next week.'

'You've been so good to him, Chris. I am grateful to you.'

'I've enjoyed it.'

'But you've been more than just a teacher to him. You've become his friend, and he's needed that in recent months.'

He shrugged dismissively. 'Oh, it's had its moments. I've never eaten so well!'

'Asking you to share the odd meal with us is hardly comparable to what you've done for Ben.'

'It's not just for him – but for me too – being here, getting to know you . . .'

'I'm not very good company, I'm afraid.'

'On the contrary, I enjoy our time together.'

'But I've dumped so much on you, all my confusion and indecision about Alan . . .'

'I'm pleased you feel you can.'

'Then I guess I'm as much in debt to the Elliott counselling service as my son is. You're a good listener, Chris.'

He grinned.

'I grew up in a house full of women.'

'And a wonderful friend.'

He stretched out his hand to cover hers. 'So are you.' He turned to gaze directly into her eyes, and for one alarming moment she thought he might kiss her. Then he seemed to think better of it. 'Is there anything good on telly, do you think?'

Back on safe ground, she got up to switch on the set, dig out the television guide – and wonder why she felt just the tiniest tinge of disappointment.

*　　*　　*

'What's this, Barratt?'

Ben winced as Michael Smith picked him up by the back of the neck, and dragged him over to the noticeboard.

'Tell me, is that your name?' Ben nodded. 'A mistake then. Better put a line through it. Here's a pen.'

'No mistake,' choked Ben. 'I'm running in the trials for Year Eight.'

'No.' Smith turned Ben round so that he could peer down into the smaller boy's eyes, only to be surprised that he could see no trace of fear there. 'I'm running for Year Eight, because I'm the best in the whole year. And the four other names on that list deserve to be there, because they're good too. You? You're a misfit, a worm with legs that aren't worth having – and THAT is a mistake.'

'Do you have a problem, Smith?' Chris's voice cut across from behind them. 'Because you will have if you don't get a move on to the next class.'

'How come Barratt's name has suddenly appeared on this list, sir? He couldn't get away from me if I just chased him down this corridor, let alone over a two-kilometre stretch.'

'Thank you, Smith. Your opinion is noted. Now clear off to your next lesson!'

Reluctantly, Smith and his small gang of friends sauntered away muttering to themselves. Ben gave them a head start before following them down the corridor, the memory of Chris's wink in his direction almost bringing a smile to his face.

'This is really very impressive, Katherine, but then I knew it would be.'

'Did you?'

'Of course. I'm far too much of a businessman to take you on face value.'

'You checked up on me?'

'Naturally, and you came out with flying colours.'

'And do you think this appeal for St Mary's will work with the big banking institutions? They must be constantly bombarded by good causes all begging for their support.'

Robert sat back thoughtfully from the desk they were sharing. 'We're putting together an appeal which is financially sound, logically argued, specifically targeted and attractively presented, thanks to you.'

'So we've done our best, and now we just have to cross our fingers in the hope that we hit a jackpot or two.'

'We need some quick answers. If we don't manage to turn around the finances of St Mary's within the month, then I fear its doors will be shut forever.'

'It's a wonderful place. Thank you for introducing me to it.'

'It was Sister Mary Lawrence who wrote to you.'

'But you were obviously behind the idea from the very start, and I'm grateful to you. It's been a real eye-opener for me to get involved with a place like this.'

Well, you've made a conquest or two. Peter stands at the door for hours on end now in the hope you'll arrive.'

She laughed. 'Yes, I've made some good friends here.'

He glanced at his watch. 'Heavens, it's gone eight – and I'm starving! Do you fancy a plate of pasta round the corner before you go home?'

Her face was suddenly serious. 'Better not. Alan will be waiting, and he's not been well, as you know.'

'That's the first time you've mentioned him to me. Did you think I wouldn't approve?'

'I'm aware of my new role as the wicked "other woman" who's wrenched a good man away from his devoted wife and family. I expect people to think badly of me.'

'And what do you think?'

'I think that all I did was fall in love, unfortunately with the wrong man. But I've remained absolutely loyal to him for years, and I've never put any pressure on him to leave his family in all that time. If our affair hadn't been discovered as it was, it probably would have gone on in exactly the same way for years to come.'

'But how could that ever be enough for you, Katherine? You deserve better than that – at the very least a man who's free to have you by his side and proud to have you on his arm. All those clandestine meetings, the weekends and holidays when Alan could never be with you, must have been very difficult for you.'

'I learned never to expect anything more than he was able to give. I lived for the times we could be together . . .'

'Sounds lonely.'

She looked at him steadily. 'Sometimes it was.'

'So you accepted invitations out to dinner by substitutes, even though your heart was never in it?'

'How could I explain? How could I tell you that I'd been in love with another man for years and years?'

'And now you're together, are you happy?'

Her head tilted to one side as she considered the question. 'Mostly. Even after all these years of knowing each other so well, I don't think either of us were totally prepared to be thrown into living together quite so suddenly.'

'And he's on your territory, the flat which has always been your own space. Does that work?'

She smiled. 'Well, he's messy . . .'

'And you are scrupulously tidy.'

'And I know that he misses HIS own space – his office at home, his workshop, even the blooming cat!'

'And his family?'

'Yes, especially his family. He's a loving, caring man, so of course he loves and cares for them. I expect that . . .'

'But it's been pretty hard for you, being the scarlet

woman, living with a man who is not totally sure where he belongs.'

'I don't doubt his love for me.'

'Of course not. Your doubts are about all the other people that he loves.'

She leaned forward to put her chin in her hands, smiling up at him. 'What a wise old owl you are.'

'Plenty of practice. Don't forget I've been the bad boy of our family too.'

'How's that going?'

'Badly. Wendy can hardly bear to speak to me now, and if it were possible for her to stop me seeing the children altogether, then she would. To be fair, I probably don't handle her very well, but I find her so infuriating.'

'Very tough when it keeps you apart from your children though.'

'So we're both outcasts?'

'You a philanderer, and me a hussy who steals unsuspecting husbands!'

'No wonder we get on well!'

'Yes – and I'm glad.'

His eyes were warm as they smiled into hers. 'So am I, Katherine. So am I.'

Emma and Matt were sprawled across the floor as they wrote the invitations for her eighteenth birthday celebration. At first Emma had been undecided about whether to have a party which was simply aimed at her own age group of friends, or whether it should be more of a family affair to include all ages of people who were special to her. In the end, she opted for the latter, and the task of whittling down the guest list to just one hundred was pleasantly taxing.

They worked out a system where Emma wrote the invitations, then Matt addressed and sealed the envelopes. As he picked up one invitation, he gave a low whistle. 'Are you sure about this?'

Emma glanced down at her attempt at copper-plate writing on the card. 'Dad and Katherine', it read. 'Look, I can't not invite her. She's my godmother. She's always been special to me.'

'Yeah, but your mum will go spare.'

Emma shrugged. 'I know it's tough, and I'm not keen on the idea myself, but we've all got to accept that they are a couple now. Of course they're going to come together. They live at the same place!'

Matt grunted, 'Sounds like trouble to me.' But he stuck the stamp on the envelope just the same.

The route was approximately two kilometres long taking the runners twice round the field, then once around the perimeter of the school building before swinging back for another two laps of the field. That Friday, six boys were lined up at the start, watched by all the members of Year 8 who thought this was a more interesting way to spend their lunch break than their usual custom of hanging around near the tuckshop.

On the way to the start, Ben had weathered a few snide comments and expressions of surprise that he should be in the line-up at all, and now he was standing second from the end with Michael Smith two places away from him. He glanced at Chris, whistle in hand, and although with such a crowd around him, it was hard to make out exactly what he was saying, Ben guessed that they should be getting into their starting positions. Head down, body coiled ready to propel into action, he waited.

What happened next, he never could quite explain. He remembered turning his head for a second to catch a venomous stare from Michael Smith, and the overwhelming feeling that his knees were turning to jelly. Then suddenly he was aware of movement all around him as the other runners hurtled away from him. The whistle must have gone, but he hadn't heard it! Confused and wrong-footed, he set off a good twenty yards behind the rest of the field.

For the whole of the first lap around the school field, Ben lagged behind the rest of the runners until just as they started the second, he was surprised to see exhaustion in the face of the first boy he reached. Smoothly overtaking him, he started his steady progress up the line. By the time they were running around the school perimeter, he had moved up into third place, with a gangly-limbed boy called Scott ahead of him, and Michael Smith way out in front. Doggedly, Ben concentrated on everything he had been taught, almost hearing Chris's calm voice in his mind as he placed one foot in front of the other. 'Stay focused! Let another runner set the pace. Keep something back for the final thrust.'

Towards the end of the third lap around the field, Ben could hear Scott breathing heavily as he began to slow his pace. Almost effortlessly, Ben was able to pull around him, until there was only Michael Smith between him and the finishing line. A cheer went up as first Michael, then the other runners passed the crowd of boys craning to see the last lap of the race. If Ben had only been able to hear, he would have realised that many of them were calling out his name to encourage and cajole him on – but he heard nothing, and saw little except the shape of Michael ahead of him, and the distance between them which he intended to cover.

Almost imperceptibly, he lengthened his stride as his feet thudded – right, left, right, left – strong and certain on to the field. The gap between the two runners was narrowing, narrowing – when suddenly Michael became aware that he had company over his right shoulder. His head swung round to see who it was, and his jaw visibly dropped. With a look that was a complete mixture of disbelief, disdain and admiration, he delved into his resources of stamina to put on an extra spurt for the last two sides of the field.

But Ben wasn't going to let him get away. His eyes firmly fixed on the back of Michael's head, he was determined to catch him, pulling out all the stops on his energy and resilience to close the gap between them. The two boys, now way ahead of the rest of the runners, were almost neck and neck as they turned the corner for the last stretch down to the finishing line. All around them, the crowd was cheering, but Ben heard nothing except his thumping heartbeat and the rhythmic pattern of his own breathing. Nearer and nearer he edged until he was only an inch or two behind Michael. Not far now! He could do this. He could do this!

Then suddenly, it was over – and it was Michael who first hurtled across the line, with Ben only a hair's breadth behind him. Ben felt himself engulfed by the crowd, as he was hugged and slapped on the back. Then the two of them, both Ben and Michael, were hoisted on to shoulders to be carried over to where Chris was waiting for them. It was as both runners were unceremoniously dumped back on to their feet that Ben found himself face to face with Michael. His protagonist looked down at him with curiosity.

'Well, you're a bit of a dark horse, aren't you, Barratt? Where did that come from?'

Ben's chin went up as he answered. 'I like running.'

'So how come you've never shown your true colours on the field before now?'

Ben shrugged.

'Not bad, Worm. Not bad at all! It would have been very bad if you'd beaten me – and now I know about you, I'll never give you that chance again – but for a slug, you did OK.'

Attention turned towards Chris as he read out the results and times of each runner. The polite round of applause for each of the other four runners was topped by a huge cheer for both Ben and Michael when their names were called out.

'Now as you know,' announced Chris, struggling to make himself heard above the clamour, 'the Midsummer Run will be taking place in just under two months' time. It's open to all the schools in this half of the county who are invited to send along their brightest runners under the age of fourteen. This is a very prestigious event, with a prize of five hundred pounds for the winning school, and a magnificent trophy for the winner to keep. The race covers a three-kilometre stretch around the Valley Park, so it's a pretty gruelling challenge for young runners. After today's trials, though, I am pleased to announce that a team of four will be representing our school, two from Year Seven and two from Year Eight – so a big round of applause please for the two boys who've earned the privilege of being the competitors from your year, Michael Smith and Ben Barratt!'

Cheering and clapping, the crowd gathered round the two boys. Ben spun dizzily as smiling faces surrounded him and hands reached out to touch him. One of them, he realised with alarm, belonged to Michael Smith who peered down on him, an unreadable expression on his face.

'Come on, Worm, I'll race you back to the shower block!'

Ben didn't need asking twice. With a grin, he turned on his heel and pushed his way through the crowd to get a head start on his rival. Then, as he looked over his shoulder to see how near he was, he found Michael right behind him, smiling broadly – and that smile was still in place as they both touched the wall of the shower block at exactly the same moment.

'You're all right, Worm!' said Michael, placing a companionable arm around the smaller boy's shoulders. 'A bit of a nerd, but you're all right!'

*　　*　　*

They planned the strategy of their campaign with great care, targeting just seven banks and finance houses at which one or both of them knew a key person. In that way, the request to help St Mary's Hospital could appeal not only on hard business terms but have the added benefit of the personal touch. After one particularly long evening when they managed to finalise all the documents and get them into the right envelopes, Katherine and Robert had stood together with their fingers crossed as they pushed the letters into the post box outside the hospital.

'That's it then', said Katherine, 'We'll just have to wait now.'

'Yes, we've given it our best shot.'

'We certainly have.'

He put an arm round her shoulder as he turned to look at her. 'Thanks, partner.'

'Thanks yourself. I've enjoyed it.'

When his lips touched hers, she was almost surprised that she didn't pull away – but then there was no threat here, no pressure for more, simply the comfortable companionship of good friends. Over the weeks of working together on the preparation of the appeal, Robert had become a very good friend – and as she felt that many more established 'friends' were avoiding her because of her relationship with Alan, Robert's easy company, intelligent conversation and astute business acumen had provided an oasis of pleasure in unsettled times.

How much more they would need to see each other would depend on the success of the appeal. Perhaps their letters would generate no interest at all, and they would have to put their heads together to come up with another approach. Or perhaps they would hit the jackpot first time, in which case once the money had been raised and the hospital made secure, there would hardly be a need for their paths to cross again.

And with that oddly depressing thought in mind, Katherine

gave him a final wave as she turned her car in the direction of north London.

Emma's invitation was lying on the doormat when Katherine walked in that evening. Smiling as she read it, she propped it up on the mantelpiece so that Alan would be able to see it when he arrived home. Much against her better judgement, he had gone back to work within a week of his angina attack. He had always been a bit of a workaholic, and she realised that the routine of working and being in the office represented familiar stability when so much was changing in other areas of his life.

Nevertheless, she worried about him, watching anxiously for any sign of weariness or pain, fussing over his diet, and trying to lessen the load of his work responsibilities. Her efforts to protect and safeguard him were met firstly by his grateful indulgence, then with a certain amount of resignation until, as he began to feel better, he was nothing less than irritable at whatever she suggested. He said it made him feel like an invalid, which he most certainly was not. In fact, she knew it brought him face to face with his own physical vulnerability – and that was a challenge he wasn't up to meeting just yet.

The subject of Emma's party didn't come up until they were having supper.

'I wondered,' ventured Katherine, 'if I could offer to help in some way? Perhaps with the decorations, because you know how much I enjoy things like that? And we must find out exactly what Emma would like for her birthday. What do you think about us buying her something gold – you know, a really special piece of jewellery which will always be a memento of her special day? Have you any idea what she'd like? A bracelet perhaps, or a gold ring?'

Alan kept on eating, not meeting her eye as he answered. 'Actually, Meg and I came to much the same decision. Meg's mother had a beautiful antique engagement ring set with five diamonds which we always intended Emma to have on her eighteenth. She's decided that the setting is too old-fashioned for her, so we've arranged to have it redesigned using all the same gold and diamonds, but in a style which Emma can decide upon herself.'

'I see.'

'And please don't take offence at this, but I wonder about the sensitivity of you and I going together to a family occasion like Emma's party. I know it will be very difficult for Meg to see us as a couple. That would spoil the day for her, and possibly for Emma too. After all, Meg and I have planned this party together, and we want it to be the best possible day for our daughter.'

Katherine stared at him for several moments before she spoke. 'It's a funny thing about that word "we". For all those years until we started living together, it was the one word which probably hurt me most. I mean, there we were very much in love with one another, spending every possible moment in each other's company – but then you'd drop into the conversation all the things that "we" were planning to do at the weekend – only of course you were talking about Meg, not me. It's a very exclusive word, did you ever realise that? Every time you used it, you reminded me that you and Meg were a unit, and that I was on the outside. But after all we've been through, and the fact that we're living together now, surely when you talk about "we", you should mean you and I. And yet you don't, do you? It's still Meg that you're thinking of when you use that awful little word.'

'Don't be ridiculous, Katherine. Meg and I are Emma's parents. Naturally we're making joint plans for this special occasion. That's only sensible . . .'

'I understand that, but I still think it's important that Meg and the rest of the family start to recognise that you and I are a unit now. I am also Emma's godmother, and she has invited US, you and me, along together. If Emma is prepared to accept that we are a couple, then why are you so reticent?'

'It's not a case of being reticent, simply sensitive to a situation which might hurt others we care about.'

'And what about hurting me? I do understand you, don't I? You don't want me to go to this party at all, so that you can play happy families with Meg?'

'We ARE a family, Katherine, and because Meg and I have two children, we always will be. That is something completely separate from the love and commitment I feel for you. There's room in my life for me to love all of you – Ben, Emma, Meg and you.'

'You still love Meg?'

'Yes, I do. We've lived together for years. Of course I love her. OK, so I've made the choice to live with you now, but I still care about her very much, and won't see her hurt unnecessarily.'

'And what am I supposed to tell Emma? What reason should I give my god-daughter for turning down her invitation to this special occasion?'

'Why don't you tell her the truth? That you think your presence might hurt her mother, so you've decided to decline the invitation.'

'That's the truth as you see it, not me.'

'For heaven's sake, Katherine, you and Meg were best friends for years. Surely you can understand her reaction to this? You can't want to hurt her any more than I do.'

'No,' she replied carefully. 'But you make it clear that I am still the outsider, and after all these years, I thought that was behind me now. I thought you were as committed to our life together as I am, but I'm obviously mistaken.'

'You're being melodramatic. I AM committed to our relationship, but on this one particular occasion, I think we should put other people's feelings before our own.'

The two of them glared at each other across the table, but it was Katherine who broke away first. Pushing her chair back abruptly, she got up and walked quickly to the bathroom where she slammed the door and locked it noisily behind her.

Chapter Eleven

Ben gasped for breath as he glanced down at his wristwatch. Good! He'd shaved yet another fifteen seconds off his newspaper round, just as he had managed to do almost every day that week. He knew it was partly because he was cutting corners and finding quicker ways to get from house to house – but he was also aware that his stamina was gaining ground day by day. Running had become a passion for him, a constant challenge against the clock which was taking over his every waking thought. He ran everywhere, timing his journey to and from school, using every lunch break to sprint around the playing field in addition to the extra training sessions which Chris had organised with the Midsummer Run now just four weeks away.

Two evenings each week, Chris took the team chosen to represent the school – that was Ben, Michael Smith and two lads from the year below them, Dave Whitaker and Simon Buxton – over to Barford Comprehensive for circuit training, alternating other nights with visits to the Valley Park so that they could become completely familiar with the course of the race. Chris watched the progress of each of the boys with interest, but it was with growing admiration that he clocked Ben's steady, determined achievement in style, strength and timing.

To his relief, Ben found that, away from his crowd of cronies, Michael became much more pleasant company. His attitude towards Ben was still rather condescending, as if he could barely stop himself laughing at the thought of 'the Worm' representing the school. Michael's own talent for running stemmed more from the fact that he was an unusually tall, big-boned boy for his age rather than any real skill or commitment to the sport. For him, qualifying for the race was a rather entertaining diversion which allowed him to be the centre of attention – while for Ben, the race had become so much more, an opportunity to prove his worth not just to his classmates, but to himself. His deafness had made him feel like an irrelevant outsider at school. His father's leaving had added to his sense of worthlessness, robbing him of confidence and ease. But all that had changed once he discovered this passion for running. For Ben, nothing matched the challenge of pitting himself against his own physical limitations. The determination to run longer, harder, faster than he had the day before became a compulsion, until he only felt truly alive with the wind in his face and the rhythmic pounding of his feet thudding in his head.

Ben's progress was a source of pride not only to Chris, but most certainly for Meg, who watched with pleasure as her young son's confidence grew daily. She found herself looking forward to Ben's return from training not only so that she could hear about his timing that day, but because Chris had got into the habit of staying for supper on several evenings. It was with some surprise that she realised how important his friendship had become to her. Chris's presence in their home felt natural and valued. There was nothing to it, of course. They were simply friends sharing an interest in Ben's running ability. The fact that they often found themselves coming out with an identical comment, or laughing at the same inconsequential thought, was an added bonus.

Their arrangement was convenient for them both. Chris

appreciated home cooked meals when his own culinary skills were basic to say the least – and Meg was grateful for the small jobs Chris took care of around the house – the squeaking bathroom door that needed oiling, the banister rail on the stairs which mysteriously came off in Ben's hand. Chris was good company – comfortable, practical and safe – and Meg dismissed as ridiculous the notion that there was something missing on the evenings when they had supper without him.

'Oh Emma, you look really lovely!'

She did. It was an elegant young woman who walked down the stairs towards her mother that evening wearing black flared trousers, and a glittering tight-fitting camisole top which left her tiny waist exposed to show the diamond stud gleaming from her belly-button.

'Thanks, Mum. You don't look bad yourself!'

'Do you really think so?' For the first time since Alan had left, Meg had abandoned her natural reserve about spending money to splash out on a special outfit for Emma's party. It was a stylishly cut suit in silken black fabric, with wide loose-fitting trousers and a sharply tailored jacket. To the suit she had added a shimmering, golden high-necked top which subtly brought out the honey-coloured tones in her hair. She had taken unusual care with her make-up too, adding a new autumnal shade of lipstick, and warm brown and beige shadow which made her eyes seem enormous in her pertly pretty face.

Meg reached out to put her arms around her daughter as she reached the bottom of the stairs. 'I'm so proud of you, love. I hope you have the truly wonderful evening you deserve.'

'You too. And thanks for all the preparation you've put in. I know it's not been easy for you having to work with Dad on this.' Emma noticed that Meg fell silent at the mention of Alan, and stood back so that she could look closely at her mother. 'I know what you're thinking – and the answer is that I really don't know if Katherine is planning to come or not. I had to invite her, you know that.'

'Oh, of course. It will just be difficult for me to see them together . . .'

'Dad must realise that. I'm sure he'll do what he feels is right.'

'He feels it's right to live with Katherine, so naturally he'll want her to be at his side on an occasion like this.'

'Well, we'll soon find out. Oh, look, here comes Chris! Just wait till he sees how gorgeous you look!'

Meg felt a sudden flutter of nerves as Emma opened the door to Chris, recognising that his reaction to the way she looked that evening actually mattered quite a lot to her. In all the months she'd known him, he had never seen her dressed in any way except at her most relaxed, usually in jeans or tracksuit bottoms with a comfy old jersey.

However, it was Meg who drew a sharp breath as Chris stood framed in the doorway. This was a man she hardly recognised; the dark navy suit accentuating his slim, long-limbed body, with his hair curling over the collar of the burgundy-coloured shirt which he wore open-necked beneath the jacket.

'Wow!' enthused Emma. 'You look tasty! Am I allowed to book you for a smoochy dance later this evening?'

Chris laughed. 'Well, you're the birthday girl. You wish is my command tonight, although I'll warn you now I have two left feet when it comes to dancing!' His gaze shifted from Emma across to Meg who was standing on the far side of the hall. 'Meg, you look . . .'

'. . . overdressed?'

'Hardly – and I know how hopeless you are at taking compliments . . .'

'I don't look too much? A bit glittery for a woman of a certain age?'

He walked over to place his hands on her arms, an unreadable expression on his face as he looked down at her. 'You look absolutely beautiful. You and Emma both do.'

'Matt should be here soon. He's late. I knew he would be.'

There was a clatter of footsteps at that moment as Ben, Gameboy in hand, thundered down the stairs two at a time to join them. He grinned as Chris registered the lurid lime green of his shirt. 'It's so you don't miss me. Darren and I are bouncers on the door checking invitations. We've decided they're going to have to bribe us with promises of alcohol all evening before we let them in.'

'I heard that!' warned Meg.

'Bad for your training regime,' added Chris, a grin belying his sternness, 'and that race is in just over a week's time. So as your coach, I'll be keeping a close eye on you, young man!'

Matt, when he finally made an appearance, looked almost unrecognisable in the dinner suit he had apparently borrowed from his father. It was a little short in the leg, and the sleeves could have done with an extra inch, but Emma was plainly impressed when she saw him.

'Right!' said Chris. 'The car's open. Hop in!' But as Meg began to follow Emma and Matt out of the front door, she found her path blocked by Chris. 'Before we go, Meg, there's something I must just do.'

She thought for a moment as he stood in front of her looking intently into her eyes that he had seen something which needed putting right, a stray eyelash perhaps. Instead his hand slipped under her chin tilting her head back until his lips met hers, featherlight at first, then deepening to become more searching and urgent as he felt a surprised but welcoming response from her. With his fingers still beneath her chin, she opened her eyes, staring at him in amazement as she felt him draw back from her.

'I've been meaning to do that for ages,' he said simply, taking her hand. 'Come on, the kids are waiting for us.'

Bemused and unsure of her feelings at the sudden unexpected shift in their relationship, she found herself smiling as she allowed him to lead her out to the car.

Alan had had a frustrating day. Having monopolised his time all afternoon, one particularly demanding client had also insisted that Alan wait to meet his colleague who hadn't arrived until gone six o'clock. A hold-up on the tube compounded the time problem, and he rushed into the flat flustered and anxious to be on the road to Emma's party as quickly as possible.

'You're late. We need to get going.'

He stared at Katherine in amazement. She looked beautiful, slim and elegantly tailored in a soft grey sequinned dress and jacket.

'Katherine, I thought we'd agreed about this. We really can't go to this party together.'

'We ARE together, Alan. I've thought about this constantly since you first made your feelings clear, and I don't agree with you. Emma is my god-daughter. She has invited US to her special evening, and WE are going – both of us together – or not at all.'

'Look, can't you just imagine how Meg will feel about this?'

'Knowing Meg, I think she'll be very practical about the reality of this situation. She may not like the thought of us together, but I know she accepts it. In fact it's not Meg's feelings that worry me about this, but yours. Why aren't you more willing to make a stand on this? This is our chance to let people see how much we love each other, that in spite of all the upset, our partnership is right and it works. Surely that's what you want?'

'But do we need to ram it down their throats? It will only cause trouble, and possibly upstage Emma on her special night.'

'Why should it? Emma invited us together, presumably because that's the way she expects us to be.'

'I can't believe you're doing this. I've never thought of you as selfish, Katherine, and I simply can't understand why you don't see the sensitivity of this situation. Think about it while I get washed and changed.'

When Alan came out of the bathroom, he found Katherine sitting stony-faced on the end of their bed. She spoke slowly and deliberately to control the tremble in her voice.

'Alan, you have a clear choice to make tonight. You can choose to consider Meg's feelings first, or mine. If you insist on going to that party without me, I really don't think you and I have any future at all.'

'For heaven's sake, you're being melodramatic. Just let me go for Emma's sake, and I promise I'll make it up to you. Perhaps we should go away or something? Would you like that? A weekend in Paris maybe?'

'If you leave this flat tonight to go to the party without me, then it's over between us.'

His smile was indulgent as he leaned forward to plant a kiss on her forehead. 'It will never be over between us. How many years have we tried to part without success?'

'Please, Alan, don't underestimate how important this is to me.'

'For me too. You are important to me, but tonight Emma is the one who matters most.'

'Then we have an impasse, and you have a decision to make. You can decide to play happy families and stand at Meg's side tonight – or you can choose to have me as your partner. Just bear in mind before you make your choice that if I am not with you this evening, then I will never be at your side again.'

Alan's smile was replaced by an expression of exasperation as he glanced sideways at the bedside clock before sitting down

heavily beside her. Tonight of all nights, he could do without
this . . .

'Steady now! Don't let it topple!'

Val backed in through the door of the reception hall, guiding
the path of Jay and Chas as they carried in their magnificent
contribution to the party. Spotting their arrival from the other
side of the hall, Emma and her entourage quickly made their way
across to join them.

A delicate balancing act later, the two men had finally
manoeuvred the three-tier cake into prime position in the middle
of the food table.

'Well!' enthused Emma. 'That is quite a colour scheme!'

'A bit of a team effort really,' explained Chas, 'Jay designed,
I baked and Val iced it. The top tier is actually one of the
layers from your original christening cake which your mum
still had. We've re-decorated it in baby pink, which seemed
appropriate. Just between ourselves though, I wouldn't touch
that cake with a barge pole even if it is liberally laced with
brandy. The middle layer is very traditional, just right for all the
mums and aunties here this evening. But the bottom tier, well,
that's different. I've baked it to my own very special recipe just
for you and your friends, Em. Guaranteed to put a zip into any
party!'

Val looked at him sharply. 'You never mentioned that before.
You haven't been up to anything, have you, Chas?'

His face was a picture of innocence. 'As if I would! Hey, I like
this record. Come on, let's dance!' And leaving Jay to put the
finishing touches to the cake decoration, Chas whisked Val on to
the dance floor.

'Where is he then?' Meg turned to see Sandy, a vision in deep
purple and cerise pink, at her elbow. 'Alan, I mean? I thought
he'd be here by now.'

Meg glanced at her watch. 'Frankly, so did I. He's talked about nothing but this party for weeks.'

'Not that you're short of company, of course. Your Chris is SO attentive.'

'He's not my Chris.'

'Well, he should be. He looks gorgeous in that suit.'

'Really? I hadn't noticed.'

'Just look at my Dave right in the middle of all Emma's girlfriends! Sorry, Meg. I've got to go before he makes an old fool of himself . . .'

'Psst! Matt!' Ben grabbed hold of Matt's jacket as he passed the entrance to the hall. 'Get us a drink, would you? This bouncing duty is thirsty business.'

'Sure. Lemonade all right?'

'A can of lager would be better. And Darren wants one too.'

'Your dad will kill me if he sees me giving you a can of anything.'

'He's not here.'

'And because he's not, I'll get a can for the two of you to share just this once. That's it though, Ben. I promised your mum I'd keep a big brotherly eye on you.'

Ben grinned. 'That's just what you're doing. Thanks, Matt. You're a pal.'

Meg, standing anxiously at the edge of the crowd, suddenly felt a pair of arms slip around her waist. 'Relax!' said Chris's voice in her ear. 'It's going fine. Everyone's having a really good time.'

She spun round to face him. 'Do you think so? Is the food all right? And you don't think the drink is going too fast, do you? I hope we've put enough money behind the bar.'

'It's all wonderful – and the disco is rather good too. Come and dance with me!'

'I shouldn't. I should be here to greet the guests when they arrive.'

'Whoever they are, they'll find you if they need you.'

'I can't understand where Alan's got to . . .'

'Well, I for one am delighted he's not here so that I can drag you on to the dance floor. Listen, dancing is not my strong point, so grab me while my offer's there. I might think better of this soon!'

She grinned at him, taking his outstretched hand to follow him into the moving mass of people on the darkened dance floor.

'Dad! You're here!' Emma hugged her father soundly. 'I was beginning to think you'd forgotten!'

'As if I would!'

'Where's Katherine?'

'She thought she'd give this evening a miss. She sends her love, of course, and I have a parcel from her for you in the car. Where's your mum?'

'In that lot somewhere.'

Alan's gaze shifted to the dance floor where he could clearly make out Meg enveloped in the arms of a tall man, unfamiliar to him, but who plainly knew his wife very well indeed. The pang of indignation and jealousy which shot through him took him by surprise. It had never occurred to him that Meg might have someone else in her life. In fact, even the thought of such a thing was quite shocking. After all, as her husband and long-time companion, no one knew Meg better than he did. She was dependable and constant – and as Ben and Emma's mother, the notion that she might be introducing some other man into the lives of their children was uncharacteristically inconsiderate. In spite of the dramatic changes in their living arrangements in recent months, he would never have thought it of her. Besides, she was far too unworldly to deal with the lecherous attentions of unscrupulous men. And bristling with the need to protect her,

Alan made his way across the room to announce his arrival to Meg — and her companion.

Robert had felt inexplicably restless that evening. He had downed a glass and a half of his favourite white wine during an hour of flicking from television channel to channel, when the phone rang.

'Tell me to push off if you're busy.'

'Katherine?' His eyebrows rose a notch at the sound of her voice.

'I'm hurt, humiliated and furious and could do with some company.'

'Alan?'

'He's playing happy families with Meg this evening.'

'Aah.'

'I was invited too, but he refused to take me.'

'So what will you do about that?'

'I've done it. I told him that if he went without me, that was the end of us.'

'I see. And do you mean it?'

'I did.'

'And now?'

'And now I need a companion who will remind me that I'm worth more than this, and that the very best thing I can do is get that man right out of my life — for good, MY good!'

'Have you eaten?'

'No.'

'Then you need something wildly extravagant and totally diverting. There's a little Greek restaurant in Belsize Park where they break plates and dance on the tables. Will that do?'

'Sounds perfect.'

'I'll pick you up in twenty minutes.'

'I'll be ready and waiting.'

'And Katherine?'

'Hmm?'

'I'm really glad you called.'

So am I, she thought, as she replaced the receiver, glanced in the mirror, then reached for her make-up bag.

Emma had opted for the minimum amount of formal proceedings during the party, but her father's affectionate, entertaining speech as he stood with her mother to propose a toast to their daughter almost brought tears to her eyes. With Matt by her side, proud, protective and heartstoppingly tasty in his father's suit, she could never remember feeling quite so happy.

'Cut the cake!' insisted Jay, handing her a huge knife – which she did, although it required quite a bit of brute force to work her way through the crisp icing on the bottom tier of very rich fruit cake. She leant down to put her nose to the cake.

'This smells delicious. What's your secret ingredient, Chas?'

'That, my darling, is for me to know and you to guess,' Chas stage-whispered in her ear. 'Suffice it to say that this cake is my little contribution to make your party go with a swing!'

Standing close to Emma with his wife, Sandy, Dave was near enough to Val to note with interest the instant suspicion in her expression as she overheard Chas's comment. And as Val picked up the cake to take it out to the kitchen for cutting, Dave watched her thoughtfully.

The moment his arm encircled her shoulders, Meg knew it was Alan without even turning to look. There was something comforting about the familiar feel of him at her side that had her leaning back against him with a sigh.

'It's gone well, hasn't it? Emma's really enjoying herself.'

'She's lovely, Meg – a credit to you.'

'To both of us.'

'It seems no time ago at all that we brought her home from

the hospital. Do you remember what a little bundle she was? And how you insisted on her sleeping right next door to our bed for months and months? And you were so constantly worried about her that even if the cat miaowed, you were convinced it was the baby!'

'Do you remember when she cut the whiskers off the cat? How old would she have been then? Four? And that picture we have of her when she first tasted chocolate ice-cream! She had more in her hair than ever got anywhere near her mouth!'

'Remember that first holiday we had in the caravan park down on the south coast, when she insisted on picking up all the snails she found in the grass to kiss them goodnight!'

'And I'll never forget how over-protective you were when her first boyfriend turned up at the door. Do you remember? He had a pushbike, and smelt of cheese and pickle sandwiches.'

'Well, he certainly sweated a lot. I couldn't bear the thought of him touching my darling little girl.'

Meg looked over to where Emma was helping herself to a piece of cake offered by Chas. 'Not a little girl any longer . . .'

Alan moved round beside her, looking first at their daughter before shifting his gaze down to Meg. 'Thank you. Thank you for Emma and Ben. Thanks for your calmness and sense of humour and love throughout all the ups and downs of family life. I know I didn't value what I had at the time. I do now . . .'

'It was good, wasn't it?' she replied softly.

'Would anyone mind if I asked my wife to dance?'

'Well, I wouldn't, and that's all that counts.'

From her table in the corner, Sandy watched Meg and Alan make their way on to the dance floor with undisguised interest. 'Look, Dave! The cheek of the man! Living with her best friend, and there he is acting as if he owns Meg!'

'Well, isn't it good that they're friends?'

'As long as he doesn't build up her hopes again. I don't trust that Alan Barratt an inch.'

'Fortunately your opinion isn't what counts. Meg's a grown woman, capable of making up her own mind.'

'And there's Chris to consider. Such a nice chap. She doesn't want him to get the wrong idea.'

'Maybe Meg doesn't think Alan is the wrong idea. After all, he didn't bring Katherine with him tonight.'

'You're right. What's going on there, do you think?'

'Just a moment,' said Dave, rising to his feet. 'There's Chas. I need a word with him.'

'Ben?' Chris folded his long frame down into the seat beside Ben who was giggling uncontrollably with his friend Darren. 'You all right?'

'Fine!' shouted Ben, his eyes distinctly glassy. 'Great party!'

Chris picked up the lager can on the table suspiciously. 'How many of these have you had?'

Ben's eyes opened wide and innocent. 'Only one between the two of us. Matt wouldn't let us have any more.' And he and Darren dissolved into peels of uncontrollable laughter.

'What's got into you?' asked Chris with concern. 'Have you been drinking that lager on an empty stomach, is that it? What have you eaten?'

'Cake,' guffawed Darren. 'Great cake. Chas gave us three pieces.'

Sticking his nose into the remains of the fruit cake, Chris's expression darkened as he picked up the plate and headed for the kitchen. He found that Dave was already there, standing with his arms crossed in front of a grinning Chas.

'What is it, your magic ingredient, Chas? Cannabis?'

'Heavens, no, as if I would! No, just a little powdered mushroom, my own recipe. Nothing illegal or dangerous. Simply a little something for the younger generation here tonight to get them in the mood.'

'I thought that bottom tier of the cake smelt odd the moment it was cut,' said Dave. 'Unfortunately a few pieces were handed round before I realised what had happened.'

'Well, Ben and Darren are high as kites for a start. And I noticed that some of Matt's friends are going round with unnaturally beaming smiles on their faces.'

'How could you, Chas!' scolded Val. 'Meg will never forgive me.'

'Does she need to know?'

They all looked at Dave, who shrugged his shoulders. 'I'm here as a friend of the family tonight, not as a police officer, so I'm turning a blind eye just for now. You make it your job to collect up every single bit of that cake though, Chas, and if I hear even a murmur of you having a private collection of magic mushrooms or whatever they are, I'll be down on you like a ton of bricks. Do we understand each other?'

Chas's smile was sweet and reassuring. 'Certainly, Dave, anything you say. Good for a laugh though, wasn't it!'

Katherine had almost forgotten just what good company Robert could be. He skilfully kept her off the subject of Alan, starting the conversation with how the appeal for St Mary's was going, then steering their discussion on to everything from music and films to childhood memories and work stories.

When the restaurant floorshow of belly dancing and plate smashing was over and the music group including a balalaika player started playing softly at the edge of the small dance floor, Robert stood to take Katherine by the hand. Without comment, she moved into his arms, their bodies comfortable together as they swayed to the rhythm.

Her head against his shoulder, Katherine found herself thinking what a very entertaining and sensitive companion he could be. And if it wasn't for the tears that clouded her eyes, and the treacherous thoughts wondering exactly what Alan was doing at that moment, the evening would have been quite perfect.

At midnight, when the music had finished and Emma and her friends were making their happy noisy way home, a small working party of Sandy and Dave, Val, Chas and Jay, Meg and Chris stayed behind to tidy the hall. Alan had left some time earlier when Ben had inexplicably turned an extraordinary puce colour and plainly needed his bed. They all agreed that the party had been a huge success. Certainly, the young people seemed to have had a great time, Meg said, not noticing the knowing looks which passed between some members of the clearing-up group.

At last Chris appeared at Meg's side with her coat over his arm. 'All done. Come on tired lady. You're ready for a lift home.'

With an arm around her shoulders, he led her out to his car, drawing up a few minutes later outside her house. He switched off the engine, turning towards her in the darkness. 'It's been a lovely evening. Thanks, Meg, for including me.'

She smiled. 'You're almost a part of the family these days.'

'I hoped you might feel that way. Getting to know you has been very special for me.'

'Well, Ben has certainly blossomed with your interest and friendship.'

'It's not Ben I'm thinking about.' She looked down at her hands, suddenly unsure of the turn in the conversation. Deliberately he stretched out to take her hand in his. 'I think Ben has extraordinary talent,' he said carefully, 'but there is no need for me to spend so much time with him when I know he'll find his own level anyway. My interest in your family may have started with your son, but Meg, it's you I come to see now. Surely you must know that?'

Her eyes were enormous as she stared at him in the light from the nearby lamppost.

'I'd be lying if I didn't admit to how much I enjoy your company too.'

'I would like to think that in time you might do more than just enjoy my company. I know you've had the stuffing knocked out of you by the break-up of your marriage, and I don't want to put pressure on you before you feel ready – but you are a very beautiful and appealing woman.'

She laughed, shaking her head with disbelief.

'You are, Meg. It would be the easiest thing in the world to fall in love with you.'

'Chris, I . . .'

'Don't. Don't say anything until you've had time to think about this. Give some thought to how well we get on together, how comfortable we've always felt even when we're not doing much at all. Then think on, dear Meg, about how it might feel if we didn't say goodbye every evening after supper – if I stayed to hold you close all night, so that you'd wake up in my arms in the morning.'

Her smile was wry. 'I look dreadful in the mornings.'

'I don't care how you look. I care what you are – and what you are is the most truly lovely woman I've ever known.'

Without another word, she reached forward to place her lips on his in a kiss that lingered with tenderness and promise. 'I'd ask you in for a coffee . . .' she said at last.

'. . . except Alan's waiting inside, isn't he?'

'Yes.'

'Is he staying here tonight?'

'No. There's been no mention of that.'

'Why didn't Katherine come with him this evening?'

'I don't know. He didn't say.'

'He seems very fond of you.'

'Of course. We've been married for so many years.'

'How did it feel to have him around at the party, Meg? Do you love him still?'

'It's been confusing.'

He traced the line of her cheek-bone with his finger. 'Take care, won't you?'

'I promise I'll try.'

'And you'll give what I said some thought?'

'Honestly, Chris, it will be very hard to think of anything else . . .' And with a final squeeze of his hand, she left the car.

It was gone midnight when Robert and Katherine left the dance floor with the waiters looking meaningfully at them as they tried to close the restaurant around them. Once in the car, Robert turned the ignition key, then looked at Katherine. 'Where to?'

'Home.'

'Yours or mine?' She considered the question. 'Is Alan coming back tonight?' he asked when she didn't come up with an answer.

'I suppose so.'

'And you've given him an ultimatum. You said that if he went without you this evening, you would no longer be there for him. So don't be. Come home with me.'

'You have to understand, Robert, I do love Alan. I've loved him for so long.'

'But does he love you enough? Do you want your ultimatum to have no substance – or would you like to give him a taste of your determination tonight?'

'And you and I are just friends, right?'

His eyes twinkled mischievously in the darkness. 'Of course. Very, very good friends.'

'Then I'm too tired to do anything except let you decide where you take me now.'

'I've a bottle of your favourite wine chilled in my fridge.'

'You smooth talker, you.'

'And music that's just right for late-night conversation.'

'And a spare room?'

He smiled. 'Of course.'

And when she smiled in return, he put the car into gear and pulled away from the kerb.

Meg was greeted by an oddly familiar scene as she walked into the kitchen that night. Alan had obviously made himself at home, as she could tell from the plate of sandwiches he'd just made. The microwave pinged to announce that hot milk was ready, destined for the two cups of Horlicks he was also making.

'I heard the car draw up, and knew you'd probably be peckish. You didn't eat a thing tonight, am I right? You never do when you're in organising mode.'

She laughed. 'How well you know me – and yes, that all looks delicious.'

Loading up a tray with sandwiches, cups and a packet of chocolate biscuits, Alan followed Meg through to the lounge where the lights were dimmed and soft music was playing from the CD.

'Harry Nilsson. I've not listened to this for ages,' mused Meg.

'It was always your favourite.'

'Ah well, life's very different now. I don't find time to listen to music much at all.'

'That's a pity.'

'It's a pity about a lot of things, Alan.'

He took a sip from his cup rather than follow that line of conversation. 'It was good tonight, don't you think?'

'Emma certainly seemed to enjoy it.'

'I did too. It was nice to see some of the old faces again.'

'Yes, now you're not living here, there must have been quite a few people there you've not met up with for months.'

'It felt good, Meg. Good to see old friends, good to be involved in a family event like that.'

'I'm glad you enjoyed it.'

'I've missed that feeling – being part of a family.'

'Your choice.'

'Yes, of course.'

'And where was Katherine this evening?'

'We decided it would be better if she didn't put in an appearance on an occasion like this.'

'And she didn't mind?'

'Of course not. She understood completely.'

'Oh, really? Conversation faltered again at Meg's dry, disinterested response, so Alan started to glance around him.

'You've changed this room. It looks better.'

'I've felt the need to change a lot of things.'

'I understand. You always did have a flair for making a place homely.'

'Untidy, you mean.'

'No. This house has a lovely feel because of you. You are a wonderful home-maker.'

'Well, you have a new home now.'

'Apparently, yes.'

'Your decision too.'

'Somehow it still doesn't feel that way.'

'Don't, Alan. I don't know how to respond when you say things like that. It's all been so painful, but I'm coming through now, really I am. Don't undermine me. Don't rake up all the hurt again.'

'What about thinking beyond the hurt, to the time when we were happy before all this happened?'

'Ten years ago, do you mean?'

'Since then too. We were happy, Meg, weren't we?'

'I was – but then I hardly knew the whole story, did I?'

'But it was good between us, you must remember that. The kids. The house. It worked well, you know it did.'

'That all seems a very long time ago – another life.'

'I find myself thinking about that time so much now, remembering what I've lost.'

'What you threw away.'

'What I threw away.' From his end of the settee, he stretched out to cover Meg's hand with his own – and she didn't pull away. 'I never appreciated what I had at the time. I was selfish and arrogant and not worthy of you and the children.'

'Well, it's all water under the bridge now. Best forgotten.'

'I can't forget.'

'Alan, please . . .'

'Do you feel nothing, Meg? Have you no love left for me at all?'

'What I feel has always been irrelevant, hasn't it? Since when did my feelings count?'

'Your feelings mean a great deal to me right now.'

'You made your choice. We've all had to live by it. Are you saying that after everything you've put us through, you're not happy?'

'I know that this evening I've been happier than I've felt in months. Being with the children and you – it's been very special for me.'

'It was important for Emma and Ben that you were there. You may have left their home, but you must never be missing from their lives.'

'And you, Meg? Have I still got a place in your life?'

'We're almost divorced. The papers are going through.'

'And that's what you want? To be completely separate from me?'

'I don't understand the question. You're living with Katherine.'

'Yes, but I miss you.' She snorted in disbelief. 'I find I miss you very much, Meg. I think about you often, wondering how you are, what you're doing.'

'I'm fine. I've had to be, haven't I? Don't do this, Alan. You asked me to accept that you and Katherine are a couple, and I do. Don't confuse me now.'

'But don't you find this confusing? As we sit here, just as we have so often in the past eating late-night sandwiches and drinking cups of Horlicks, isn't it confusing? Doesn't this feel good to you? Isn't there a rightness about the two of us sitting here as if we were married again?'

'What are you saying?'

'That you never know the value of what you have until it's no longer there. Perhaps I have lost all this, and that would only be what I deserve. But I need you to know that the nearer we get to being divorced, the more I realise I don't want it.'

'You're living with Katherine, but you don't want a divorce?'

'I don't have to live with Katherine, not if there is even the remotest chance of you giving our marriage another chance.'

She shook her head, 'How could you ask that? How could you ever expect me to trust you again?'

'Because I'm a different man now, wiser for having learned the hard way. I'm not asking you to turn the clock back to what we were before because that's gone for ever. What I'm hoping for is a new start where I have to earn your love and trust. I take nothing for granted. I simply ask for the chance to prove how sorry I am, how much I love you.'

'I don't know . . .' In spite of herself, Meg realised that her eyes were pricking with tears.

'Oh, Meg, darling, I am so sorry . . .'

He was beside her then, pulling her close to him, his lips on her hair and forehead and cheeks — and in spite of herself, she found she was responding, lifting her face until her eyes were level with his. What he said was true. There was a sense of rightness in having his arms around her again. This man was the love of her life. For as long as she could remember, he had been her reason for waking and working and being alive. And now he was sorry for ever leaving her. During all those long hours and days and weeks when she had ached for the loss of him, he had been missing her too. He loved her! And didn't she still love him? Wasn't that why the past few months had been such hell — because she was without the presence and support of the man she loved above anyone in the world?

She could feel salt tears on their lips as he kissed her, her mouth moulding into his with a mixture of familiarity and desire. And then all coherent thought disappeared as she melted into the feel of him, the strength and hardness of his body, the faint scent of the sharp citrus aftershave he always wore, the touch of his hands upon her face, her shoulders and finally her breast. She should pull away. She should remember her dignity, the hurt he had caused her, the danger he posed to her delicate heart . . .

But when he gently leaned her back so that their bodies touched along the length of the settee, she gave herself up to the passionate longing which soared through her as she clung to him with relief and overwhelming joy.

Robert had just stepped out into the kitchen to make coffee when Katherine succumbed to the temptation of ringing Alan. She knew she'd given him an ultimatum, that she should remain aloof, but she found herself ringing his mobile number all the same. It immediately clicked into his answering service.

He always had his mobile phone on, even overnight. So why was it off now? She replaced the receiver thoughtfully. Perhaps because he was already at home? Of course, that was the answer! And if Alan was at her flat, did she really want to be here in the home of another man? In spite of her ultimatum, didn't her confusion and guilt tell her she was with the wrong person?

Fumbling with the numbers, she rang the flat. Four rings later, she heard her own voice telling her there was no one there to take the call.

Damn him! Damn the man! Damn Alan Barratt for everything she found in him that made her fall hopelessly in love with him! And damn her foolish heart for caring so much and hurting so badly!

Meg arched her back to draw closer to him, marvelling at the ease with which they resumed the familiar, comfortable role of lovers. Deliberately, she put all rational thought from her mind, allowing herself to follow the instincts of her body. There was so much wrong with what was happening – but she would think about that later. For the moment, all that mattered was the magical spark of desire between them, long forgotten and buried in the routine of marriage and family life – and the undeniable truth that Alan was the man she loved, had always loved, and longed to love again.

Years of partnership had made them practised in the art of pleasing each other, and Meg gave herself up to the reassurance of his knowledge of her, his skill at drawing out a depth of passion that she had only ever found with him.

Then it was over, and she fell back damp and spent, mellow and contented, relishing the soft touch of his fingers as he stroked the curve of her shoulder, aware of his breath on her face, relaxed and sleepy as he held her close.

'What time is it?' His eyes shot open.

'I'm not sure.' His question surprised her. 'After one, I should think. Does it matter?'

He was already getting to his feet, reaching for his clothes. 'Meg, I must go. Forgive me, but . . .'

'. . . Katherine's waiting.'

'I wasn't really truthful about her reaction to me coming alone this evening.'

'She was furious.'

'I didn't want her presence at the party to hurt you – and I don't want me being here now to hurt her.'

'I see.'

'We'll sort this out, Meg. We'll have to – but I must go.'

She didn't answer. And if he noticed her silence as he quickly dressed, collected his keys and grabbed for his coat, he made no comment about it. With a swift brush of his lips across hers, he was gone leaving her numb and naked in the circle of light from the lampstand.

Chapter Twelve

Getting back to the flat in the wee small hours to find Katherine wasn't there was quite a shock for Alan. He'd driven through the night like a dervish, anxious not to compound her unhappiness by being any later than necessary. More than that, his mind was in turmoil about what had happened with Meg. Dear Meg, his wife for so many years, the mother of his children. There was such a feeling of coming home to be in her arms again. But then Katherine's face fought its way into his thoughts – trusting, accepting, committed and loving – and the thought of hurting her tore him apart.

But she wasn't there. The flat rang with eerie emptiness as he quickly checked the lounge, bedroom and bathroom. For the first time, he wondered if she had actually meant what she'd said about no longer being there for him if he went to the party without her. He hadn't taken her threat too seriously because they'd made decisions about splitting up on so many occasions in the past, and nothing had ever come of it. Neither of them had been strong enough to break apart, and he hadn't honestly expected this occasion to be any different, especially not now when their relationship was out in the open and they were living together as a couple. As everyone around them seemed to accept them as a couple, there seemed less reason for them to talk about pulling apart.

He undressed and climbed into her side of the bed, sure that sleep would overcome him immediately. When it didn't, he tossed and turned for what seemed like hours, trying to analyse his feelings.

The sense of relief in knowing that Meg still loved and wanted him was overwhelming – and yet the thought that Katherine, who had stood so patiently and lovingly in the shadows behind him for years, might have reached the point of choosing to leave him, sent waves of alarm through him.

He was aware of an ominous ache in his chest as he groaned and thumped the pillows into submission. The doctor had warned him against both over-exertion and stress. The party, and the events after it, had been exhausting, physically and emotionally. It was little wonder that he felt so dreadful. What was happening to him? Just hours before he had told Meg he wanted to resume their marriage – and now he was distraught with worry because he had no idea either where Katherine was, or what state she was in. She was not a woman who had particularly close girl friends – except Meg, of course, and they were barely able to speak to each other these days. Where could she have gone? Where would she turn when she was unhappy and alone? Who might know? Who could he ring when her own mobile was switched off? Where could she possibly be?

The church clock down the road struck five before he finally abandoned his attempts to sleep, and got up to turn the television on. For minutes he flicked across the channels, finding nothing to hold his attention. It was as he reached over to switch off the set that he spied the little jewellery box. Opening it, he gently picked out the elegant band of gold set with its row of shimmering diamonds. Turning it over in his fingers, he read again the inscription engraved inside: *Forever, Alan.*

And at the sight of those words, Alan's body curled over as

he closed his fingers around the ring, unsure if the sadness which engulfed him was for himself, or the women he loved.

To Alan's concern and surprise, Katherine did not return the next morning. Her mobile remained off, and there was no word from her. However, when he had to go out for a few hours in the afternoon, he was relieved to see she'd obviously been home as the kettle was hot, and her coat was hanging behind the bedroom door when he got back. He found her note on the dressing table.

> *Alan,*
>
> *It is obviously not appropriate for you to stay here any longer, as I cannot return to my home until you leave. Please make alternative arrangements for tonight and from now on. You don't have to take all your belongings straight away, but I would appreciate you removing them as soon as you have a forwarding address.*
>
> *I am sorry it's had to end this way.*
>
> *Katherine*

He sat down heavily on the bed reading and re-reading the note. Then he took his filofax from the dressing table, looked up the right number, and crossed his fingers that Colin would be in to take his call.

Minutes later, he made a second call to the number he knew so well. He wanted to speak to Meg, needed to know her reaction after the events of last night.

But her line was engaged.

'Meg?' She recognised Chris's voice immediately, although it had crossed her mind as the phone rang it might be Alan. He hadn't rung – and she wasn't quite sure whether that was something which made her relieved or angry. He SHOULD have called, of that she had no doubt — but if he had, would she have known what to say?

'How is everyone? How are you after last night?'

Confused, she thought, in a way that Chris could never know or understand. Whatever would he think if he realised what had happened between her and Alan at the end of the evening? He'd despise her. Dear, honest, straightforward Chris who had shown her and the children nothing but kindness and consideration since Alan had left them, could never be expected to understand the treacherous way in which her body had responded to her former husband. Her reaction was too inexplicable, her emotions too complex for her to understand, let alone explain to anyone else.

'Ben is exhausted, and definitely still a bit queasy. You don't want him to go running this afternoon, do you?'

'The race is next Friday. He should train really.'

'He's not even got up properly yet. That's most unusual for him.'

'Then perhaps he should have today off. What about Emma?'

'Matt's here, and they're just planning a quiet day.'

'Then would you consider coming out for dinner with me tonight?'

'Oh, Chris, I don't know. I'm not sure I should leave them . . .'

'They're fine. Emma is eighteen, you know, and perfectly capable of keeping an eye on Ben.'

'I suppose you're right.'

'Oh dear, you don't sound very keen.' She could hear the smile in his voice.

'Chris, I'm sorry — how rude of me. It's a very kind offer.'

'Not kind at all. I'd like to see you.'

'I'd like to see you too.' And in that instant, she knew it was true. She needed Chris's solid, reassuring company.

'Chinese be all right?'

'Lovely.'

'I'll pick you up at eight then.'

And minutes after she replaced the phone, she caught sight of herself in the hall mirror and realised she was still smiling.

My dear Katherine,

With great sadness, I have done as you asked, and will be based at Colin's for a few days while I sort myself out. I wish so much that we could have talked about this today. You have no idea how worried I was when I came back to find you gone last night.

I realise that I've hurt you, and that I regret with all my heart. Surely, though, we have been through such a lot, and loved one another for so long, that we owe it to ourselves to meet up. Then you can look me in the eye, and tell me how sure you are that it's really over.

I love you. I always will. Please ring me.

Alan

When Katherine came back that night to find Alan's car gone and his note on the table, she helped herself to a glass of wine before she sat down to read it. Then, resting her head against the back of the settee, she closed her eyes tightly – and even then the tears still managed to squeeze their way through to slide down her face unchecked.

By the time they got there, the Chinese restaurant was surprisingly full, although Chris and Meg managed to find a quiet table tucked around the corner where they could pore over the menu and discover that their taste in Chinese food, as in so many other things, was comfortably in tune.

What she remembered of that evening later was the laughter. Even though Chris realised she was tired, he kept her entertained with delightful stories of growing up in a house of women – his delicate, unworldly mother and Gilly, his dance-mad sister.

'I often got dragged along to watch Gilly's shows, and before she grew too tall for classical dancing, it was always a ballet display. I remember one time when she had just done a duet performance with another girl, then they both had a quick change to be in the next number which was a scene from *Swan Lake*. The curtains opened to reveal sixteen little girls sitting there in their frilly tutus – when suddenly the one right at the front, my sister, wailed in pain. It turned out that in the rush at the side of the stage when Mum was helping with her change of costume, they'd forgotten to take the wire coat hanger out of her tutu. Her performance from then on was partly Dying Swan, partly Sugar Glum Fairy!'

'Do you see much of them now?'

'Gilly and her partner are constantly travelling the globe doing demonstration ballroom dancing, but I do see Mum and Hubert whenever I can. You'd think she's made of porcelain when you see the care he shows her. My mother was born to be cherished and cosseted. Hubert does all that, so she's blissfully happy.'

'They sound nice.'

'I hope you'll meet them.'

'I hope so too. Families are important.'

'Yours are – to me.' She stretched out her fingers until they intertwined with his. 'Have you thought about our conversation last night?' he asked, looking at her steadily.

'A great deal.'

'And?'

'And . . . I think you're incredibly special.'

'That sounds boring.'

'You could never be that.'

'Desirable would be nice. Irresistible would be better. Sexy would be terrific.'

She laughed. 'Caring. Sensitive. Good fun. Very attractive . . .'

'VERY attractive? That's hopeful.'

'I'm scared, Chris. The whole idea of getting to know someone else after so many years with one man is terrifying.'

'And I guess you're still not clear about exactly what you feel for Alan, am I right?'

She wondered if her cheeks reddened as a hot flush of guilty embarrassment flooded through her.

'Don't worry, Meg, I understand. But I need you to understand how I feel about you. I think you're brave and practical and tough and vulnerable, all at once. I think you hide the hurt well, but the confidence has been knocked out of you by the break-up of your family. And I think you are a beautiful person – lovely to look at, even lovelier to know.'

'Oh, Chris . . .'

'And,' he said, squeezing her hand as he spoke, 'I love you. I can't help it, I just do. And even if you're not ready for another relationship, even if you feel I'm totally repulsive – nothing will change the way I feel about you. My love is unconditional and infinitely patient. You need to know that.'

Looking into his eyes, the grip of his fingers on hers, she became aware of a warm, exciting glow of contentment creeping through her. It would be so easy to sink into this, to let herself respond to him. She stared at him, wondering how it would feel to kiss those lips with passion, to feel his hands on her body just as Alan's had been the night before. Did she want him? Could she long for him physically as she apparently did for her husband?

But Alan had taken what he wanted, then rushed off with hardly a word, no sign at all of care for her. And he'd not rung all day, tossed her aside again, just as he'd done when he left her for Katherine.

'I think perhaps we should go home.' Her voice was barely more than a whisper as she spoke – and with a nod of understanding, Chris signalled to the waiter that they'd like the bill.

Outside the door of the restaurant, Chris gently turned her to him and kissed her. As he opened the car to let her into the passenger seat, he kissed her again. And when they arrived back at the house, they had barely got inside the hall before he was drawing her close.

'Mum!' Ben's voice came ringing down the stairs. 'Is that you, Mum? Dad rang.'

She slumped back against the wall. 'Did he?' she called back.

'Can you call him on his mobile?'

'Tomorrow. I'll do it tomorrow.'

'Tonight, he said.'

'Are you all right, Ben? How are you feeling?'

Her son walked down the stairs to join her, grinning broadly when he saw that she was locked in Chris's arms. 'Hello sir! Nice meal?'

'Fine thanks, Ben.'

'I'm just getting a Coke, by the way, then I'll leave you two to it.' Meg stiffened.

'Do you know, Ben, I think your mum is absolutely beautiful.'

'Fancy her then, do you?'

'Quite a lot, yes.'

'Oh.' Ben yawned. 'I'm watching a film upstairs. Night Mum!' And with a definite wink in their direction, he and his drink disappeared upstairs.

Guiltily Meg pulled away, and with a chuckle Chris planted a kiss on her forehead. 'Look, I know you're uncomfortable about this with Ben around, and I can see you're bushed after last night. So I'll leave you to your beauty sleep now. Training re-starts for Ben tomorrow. Eleven o'clock OK?'

'Come for lunch. I'd really like that.'

He bent his head to kiss her gently. 'I'd like that too. I love you, Meg. Get used to the idea, because I'm not going away.'

Minutes later when she'd waved goodbye as his car pulled away, she thought about giving Alan a ring on his mobile.

When she didn't, she realised that she simply didn't want to. Pouring herself a glass of milk, she went instead to bed and slept deeply for the first time in days.

'Here, Barratt!'

'He won't answer. He's as deaf as a post!'

'Barratt!' Steven Manson lumbered his round frame right into Ben's path so that he was surprised into stopping suddenly. Ben didn't know Steven well. He was an amiable skiver with a reputation for being able to wriggle out of anything he didn't want to do. What he wanted least of all was anything to do with sport or exercise, and he came up with all sorts of excuses for getting out of lessons, most of which Chris Elliott, like everyone else, immediately saw through. His almost constant companion, Stuart Golding, as small and wiry as Steven was tall and wide, was at his side as the pair barred Ben's way.

'Is that right, Barratt, you can't hear anything?'

Wincing inside, Ben managed to keep his face composed. 'Not a lot. I need to be able to see your lips to be sure what you're saying.'

'Are you going to be able to hear the whistle on Friday then, Barratt?'

'They're going to use a flag.'

'So you'll have a chance of starting when everyone else does this time?'

'I hope so.'

'We hope so too. Just wanted to say that. Didn't believe you could run. Could have knocked us down with a feather when we saw you.' Ben said nothing, unsure what would be appropriate. 'Anyway, just thought you'd like to know we've got a bet on you.'

'Who has?'

'We all have. Not sure who's behind the whole idea, but

there's a lot of stuff riding on you, so don't trip over your feet, you understand?'

'I'll try my best.'

'Yeah, it's not just money. There's an extra prize if you actually WIN! Spoogy's sister, Sharon, has offered to go out on a date with whoever makes the highest bid before the race – and everyone knows she's really fit, up for anything!'

'Wicked!' breathed Ben. Even he was impressed with that. 'So how's it going to work?'

'Either you or Michael Smith have got to win, or Sharon withdraws her offer. Got that?'

Ben nodded.

'Are you coming to Maths?'

'Yes.'

'So are we.' Steven and Stuart stationed themselves one at each side of Ben, until he felt he was forcibly escorted down the corridor. But by the time they had reached the Maths room, their trio had grown to a small group of about seven boys, all walking around Ben as if he were the most impressive person they knew.

'I just wanted to be the first to congratulate you.'

Katherine smiled to recognise Robert's voice when the phone rang in her office that morning. 'Well, thank you. What have I done?'

'Probably saved St Mary's.'

'You've had a reply?'

'Not just one. Three responses so far – one offering a package of financial help over the next two years, the others asking for us to go in to talk to a member of their board to tell them more.'

'Oh, Robert, that's wonderful – and so quick!'

'Well, we did target those letters very carefully. Writing only to chief executives we know personally obviously makes it easier.'

'But do you think the money will come in quickly enough to save the hospital?'

'That's the big question. I'm sure their bank will be a little more lenient with them if they know they're likely to get major sponsorship. I'm going to suggest, though, that the hospital changes its account to one of the banks which sponsors them. That gives the bank a real involvement, and should mean the hospital will find money much more forthcoming in the future.'

'Well, don't thank me, Robert. You're the powerhouse behind all this.'

'I couldn't have put that presentation pack together without you.'

'It's been fun.'

'So where shall we celebrate? And when? Are you free on Thursday night?'

'Alan's coming round.'

'First time since Fateful Friday?'

'Yes. He left the flat as I asked him, and in fact he's been working up north most of this week, so tomorrow is the first convenient time for us to meet.'

'Are you sure you should?'

'There's a lot of water under the bridge between Alan and me. Nothing has ever been simple between us. Yes, we do need to talk.'

'You're missing him?'

'The flat does seem very empty.'

'Remember how he hurt you, Katherine.'

'How happy he makes me too.'

Robert sighed. 'OK, I give in. It will have to be Friday for our celebration then.'

She laughed. 'Sounds wonderful.'

'I'll ring you that morning to sort out the details.'

'I'll look forward to it.'

'And Katherine?'

'Hmm?'

'Just remember to let your head get a look in as well as your heart where Alan's concerned.'

'Warning taken.'

'And probably ignored.'

'Well done on the appeal, Robert. That's great news. Until Friday then!'

And the phone clicked dead.

'You look a bit peaky. Are you all right?' Val spoke quietly in Meg's ear as they both helped themselves to coffee in the staff room that Wednesday lunch-time. With a flick of her head, Meg gestured that the two of them should head for the seats tucked in one corner of the room slightly apart from the rest of the teaching staff.

'Well?' asked Val kindly, once they were both settled.

'You won't think very much of me . . .'

Val chuckled. 'Sharing my life with two ex-husbands? I'm hardly in a position to criticise anyone!'

'But once you're going through a divorce, isn't that what they should be — EX-husbands?'

'Aah,' nodded Val with understanding. 'Alan wants to come back, does he?'

'He says so. Well, he did on Friday.'

'And how do you feel about that?'

'Relieved. Exonerated, in that if he chooses to come home having left me, then it gives me back a sense of worth, and I haven't felt much of that since Christmas.'

'Do you love him?'

'Yes. I suppose I must do when I think how I behaved that night . . .'

'After the party?'

'Hmm. He brought Ben back early, do you remember?'

Val gave a wry smile thinking of Chas's little birthday gift about which Meg still knew nothing. 'I remember.'

'So he was there when I got back.'

'And?'

'And – it felt very natural, a bit like old times really. He'd got sandwiches ready, and we sat there drinking Horlicks . . .'

'And one thing led to another?'

'Whatever must you think of me?'

'Why should I? What's more important is what you think. It had been an exciting evening, a family night together. It would be easy to find that beguiling, to confuse a sense of familiarity with attraction.'

'I worry about that.'

'But perhaps you actually do love him. You've been together a long time, Meg. You always seemed to have a very good marriage, from the outside at least. I know being single and having to bring up the family on your own has been very hard for you.'

'I've managed though, haven't I? In the end, as frightening as it was, I've coped. More than that, I've enjoyed it. There! I never thought I'd say that – but it's been good to make decisions all on my own – to change the room around if I want to, spend money or save it without asking permission, wear whatever I feel good in without having to take Alan's opinion into account.'

'Well, I have to say I've seen a change in you. You seem much more confident in your own ability these days.'

'It feels almost as if I've crawled out from under his shadow to find that I'm a perfectly capable woman able to solve problems on my own. I've been wiring up plugs which always used to terrify the life out of me. I even mended the tap in the bathroom sink the other day! I'm fairly organised with money. During the divorce settlement, I've fought for a fair share for the children and me, and not allowed him to bat me down. More than that, I have found confidence in my own opinion. I got into the habit of agreeing with Alan's view on everything, as if he spoke for us both. Since I've discovered that he lied and lied and lied to me over the years, why on earth should I take what he says into account when my own thoughts are not only every bit as worthwhile, but based on honesty too?'

'Exactly.'

'So if I feel like that, if I've felt like that for months, why did Friday night happen?'

'Because you're only human. Because you still have feelings of love for this man with whom you shared so much. Because it was an opportunity to score one over on the woman who deceived you. After all, you'd loved and trusted Katherine all those years too, then she stole your husband and broke up your family. Don't tell me you didn't feel a thrill of triumph when he came crawling back to you?'

Meg grinned. 'Perhaps. Actually, I really couldn't tell you what I felt.'

'Do you want him back, Meg? Could you re-build your marriage?'

'Maybe. I've been thinking about that a lot this week.'

'And what does Alan say?'

'No idea. I've not actually spoken to him. After it happened, he was up and out the door mumbling something about getting back to Katherine before I'd even got my breath back.'

'How sensitive of him. And he's not been in touch since?'

'He has, but I've always managed to miss his calls. I know he's working away this week so I don't feel I should ring him. In fact, I don't want to. I don't know why, but I'm not sure what I should say to him, how I want to react.'

'How much has this got to do with Chris? You two seemed very close at the party.'

Meg couldn't help smiling at the mention of his name. 'He's such a lovely man, a very dear friend.'

'And he's keen on you?'

'So he says.'

'And you?'

'I think I'm pretty keen on him too. He's sort of crept up on me, if you know what I mean. He's been around so much because of Ben, and yet I always found it was Chris and I who ended up talking for hours when he came back to the house.'

'I chatted to him for quite a while during the party too. He struck me as a good listener, very caring. I liked his sense of humour.'

'We do seem to laugh a lot together. He's very easy company.'

'Do you fancy him?'

'After Alan, I never thought I could be drawn to anyone in that way again – but yes, there does seem to be a real pull between us.'

'Then go with it, Meg. Alan's messed up your life once. Don't let him do it again.'

'But what about Ben and Emma? He's their father. If he came back, we could be a family again. Surely I owe that to them?'

'If you and Alan resume your role as a couple, it must be because the two of you are both totally sure your relationship is right, and you know you don't want to be apart from each other ever again. Emma has almost left home. Ben isn't far behind her. Children grow up and move away, and you'll be left with years and years of your own life to live. Don't compromise, Meg – not with Chris and not with Alan. Just make sure that whoever you choose, and even if you choose simply to be alone, that it's what you're certain you really want.'

Meg jumped at the piercing sound of the school bell as it rang to announce the start of afternoon lessons. 'Thanks, Val.'

'You're a smashing lady, Meg Barratt. You have choices. Remember that.'

Meg could have hugged her – but she didn't as the two

women gathered up their bags and books, and hurried off to
their respective classes.

The moment she saw Emma that evening, Meg knew something
was dreadfully wrong. Her daughter had slammed the front door
shut behind her, then scuttled upstairs to her room – but not
before Meg had noticed her red-rimmed eyes and smudged
mascara. Meg reached for Emma's favourite mug from the
cupboard, boiled and frothed milk for drinking chocolate which
she topped liberally with cinnamon, grabbed a handful of
chocolate biscuits, and tiptoed up the stairs to knock on Emma's
bedroom door. There was a mumbled reply which might have
been 'push off' – but Meg went in all the same. Emma was
stretched out face down on her bed, a soggy paper hankie in one
hand, and Matt's framed photo in the other. She opened one eye
to take a look at what her mother was carrying.

'I'm on a diet.'

'You're also upset. This is comfort food.'

'Are those biscuits plain or milk chocolate?'

'Plain. Your favourites.' Slowly Emma curled her legs up
towards her and swivelled into a sitting position propped up
against her pillows. 'Care to talk about it?'

'He's not worth the bother.'

'He?'

'Matt can be such a git sometimes.'

'Aah . . .'

'Really selfish.'

'Well, he's a man . . .'

'So he tells me, but he acts more like a big kid. He knows
how much work I've got to get through for these "A" levels, and
all he does is whinge about how he expects me to spend more
time with him.'

'Would you like to?'

'Yes! Of course I would, but I've got to work, haven't I? He was happy for me to go back to finish my exams after all the trouble at Christmas because he thought that might mean I'd get a better job and earn more money for us when we get married, but now he's just a pain. If I don't ring him every half-hour, if I'm not round at his flat by eight o'clock every night, he gets the hump.'

'You're still planning to get married then?'

'He is.'

'And you?'

'I love him, Mum, I really do — but he's getting right up my nose at the moment.'

At the tragically dramatic expression on her daughter's face, Meg had to bite her lip to stop herself chuckling. It took one look at her mother for Emma to realise what was happening, and for a moment it seemed certain Emma was going to throw a wobbly — until suddenly, surprisingly, she grinned instead.

'I think right now I'd rather tuck myself up for the night with a packet of these biscuits than Matt.'

Meg laughed out loud. 'At least you wouldn't have to share them.'

'Or do the washing up when he leaves cups and plates everywhere.'

'It was socks that used to drive me mad. Your dad would stand in the middle of the room and just chuck his socks wherever he felt like flicking them. Then he'd complain that socks never arrived back in his drawer in pairs.'

'Your fault obviously, because you should have got on your hands and knees and gone looking for them.'

'I used to marvel at how many odd socks I was always finding in the bottom of the wardrobe. I developed a theory that single black socks are a kind of caterpillar form that disappear into the bottom of wardrobes and emerge weeks later as empty wire coat hangers!'

'Do you miss him, Mum? Dad, I mean?'

'A bit.'

'He misses you.'

'What makes you think that?'

'I was watching him at the party on Friday night. He couldn't take his eyes off you when you were dancing with Chris.'

'Really? I didn't get much chance to dance with anyone after your dad arrived because he seemed to monopolise my time a bit after that.'

'Exactly.'

'What about you? Do you miss your father living here?'

'Not really. Oh, I did at first. I really hated him for all the upheaval he was putting us through. And knowing we might have to sell this house when you two divorce cheesed me off too. He was quite good about the party though.'

'Just so pleased you were speaking to him again, I think.'

'Has he talked to you about coming back?'

'Why do you ask?'

'Because he mentioned the idea to me during the party – you know, asked what I'd feel about it?'

'And?'

'I don't feel anything really. It's up to you.'

'Has the atmosphere here changed much since Dad left?'

Emma hugged her knees while she thought about the question. 'Yes, yes it has. You and I are closer for a start.'

'I'm glad you think that. I do too. You've been great when I've been feeling inadequate and rejected.'

'You're over that now.'

'Do you think so?'

'Definitely. Well, that's because of Chris, isn't it?'

'Is it?'

'You're good together.'

'We are?'

'You do a lot of smiling when Chris is around.'

'That's a nice thing to say.'

'So what are you going to do — about Dad, I mean, if he wants to come back?'

'Honestly, Em, I don't know.'

'He did go off with your best friend.'

'He's the husband I loved for years and years.'

'He betrayed you.'

'He supported me too all the time we were together. Ours was a good marriage on the whole, Emma.'

'So good he had an affair right under your nose for nine years?'

'Wouldn't you like to have your mum and dad living under the same roof again?'

'Not unless it's right for you. You'd go back to odd socks all over the floor and Dad making pronouncements and you having to go along with them. You're past that now, more your own woman, I'd say.'

Meg smiled as she reached out to touch her daughter's cheek. 'What a wise young woman you are.'

'Not much good with my own relationships though, am I?'

'What do you want more — Matt or good "A" level results?'

'Good results probably.'

'There you are then.'

'And,' added Emma with a grin, 'there is this really cool guy in my Psychology tutor group . . .'

Laughing out loud, mother and daughter hugged with delight and complete understanding.

Chapter Thirteen

'Come in.' The formality of Katherine's greeting took Alan by surprise as she stood back to allow him into the flat. 'Coffee – or would you prefer a drink?'

He smiled. 'You know me. White wine would be nice.' He didn't follow her into the kitchen but went through instead to the lounge, looking around the room which had become so familiar to him over the years. He turned to take the glass she offered him before she took a seat on the far side of the room.

'Katherine, I won't bite.'

'I prefer it this way. I can think more clearly.'

'And I could think more clearly if you were closer. Please?'

'I've made my decision, Alan. It's over. It's sad, heartbreaking, in fact, but you know as well as I do that this just isn't working.'

'That's it? No discussion? After all we've been through, all we've meant to each other, you can end it so abruptly?'

'It's not been like that. The thought has been creeping up on me for months, long before our disagreement on Friday night.'

'I was right not to let you come to the party. It was kindest to Emma and the family, and it would have been extremely difficult for you.'

'Perhaps. We'll just have to agree to differ on that one.'

'I love you, Katherine. You know that. I can't bear to see the hardness in you now. This isn't the you I've come to know so well.'

'Well, maybe we didn't know each other well enough. Being lovers for all those years didn't prepare us for everyday life together, did it? We were used to romance and privacy and wonderful love-making. We had candlelit dinners and discussions into the night and talk of being soulmates for eternity. Now we worry about what's in the fridge and dripping taps and who pays the bills and mess left all over the place . . .'

'I'm not untidy. I resent that. It's just that you are inordinately precise about everything.'

'I like order. I like to see my things in their place.'

'YOUR things. YOUR place. Isn't that where we went wrong? I have been trying to live on your terms in your home. What we needed was a place we chose together.'

'No chance of that until your divorce settlement comes through . . .'

'These things take time.'

'And in the time it's taken, we've grown apart, Alan. We both know it.'

He looked at her helplessly. 'Is there someone else?'

'YOU can ask me that? You who shared your life and bed with another woman for nine years before our relationship became public knowledge?'

'Is there?'

'Why do you ask?'

'Where did you go on Friday night? I rang round the obvious people you might be with, and no one had any idea where you were.'

'That's my business – just as you made it your business to go to that party on your own.'

'Is it Robert Masters? You've been seeing a lot of him over this appeal thing. Is he making a play for you? He thinks he's God's gift to women, so I wouldn't put it past him . . .'

'I think you'd better leave.'

'Katherine, I didn't mean that. I'm just jealous. I don't understand what's happened to us. Where did it all go? All that passion and commitment and connection between us. Do you feel none of that now?'

Her face softened. 'Of course I do. What else but the most devoted love could have kept me standing in the shadows beside you for all those years. You have been my life. I couldn't help but love you, and I couldn't leave as long as that love remained.'

'And now?'

'Now I realise I must move on. So must you.'

'I already have, or haven't you noticed? I've left my wife, split up my family, and broken some very tender hearts on the way. I've wrecked lives and loyalties and futures for Ben, Emma and Meg. I did all that for you.'

'But I only ever wanted that to happen if you were sure you were doing it for YOU – because I was the only woman you wanted to be with, because your love for me was strong enough to bear the hurt we knew it would cause. And in the end, Alan, you only moved in here once we were discovered. This wasn't a positive move in my direction. It was a knee-jerk reaction out of guilt and necessity.'

A bleakness crossed his face as the fight seemed to go out of him. He leaned back against the sofa and closed his eyes. Quietly, she got up and came to sit beside him, taking his hand in both of hers as she spoke.

'Would you like to try and make another go of it with Meg?' His eyes opened. 'It's OK. You can tell me. I couldn't bear the thought of you being with anyone else – but Meg? Well, she's rather special, isn't she? I never realised just how much her presence in my life meant to me until suddenly it's no longer there. She'll never forgive me, of course, and that's a loss I'll regret all my life. But if I feel that way about her, why shouldn't you?'

'It's not just Meg. It's the kids too. It hit me hard this week —
preparing for the party, and the night itself with all those old
friends and neighbours . . .'

'You felt you'd come home?'

He looked at her sharply. 'That's exactly how it was. It made
me realise that swopping one woman for another is only a small
part of the story. What I'd actually done was leave behind the
whole context in which I existed — the home we shared, the
memories we had, the jokes and stories we both knew, the
children we brought up, the future we planned, the friends we
loved. And I felt condemned by them all, even though I honestly
don't think people are surprised by marriage break-ups any more.
It was my own guilt that challenged me, of course, but I found
myself actively avoiding people I assumed would disapprove.'

'And on Friday night,' she asked softly, 'you realised that you
still have a place there. It's where you belong.'

He sighed, sad and accepting. 'Kathy, I'm so sorry. Sorry I
couldn't make it work for you, that I've wasted all these years of
your life . . .'

She cupped and tilted his face in her hands until their eyes
were level. 'I wouldn't change a second of it. Loving you has been
wonderful . . .'

Suddenly he was kissing her — hungry, bruising kisses of
passionate desire, then softer and more tender, tinged with
sorrow and regret. It was Katherine who first pulled away,
her breath short, body trembling. For seconds their eyes locked
in longing and understanding — acknowledging the painful,
inevitable truth that this was the end.

'Will you be all right?' he said. She nodded. 'Be happy,
Katherine. You deserve it. Perhaps with Robert? I'd be jealous as
hell — but I care enough about you to want your happiness.'

'You too. You and Meg. You belong together. I always knew
that really.'

'I love you.'

'I love you too.'

She didn't look at him as he stood up. She felt his hand upon her shoulder, his lips on her hair – and then the soft thud of the front door as it closed behind him.

Ben leapt out of bed on Friday morning, and tore back the curtain. It was a perfect day for the run, cooled by an overcast sky. Within minutes he was out of the bathroom, into his shorts and T-shirt, and over the garden gate.

He glanced at his watch as he emerged from the newsagent's, the bulging bag heavy on his shoulder. Today was the day. What better way to start than by getting through his round faster than ever before!

And after that, he'd try and do exactly the same along the Valley Park course of the Midsummer Run . . .

He was back and on his second bowl of cereal when the phone rang. Meg stiffened to hear Alan's voice. For a whole week she had either missed or avoided the few calls he'd made. Plainly that fact hadn't bothered him much as he sounded buoyant, almost excited.

'Just wanted to let you know that I'll be there for the race this afternoon!'

'Ben will be pleased. He's here. Why don't you tell him yourself?'

'Meg, in a minute! I need to talk to you first. In fact, there is so much I need to say to you, but not on the phone. This afternoon would be best – after the race, would that be OK?'

'Well, it depends on Ben, how he's feeling.'

'Of course. I understand that he might need cheering up, and we can do that together. I can't wait to see you all. Is Emma going too?'

'The race is timed for four fifteen so that as many pupils of the senior schools as possible can be there to cheer on their own competitors. It's always a big event, and Emma is as proud as punch that her little brother is in it!'

'I'm looking forward to it – being with the family, with you . . .'

'Here's Ben.' Annoyed with herself for sounding flustered, Meg handed her son the phone and went back to making packed lunches.

Ben was about to leave and Emma already on her way when the phone rang again. 'Just wanted to see how Wonder Boy is feeling today?' The warmth in Chris's voice was unmistakable.

'Broke his own record on the paper round this morning, so he's pretty pleased with himself.'

'Not worn out, I hope?'

'He's raring to go. I can't recognise the boy I see today with the scared little rabbit he was just before Christmas.'

'That's all behind him now, and today will prove it.'

'Where will you be this afternoon? Will we see you?'

'The runners start and finish on the same line, so that's where I'll be – where I hope you'll be too.'

She smiled. 'I'll leave school as soon as I can, so Emma and I should be there by four at the latest.'

'Cheering him on.'

'You bet! Although you know what they say about it not being the winning that counts, but how the race is run.'

'Stuff that! We're out to come first! Unashamed and ambitious, that's us!'

'Well, you've worked hard enough with all four boys from your school. So good luck to you too, Chris. You deserve success.'

'Let's hope after the race, I can share some of that with you . . .'

'Heavens, is that the time?' Meg stared at the clock. 'I must fly!'

'Me too! Four o'clock it is then!'

Grabbing her bulging briefcase and the last packed lunch from the work surface, Meg checked for her keys and ran out of the house.

Alan had to visit a client in Oxford that morning. With the all-important race in the afternoon, he had considered rearranging the meeting, but it was a fairly straightforward piece of business which would be concluded by one o'clock at the latest, leaving him ample time to get across country to join the family at the Valley Park.

Whistling softly as he threw his briefcase into the car, his fingers fumbled for the package in his jacket pocket, checking for the umpteenth time that it was safely there. He felt good about this, good about the burden of guilt and regret which seemed to have lifted at last from his shoulders. With blinding clarity, he now realised where he belonged. He was going home.

Speaking to Meg that morning had been a good start to the day. She sounded defensive and wary, which was only to be expected in view of everything that had happened. There was so much for them to talk about, unhappy memories to lay aside, and a bright future to build together.

And with that thought in mind and a smile on his lips, he headed west out of London.

'Ready, lads? In the car then!' Chris led the way as Ben, Michael Smith, Dave Whitaker and Simon Buxton carried their kit bags out to the Mondeo Estate.

'Good luck, Simon! Knock 'em flat, Michael!' Shouts of encouragement greeted the four boys who grinned sheepishly as they climbed into the car.

'Anyone nervous?' asked Chris, his eyes peering at each one of them in the rear-view mirror.

'Terrified,' said Dave.

'Actually I feel sick,' added Simon, who definitely did look a bit peaky. 'I've been ill, you know.'

Chris glanced at him. 'I noticed you've been off this week. Well, Simon, it's only a race.'

'Yes sir,' agreed Simon glumly.

'Michael, are you confident?'

'Sir?'

'I asked how you're feeling about the race. You've missed a lot of training.'

Michael shrugged. 'It's all right.'

'Looking forward to it?'

'Not bothered really,' was the slightly bored reply.

'And Ben? Raring to go?'

'You bet!'

'Well, best of luck, all of you. The hopes of the school are riding on you, and I think you'll do them proud!'

'How are you, Katherine? Was it rough with Alan last night?'

'Yes.'

'Then you'll need to be cheered up this evening,' said Robert. 'And I can do that partly by telling you we've had another very positive reply to our appeal. Sister Mary Lawrence is whooping with joy!'

Katherine's lips twitched with amusement at the thought. 'I'm glad.'

'And as you sound like a girl in desperate need of a hug, a bit of TLC is the other way I aim to cheer you up.'

'Robert, I . . .'

'Oh, I know. You're very raw – but I'm a patient man, and I happen to think you're worth waiting for.'

'Don't expect too much of me.'

'I expect nothing – but you know me, ever the optimist. Where you're concerned, I live in hope . . .'

'Even if I'm rotten company tonight?'

'I'll cope. I've got broad shoulders.'

'And a kind heart.'

'Well, there's something about you that seems to do very alarming things to my heart.'

'Then it sounds as if you need a little TLC too.'

'Oh, I do, Katherine. I really do.'

The client wasn't in his Oxford office as arranged when Alan arrived.

'Where is he?'

'Mr Stack has been held up over at our Witney branch,' said the glamorous but obviously efficient receptionist. 'A bit of an emergency. He says he should be back within the hour.'

Alan glanced at his watch. Half past ten. That would mean they would start their meeting at half-eleven, finish probably by half-twelve, maybe one o'clock, and he'd be on the road in plenty of time after that.

'Take a seat, Mr Barratt. Can I get you a coffee or anything?'

A boss who keeps his appointments, thought Alan grumpily as he settled down to wait.

'Wish him luck from us!' Val caught Meg as she raced out of the building at the end of afternoon school. 'Jay said that speed has nothing to do with leg length or height, but is all about pace, stamina, technique and determination – and he was schoolboy cross-country champion of Kent or something when he was a teenager.'

Meg laughed. 'Then he should know! Thanks, Val – not just for remembering Ben today, but everything.'

'Chas sends his love too. He says he'll ask Ben to take his overweight labrador for regular runs round the block if he does well in the race today!'

'I'll tell him.' She gave Val a quick hug, watched with giggling interest by the group of seven-year-olds who were walking through the door at the same time – then crossing her fingers in the air, she headed for the car.

Alan couldn't believe it. Having waited more than an hour for his client to return, he made the mistake of believing the receptionist when she said he was on his way. Half an hour later, there was still no sign of him – and with the time ticking on, Alan stood to pick up his briefcase.

'It's for you, Mr Barratt,' she said holding out the phone towards him.

'Alan,' said Ralph Stack apologetically, 'One of those mornings, I'm afraid. But I do need to speak to you, and I'm on my way over now. The least I can do is take you out for a late lunch.'

'That's kind, Ralph, but I'm on a tight timetable today.'

'Then I'll drive quickly, and be with you a.s.a.p. Bye!'

'Over there! There's a space behind that green car!'

Meg swung her old Fiesta over towards the direction in which Emma was pointing, then backed neatly into the gap.

'It looks as if everyone is walking over that way', said Emma, gazing into the distance. 'Come on, Mum, we'll be late!' Five minutes later, they arrived panting at the start line.

'There's Ben!' Emma spotted him first, limbering up in his

school tracksuit, his face a picture of concentration. 'Doesn't he look grown-up? That's my little brother out there, and just look at him!'

Meg and Emma pushed their way forward to the front of the crowd so that they could see him better. They could see Chris too, deep in conversation with a couple of lads wearing identical tracksuits to Ben.

'Honestly, sir, I feel awful,' wailed Simon Buxton. 'I've just been sick again.'

Chris studied the boy with concern. This wasn't just nerves. Simon was deathly pale except for hot spots of colour in the middle of his cheeks and eerily glassy eyes. 'You can't run like that. Have you got anyone here, Simon? Your mum or dad?'

'She's there, sir.' Simon pointed in the direction of a tall, sandy-haired woman who was hurrying over to join them. Within minutes the decision was made that, disappointing as it certainly was, Simon was in no fit state to be standing, let alone running in the Midsummer Run. Clucking like an over-protective hen, his mother led Simon away.

'The pressure's on you now, lads!' said Chris as the other three team members forlornly watched their fellow competitor disappear from view. 'Keep warm now! Get limbered up. The flag goes up in just over ten minutes.'

'Psst! Smithy!' Michael looked round to find Spoogy had crept under the tapes designed to keep back the crowd so that he could beckon his friend over for a quick word. 'Is the plan still on?'

Michael tapped his fingers confidently on his freshly gelled hair. 'It's in hand.'

'And he still doesn't know a thing about it?'

'Our little Barratt? Course not.'

'It's all riding on you then, Smithy. May the best man win!'

A slow smile spread across Michael's face. 'Oh, he will. If I have anything to do with it, he definitely will!'

Alan was livid. Ten minutes to go, and the motorway had ground to a halt in front of him with more than five miles still ahead before he even reached the outskirts of the town.

Ralph Stack had a lot to answer for! When he fnially did get back to his office, he found he had several urgent messages to respond to before they could begin their meeting. It was desperately late when Alan raced towards the Oxford ring road, hoping that the Friday evening traffic would be kind to him.

No chance! It was worse than ever. Furiously he groped for his mobile phone, plugging in his earpiece as the car stopped again at the back of the queue. Would Meg have thought to take her phone with her? At least she might be able to let Ben know that dad was on his way, and would be there very soon.

But Meg's phone rang three times before the answerphone cut in.

Suddenly a gap appeared in the lane before him as the traffic began to move forward. Drumming his fingers on the steering wheel, he hurried to catch up, only to come to a complete standstill again almost immediately.

'Meg! Coo-ee!' Sandy was waving enthusiastically towards Meg as she and Dave, arm in arm, made their way over to join them. 'We couldn't miss Ben's big moment! He looks really cool and confident, don't you think? It's so exciting.'

'Have you got your youngsters with you?' asked Meg.

'They've taken themselves off to the adventure playground. They're not really interested in races unless they're doing the running!'

'It's good of you to come, Dave. Aren't you working tonight?'

'I've been on duty since five this morning, so the answer, I'm delighted to say, is no.'

'Busy day?'

'You could say that. It's had its moments though. Some old duffer rang into the station when I was on the desk this morning to say that his elderly sister had died in the night, and could we organise an undertaker to pick her up? Well, obviously any death needs a proper investigation, so I enquired where he lived. He said it was something like Eucalyptus Crescent, which I've never heard of, so I asked him to spell it for me. He went quiet for a moment, then asked if it would help if he dragged her round the corner to Oak Street!'

Sandy laughed loudest putting her arm around her husband's waist and gazing at him lovingly. Meg watched with interest as Dave looked down at her with undisguised affection.

'You know, Meg,' he said, 'my wife doesn't trust me an inch, when for me there could never be a woman to compare with her. If I leave her a note with three kisses on the bottom, she'll complain that the last one I wrote had four! If I ring in the afternoon from the station to check how she is, she'll want to know why I didn't ring in the morning. If I say she's got a gorgeous figure, she'll tell me she's fat and I'm lying.'

'I don't care about that any more now,' retorted Sandy, her eyes not leaving his. 'I'll just be fat and happy . . .'

' . . and pregnant!' added Dave proudly.

'You're not!' exclaimed Meg, 'That's great news, a wonderful surprise!'

'It's due early next year. Heaven knows what the kids will make of it. Joely will be six by then, so I thought my days of wiping bottoms and sleepless nights were behind me.'

'Well, Sandy, you'll have plenty of willing hands around you to help you, including mine. I'm delighted for you both. Congratulations!'

'Mum!' interrupted Emma. 'It's about to start. Look the flag's up!'

They crammed up as close as they could to the tape, all eyes on the small figure of Ben at the end of the long line of fifteen runners.

Bent forward in his starting position, Ben was determined not to make the same mistake again. His eye was firmly fixed on the flag as it fell – then he was off like a pellet from a catapult!

At last! The traffic ahead cleared enough to allow Alan to pull into the outside lane at a half decent speed. Ahead of him he could see the start of the town, but he had either to go straight through the centre, or round the inner ring road to reach the Valley Park on the other side. Whichever way he chose, it was clear the rush hour was building up fast.

It was well past four – and he had never felt such furious frustration in the whole of his life.

Ben concentrated on positioning himself in the middle of the field with about four runners in front of him. He wasn't yet one-third of the way into the race, his breath steady, mind clear as he pounded round the course.

He could only see one runner whom he recognised, and that was Michael Smith next but one ahead, his stride strong and confident. Of Dave Whitaker he had seen nothing, so he assumed that he'd been left behind quite early back at the start.

From the practice runs that Chris had made him do around the course, Ben recognised the tree they'd identified as being the one-kilometre mark on this three-kilometre length. Ben dug into his energy resources to lengthen his stride and quicken his pace, easily overtaking the lanky, rather surprised runner ahead of him.

Michael Smith's back was dead ahead of him now, com-

fortably keeping up with the two runners in the lead. As if he
sensed the change of positions in the field behind him, Michael's
head snapped round so that for just a second he looked directly
into Ben's eyes.

And what Ben glimpsed there was not so much venom, or
even rivalry – but sheer mischief!

Once the race was underway, Chris came across to stand
beside Meg, his binoculars and stopwatch in hand. Way across
the other side of the park, the straggling line of runners was just
visible to the naked eye.

'They've covered that first kilometre in great time. That's not
bad. And Ben is right up near the front. Mind you, I think that's
Michael Smith ahead of him, so he's doing really well too.
Tiredness can set in now though. We'll see who has the stamina
to stay out in front after the next stretch!'

Thank goodness Alan knew his old home town well enough to have
a few back doubles up his sleeve. Swinging away from a static line of
cars, he turned right down a narrow one-way street at the start of a
shortcut he'd used to trim off that corner for years.

Two minutes later, he went as fast as he dared down an
avenue newly lined with speed bumps to find he was at a dead
end. A series of metal posts had been sunk into the road to
ensure that the tree-lined area remained upmarket and residential
and not the rat-run that Alan and others like him had always
thought it to be.

Thumping his fist furiously against the dashboard, he spun
the steering wheel until he'd turned the car round, then sped off
regardless of the bumps with his foot jammed against the floor.

It struck Ben that not being able to hear clearly was a distinct
advantage when it came to running. There was only silence

around him. No distraction from others' footfalls or laboured breathing. He sensed rather than heard his own heart thumping in his chest, felt the jar of his feet on the hard grass surface as they thudded rhythmically one after the other — left, right, left, right . . .

He remembered what Chris had drummed into him. At this point — two kilometres on — it was time for him to make his move. Ahead of him, Michael Smith was relying on sheer strength rather than style — a great, lumbering powerhouse in motion. But as Ben started to plan his move to overtake Michael, he realised that his rival was obviously in the middle of a plan of his own. Michael's eyes were focused firmly on the runner ahead of him as he not only closed the gap between them, but actually moved across until the two boys were almost trying to run on the same strip of ground. In alarm the runner in front turned round to glare at Michael, who grinned amicably as his shoulder went down as if he planned for the two of them to collide. In fact, their bodies didn't touch — but the other boy was sufficiently distracted to lose his footing, stumble and fall as the rest of the field sped past him.

Ben gasped with shock which quickly became fear when he saw Michael turn to stare at him. But he was still smiling. More than that, he was plainly slowing down. Not waiting to wonder why, Ben put on a spurt which took him round Michael and several yards ahead of him, so that there was now only one runner between him and the finishing line.

And as he ran on, Ben wondered if he could believe what he'd seen. Had Michael Smith deliberately sabotaged another runner? And rather than get in the way, was it possible that he had actively moved aside to allow Ben to come through?

The entrance to the Valley Park at last! Alan swung in through the gate, then turned towards the car park. The race had obviously attracted a lot of onlookers as it took him another frustrating couple of minutes to find a space, park and lock the car. Then he started running, realising from the distant sound of cheering encouragement that he still had quite a way to go before he'd reach the crowd gathered round the finishing line. Hot and panting, he ran as he hadn't run for years.

The boy ahead was good. He was really good. He glanced over his shoulder, aware that Ben was moving up behind him before picking up pace in his determination to cross the line first.

As the two boys, now way ahead of the rest of the field, turned the last bend for the home run, Ben suddenly became aware that there was a crowd lining the side of the course. Their mouths were open, their arms in the air, but the sound was muffled, drowned by the pounding of his own heart and the thumping of his trainers. Then faces began to make sense to him. There was Spoogy, Steven Manson, Stuart Golding – even Darren was there, all of them watching him, mouthing his name as they cheered him on.

Ahead of him, he could just make out Chris and his mum standing together, and something stirred within him, a steely determination, a commitment to himself and everyone else that he would never again be the underdog. Fixing his eyes on the shoulder blades of the boy in front, Ben pulled out every ounce of energy he could muster. He could hear the cheering now, hear his name called out over and over again as the excited crowd screamed encouragement. So he ran. He ran like a person possessed. He ran as if his life depended upon it, as if death itself was chasing him across the line.

They were neck and neck. The front runner turned in alarm when he saw Ben draw level – and in that split second, the younger boy shot past him. With only a matter of yards to go, his head went back, his chest forward, and the tape split in two as he thundered across it.

Euphoric and breathless, he would have fallen to his knees had it not been for the army of hands around him – hands that patted his back, touched his hair, hugged him and finally lifted him off his feet and into the air. Shoulder high, he was carried across to the winners' podium, where he was unceremoniously dumped near enough to be grabbed by his plainly delighted mum in a huge, relieved, elated, loving hug. Next it was Chris who hugged him, his face a picture of unashamed pride. And because the next hug came from Emma, who was in floods of uncontrolled tears as she held him, Ben didn't see what happened behind him as in full view of a very interested crowd of onlookers, Chris drew Meg into his arms and kissed her soundly.

'I do love you, Meg Barratt, very much . . .'

Meg looked up at him, seeing the love and hope in his eyes, knowing in that instant not just where her heart but also her future lay. 'And, Chris Elliott, I love you too,' she shouted over the noise of congratulation and applause before slipping her arms around his neck to kiss him again.

On the other side of the crowd, unable to fight his way through, Alan caught sight of his family. He watched as Meg first hugged Ben, then another man – the one who had spent so much time dancing with her at the party the week before. Then, as Emma sobbed on Ben's shoulder, Alan kept watching as Meg looked up to kiss the man beside her, an expression on her face which spoke of affection, promise and belonging.

In all the years they'd been together, she had never looked at Alan quite like that – and the sight of Meg, his own dear Meg, plainly in love with another man rooted him to the ground as surely and painfully as a bolt of lightning.

Suddenly Ben was swept up on to the podium to collect his cup and a handsome cheque for the school. Even he could tell the noise around him was deafening as his classmates hoisted him up on their shoulders yet again.

When his feet finally touched the ground, a shudder went

through Ben as he realised he was only yards from Michael Smith. What would his mood be? Surely he had wanted to win the race himself?

'Don't look so worried, Worm!' Michael hissed in his ear. 'We all knew you could win, even if it did take a little helping hand – or should I say shoulder? Everyone in our form bet on you – and persuaded all the other forms that you didn't have a chance, so they would bet on me. That means the guys in our form get all the sweepstake money – and I win the top prize, a night out with Spoogy's sister – we both know what that means!' And with a wink and an enormous thump on Ben's back, Michael sauntered off.

Savouring the comfort of Chris's arm around her shoulders, Meg welcomed Emma and Ben as they finally came back to join them.

'Right!' said Chris, 'Time for a celebration, don't you think? Who fancies a pizza tonight?'

With delighted agreement all round, the four of them started to follow the crush of people out of the park, with Ben collecting constant congratulations on the way.

Suddenly, Meg looked up to find herself staring across the crowd into Alan's eyes. In the excitement, she had completely forgotten he planned to come. She thought back in panic to what he might have seen. Did he watch Ben win? Did he see his son proudly take the cup and cheque for his school? And did he spot her with Chris, and recognise the depth of commitment there?

In an instant, she knew the answer to those questions. Alan had seen it all. The gaunt sadness in his face told her so. He continued to stare at her, his eyes saying what words somehow could not. It was over. Their marriage was truly at an end. Their family were no longer his family. Another man now held their love and affection, and stepped into the place he had always assumed would be his. He had lost them. Time to let go.

The crowd started to move again, and Meg found herself

pulled abruptly to one side. When she looked back again, Alan was gone. For a second or two, she breathed deeply, shocked at seeing him. Then Chris noticed she was lagging behind and looked back at her with such infinite tenderness that all doubt was swept from her mind. Grabbing his hand, she allowed herself to be carried along by the happy, chattering mass of people around her.

It was when Alan got back to his car, shaken and alone, his fingers found the precious package in his pocket. He slowly drew out the box, then flicked it open to reveal its contents. The eternity ring with its line of shimmering diamonds caught the evening sunlight. Picking it out carefully, Alan read again the inscription inside the band: *Forever, Alan.*

For several seconds he stared at it until his eyes misted over and pricked with tears. He walked round to the front of the car, and standing beside one of the tyres, deliberately dropped the ring into the mud. Then he got behind the wheel and pulled away, a wave of grim acceptance seeping through him as he felt the tyre bite deep into the ground beneath it.